W9-AUT-355

Eye of the STORM

ALSO BY KATE MESSNER

The Brilliant Fall of Gianna Z.
Sugar and Ice

Eye of the STORM

KATE MESSNER

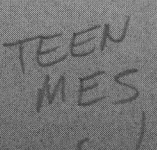

WALKER & COMPANY
New York

First published in the United States of America in March 2012
by Walker Publishing Company, Inc., a division of Bloomsbury Publishing, Inc.
www.bloomsburykids.com

For information about permission to reproduce selections from this book, write to
Permissions, Walker BFYR, 175 Fifth Avenue, New York, New York 10010

"Geometry" from *The Yellow House on the Corner*, Carnegie Mellon University Press, Pittsburgh, PA.
© 1980 by Rita Dove. Reprinted by permission of the author.

Library of Congress Cataloging-in-Publication Data
Messner, Kate.
Eye of the storm / by Kate Messner. — 1st U.S. ed.
p.   cm.
Summary: Jaden's summer visit with her meteorologist father, who has just returned from
spending four years in Russia conducting weather experiments not permitted in the United States,
fills her with apprehension and fear as she discovers that living at her father's planned
community, Placid Meadows, is anything but placid.
ISBN 978-0-8027-2313-0 (hardcover)
[1. Fathers and daughters—Fiction. 2. Storms—Fiction. 3. Weather—Fiction. 4. Climatology—Fiction.
5. Mystery and detective stories.] I. Title.
PZ7.M5615Ey 2012   [Fic]—dc22   2011006393

Book design by Nicole Gastonguay
Typeset by Westchester Book Composition
Printed in the U.S.A. by Quad/Graphics, Fairfield, Pennsylvania
2 4 6 8 10 9 7 5 3 1

All papers used by Bloomsbury Publishing, Inc., are natural, recyclable products
made from wood grown in well-managed forests. The manufacturing processes
conform to the environmental regulations of the country of origin.

For my aunt, Maureen Lahue,
and for all librarians
fighting the good fight
for books and knowledge

Eye of the STORM

Chapter 1

There are no words to describe this sound.

In the old days, they said tornadoes sounded like freight trains. I've seen video archives of survivors being interviewed, all out of breath. They describe an approaching rumble and then a roar. Wind pouring out of the sky. Buildings shaking. And finally, the train rumbling off, fading away as the storm lumbers on.

But that was then.

There are no words for the sound of what is happening now.

A thick, dark shadow is snaking down from the cloud that followed us from the airport. It's wider and stronger than anything those people in the video archives had ever seen. Bigger than anything they could have imagined.

It is headed straight for us.

"No worries, Jaden," Dad says, but both our DataSlates are wailing with high-pitched storm alerts. His eyes dart to the rearview mirror as he pulls the HV into a safety lot.

I've heard about these huge roadside shelters, but we don't have them at home in Vermont. The one time Mom and I got caught out with a storm coming, we just knocked on somebody's door. It goes without saying in New England: on storm days, you let anybody who needs help into your safe room.

But in this part of Oklahoma, there are fewer houses now, hardly any doors to knock on. This huge concrete structure is the first building we've seen for miles. It's almost full, but Dad maneuvers into one of the last spaces. "We'll be fine here."

"Good timing, I guess." My voice shakes, even though I try to pretend it's no big deal; Mom warned me the storms would be more frequent here, but I never thought I'd see one before we even got to Dad's house.

"That good timing's no accident." Dad leans back in his seat and picks up his DataSlate. The glow of the screen lights his face an eerie blue, even as the sky outside grows darker. "When StormSafe got the government contract to build these lots, we put one every fifteen miles on major roads so you'd never be more than a few minutes from safety."

"That's how much warning you get when a storm's coming?"

"Give or take."

They're like the Revolutionary War–era taverns I learned about in my online history course, spaced fifteen miles apart because that's how far a traveler could ride in a day. Here we are, 275 years later, driving hydrogen vehicles instead of horses, and we're back to needing shelter every fifteen miles.

Lightning flashes outside. I tug my backpack from the floor into my lap and run the strap between my fingers, over and over, so I can concentrate on that instead of the pounding in my chest. I can't freak out. Not on my first day with Dad in four years. He lives for storms like this.

A plastic chair tumbles, legs over arms over legs, past the entrance we came in.

"This is turning into a good one." Dad cranks the volume on his DataSlate so we can hear the regional news feed over the screaming wind. If they mention the storm, we'll know it's big. Normally, they send out the DataSlate alerts that replaced the old tornado sirens and leave it at that. Mom said when she was growing up, her town got on national news once when a tornado wiped out half a mobile home park. *National* news!

Now the news feeds only report the biggest of the big, the true monsters. It sounds like this could be one of them.

"The National Storm Center confirms a tornado warning for all of eastern Logan County," the voice on the DataSlate says. "NSC meteorologists say the system that developed this afternoon has spawned three separate tornadoes—the latest, a possible NF-6. Residents are advised to get to safe rooms immediately."

"NF-6?" I swallow hard. We have our share of storms back home—who doesn't?—but the worst I've seen was the NF-4 that ripped the roof off Mom's environmental science lab at the University of Vermont.

"Could be." Dad leans to see past me, out the shelter door. The tornado doesn't even have its funnel shape anymore; the thick, jerking rope has swelled into a churning blur of brown-black wind.

"It's rain-wrapped!" Dad shouts over the roaring. "Tough to see how big it's grown. But at least it's not a Niner!" That's weather-geek slang for an NF-9, the second highest rating on the new scale they developed a decade ago when it became clear the storms had outgrown the old Enhanced Fujita Scale that went from one to five. When I was a baby, EF-5 was the worst a tornado could be. The New Fujita Scale goes up to ten, though nobody's ever seen a ten touch down. What would they call it? A Tenner?

The lights flicker, and I grip the door handle.

"Relax, Jaden." Dad punches me lightly on the arm, and it sets something off inside me. All the swallowed-up storm jitters rise in my throat, and I want to scream. Instead, I swallow that, too, and my eyes fill with tears.

I've been on the ground all of two hours, and I'm not used to it here. None of it feels like home.

Not the desolate brown flatness of the land.

Not the stark concrete gray of the shelters.

And not the storms. Especially not storms like this.

Dad should know that.

Maybe he'd understand how I feel, understand *me*, if he hadn't spent the past four years in Russia, doing weather experiments that weren't allowed in the United States. Maybe he'd ask how I'm doing now that—

"Jaden, look!" He holds up his DataSlate and turns the radar screen my way. "This hook echo is incredible!"

He points to the blob on the screen. It's churning, growing, hungry enough to swallow half of Oklahoma. A curled-up green extension sticks out one side of the storm, like a witch's finger calling us in.

I know what he wants me to say. He wants me to *ooh* and *ahh* and talk about the rotation like we used to when I was little and I'd sit on his lap, and he'd laugh because I knew how to read a satellite map before I was five. He wants me to be WeatherGirl, the nickname he gave me before he left, before he and Mom split up, before the storms got this bad, before everything. He wants me to say how awesome it is, how fantastic and powerful. How amazing.

But it's not. It is terrifying and loud, pounding the concrete shelter we're hiding in with uprooted hackberry shrubs and tree trunks and God knows what else. I grab the door and hold on.

"Relax, Jaden. This is no big deal around here. You're safe. I designed this shelter model myself. StormSafe tested these things under conditions that were far more—"

He's trying to comfort me, but he is screaming, *screaming* over the storm he says is no big deal. So I scream back.

"Dad, *stop!*" I put my head down on the dashboard and press my hands into my eyes, but I still can't escape from the sound. Forget the passing freight train. This is like being *inside* the engine of the train, inside the throat of some ancient Greek monster that's roared down out of the sky. It's throwing recycling bins and branches, torn-off roof tiles so frantic and flapping they look like huge tortured birds, all flying past the entrance to the lot. I scream again, "Just stop! Stop!" And I don't know if I'm screaming at Dad or the storm or both. But neither responds.

Finally, I sit up and open my eyes. Dad is ignoring the weather outside, staring at me. He closes the radar image—the storm looks even bigger in the glimpse I catch before it's sucked into a folder on his screen—and pulls up his StormSafe corporate log-in page. He turns the slate away from me as if I'd be able to see or remember his stupid password in the middle of this and pokes at the onscreen keys. "Relax," he says. "It's weakening now."

I squeeze my eyes closed against the pounding, against the attack from the wind and debris, and I don't answer him. But as if by magic, the roar of that monster-from-the-sky fades back into something more like an old-fashioned freight train and then dissolves altogether.

I don't open my eyes.

I sit, listening to the train rumble off. I squeeze my eyes shut tighter and think.

This was not a storm. It was a monster.

This is not home.

And this is not the same father I used to have, the one who tucked me into bed, singing songs about the wind.

That father took me out for ice cream on a summer night four years ago. He ordered rainbow sprinkles on his cone, right along with me, and he told me why he had to go on another trip. Why he wasn't coming home anytime soon. Why he needed to open a new StormSafe headquarters in a country that would allow him to do his research. And he left.

This father who has come back to me . . . I open one eye a crack. His fingers fly over the DataSlate. His eyes focus on the scrolling columns of numbers, laser-intense. Fierce.

He feels like someone I don't even know.

Chapter 2

No matter how bad things get in Logan County, no matter how the clouds swirl, how the radar screens light up, I'll be safe in Placid Meadows.

Perfectly, one hundred percent safe.

That's what Dad promised Mom, how he convinced her to send me here, to the heart of the storm belt, for the summer. And his new, self-sufficient StormSafe community does sound impressive. Safety. Higher water and kilowatt allowances, thanks to Placid Meadows' private solar and wind energy reserves. Eye on Tomorrow Science Camp, the state-of-the-art program Dad's corporation runs for "the best and brightest young minds" in the world. Dad said it went without saying that I was one of them and sent me admissions papers, but I still wanted to take the official entrance exam. When I answered the last question on my DataSlate and pressed the SUBMIT button, the score that appeared on the screen put me in the top five percent of applicants. I couldn't argue that I didn't belong there.

Plus Mom had her own research project waiting in the shadow

KATE MEJJNER

of an active Costa Rican volcano. Not to be outdone by my father's adoration of storms, Mom's had her own love affair . . . with frogs. While Dad's been studying the effects of global warming on storm formation, she's been researching its impact on wildlife in sensitive ecosystems, particularly rain forest amphibians like the poison dart frog. Mom's wanted to take this trip for years but had nobody I could stay with until now.

"This must be WeatherGirl!" As we pull up to the Placid Meadows gate, a beanpole of a man leans down into the HV window.

Dad nods in my direction. "This is indeed my daughter Jaden, the infamous WeatherGirl." My stomach's still tangled from the storm, but I smile; nobody's called me that in four years, and even though I'm a total science geek, I'm surprised Dad still thinks about me that way. Surprised, and I guess a little pleased.

"Hi, Jaden. I'm Lou." He points to the shiny silver name tag on his navy blue uniform. There's a StormSafe emblem above his name. Does everybody here work for Dad? "Any update on the expansion, Dr. Meggs?"

"Unfortunately, no," Dad says. "Looks like Phase Two is going to be delayed a bit."

"What's Phase Two?" I ask.

"Phase One of Placid Meadows is full, and we have two dozen families waitlisted, so we're going to expand the development. *If* we can get the land we need."

Lou chuckles. "Those farmers getting you down?"

Dad isn't smiling anymore. "Honestly, why someone would be crazy enough to stay here to run a dying farm is beyond me. And why *anybody* would turn down an offer that's five times what the property is worth . . ." Dad shakes his head, then looks at the dashboard clock. "I'd better get Jaden home." He lifts two fingers from the steering wheel in a wave.

When he drives through the Placid Meadows gate, it's like driving from Kansas into the Land of Oz.

From the minute I stepped off the plane, Oklahoma has been a place of charcoal skies and yellow-gray clouds. It's like Florida when the hurricanes started getting bigger; no one lives here anymore unless they're too attached to family farms or they can't afford to leave. The oil wells were abandoned a decade ago when the international fossil fuels ban took effect. The sprawling cattle ranches are ghost towns. It's a state abandoned, except for a few farms, storm-torn mobile home parks, and corrections department energy farms, where convicted criminals ride generator-cycles outside in the daytime and sleep in StormSafe bunkers at night. It's a black-and-white world, with shades of brown.

But Placid Meadows blooms in full, all-of-a-sudden color.

A billowing garden of bright flowers divides the street. In the middle is a fat boulder with a bronze plaque affixed to it. WELCOME TO PLACID MEADOWS, A STORMSAFE COMMUNITY, it says in calm, loopy cursive. All around, the garden bursts with reds and pinks and fuchsias. Tall purples tip their heads, and spreading silver-blues creep along the curb.

"It's beautiful." I lower my window to breathe in all that brightness, and for the first time since I said good-bye to Mom at the airport in Burlington, I almost feel calm.

Dad pulls over and smiles, and his face relaxes into something I almost recognize from the Dad I had before. "Isn't it the most gorgeous garden you've ever seen?"

I nod, but this new glimpse of Dad is more interesting than the plants now. The DataSlate man from the car seems to have been sucked into a folder deep inside him. Now he looks like someone who might order rainbow sprinkles on an ice cream cone again someday. Between that and the flowers, I feel my heart lift. Maybe this summer will be all right.

"The flowers are so perfect." I lean out my window.

"Of course they are. Everything we plant is DNA-ture; it's the best." He puts the HV back in gear. "We better go. Mirielle's making an early dinner."

Mirielle. The stepmom I've only seen on my DataSlate videophone, and always with my new half sister, Remi, in her arms.

Dad pulls away from the garden, farther into the development.

The street is lined with StormSafe houses, concrete structures tinted mauve, slate blue, and sea green. They have windows, which surprises me a little; they must be made of glass that's engineered not to shatter under pressure. And there are bigger buildings, without windows.

"Are those houses, too?" I ask.

"Nope—that one's the community warehouse." Dad nods toward a big brick-colored structure as we pass. "DNA-ture delivers food orders once a week so we don't need to go out to the regional grocery store."

No wonder the farms Dad mentioned to Lou aren't doing so well.

Dad points out my window. "Here's the entertainment dome."

He slows down as we pass a building that looks like the big skating rink at home. The electronic sign outside has a schedule of showings. Movies. Sporting events. Ballet and theater streamed in live from the National Arts Center in New York. And something called Museum Night, with Natural History: Jurassic Period on Tuesday and American History 1900–2050 on Thursday.

"What's Museum Night?" I ask as Dad pulls away.

He smiles a little. "Do you remember when you were really small—I think you were three—when we took you to closing ceremonies for the American Museum of Natural History in New York City?"

"Kind of." I remember walking through a room with huge dinosaurs and another one with all kinds of rocks and gems. And Mom was crying. "Mostly, I remember Mom being sad."

Dad nods. "It broke her heart when the government decided most of the major museums needed to close so artifacts could be protected in underground bunkers until the storm crisis is resolved. But this place"—he looks in the rearview mirror—"is the museum of the future. It's all holograms, so it changes every night. What did it say for this week?"

"Jurassic and American History."

"Great shows; you should go," Dad says. "You walk a path through the dome, and you'll see dinosaurs approaching. The T-Rex looks like it's about to eat you for dinner." He chuckles. "They're just holograms, so they don't bite, but they're realistic. American History is fascinating, too. You meet history makers of the twentieth and twenty-first centuries—Martin Luther King, Steve Jobs, Al Gore—and former presidents, too. I think they have Barack Obama and Grace Farley in this show."

"Interesting," I say, and it is. But then I have another flash of memory from the museum's closing night—the feel of a cool, rough dinosaur tail under my hand when I ducked under the velvet rope to touch it, even though the signs said not to. It felt real, like it might come alive and roar any second. A hologram could never feel like that.

We turn a corner, and Dad slows down. "That's Risha Patel, the girl I told you about on our video-call last week."

The girl looks about my age. Her long black hair has a bright green streak along one side. She must have a BeatBud in her ear because she's bobbing her head back and forth to something fast and playing imaginary drums in the air, right above the handlebars of her bicycle as she rides along, hands-free.

Dad speeds up again, but I turn in my seat and stare.

She is riding a bike.

Nobody rides bikes anymore at home. The storms churn up so fast, there's not a kid in our neighborhood who's allowed to ride more than halfway down the block, so why bother? Amelia was the last of my friends to give hers up. She held out right through last summer and never cared how ridiculous she looked riding up and down the street, back and forth, alone. When we laughed, she told us that in her mind, she was going all over town, through the woods past the big tree house where our moms used to camp out when they were little, branches brushing her cheeks as she flew down the trails. But at the end of the summer, we got our StormSafe Mall and Teen Center, and even Amelia figured that was better than imaginary trails. The recycling crew picked up her bike at the beginning of October.

Was this girl imagining faraway places, too?

"Does she live right around here?" I ask Dad.

He shakes his head. "The Patels live on the other side of the development. Closer to the Eye on Tomorrow campus."

"Wow." I scan the horizon. The storm we just saw has already barreled off, but there are more clouds churning in the west. "She's far from home for a storm day."

Dad laughs. "I see it's going to take you a while to get used to being a StormSafe kid." He slows down and pulls into the driveway of an adobe-colored concrete box. "It's different here." He presses a button on the dashboard, and a dome-shaped mouth yawns open on one wall. He pulls the HV forward into what must be the Storm-Safe version of a garage. Three bicycles are lined up inside, one in my favorite color, electric blue.

"We ride bikes all over the place here. In fact," he says, nodding to the fleet along the wall, "it was supposed to be a surprise, but the blue one's yours. You'll love having that freedom again."

"But . . . how can that be safe? I know the *houses* are safer here, but if you're outside . . . I mean, the storms are even worse than at home, so—"

"How many times do I have to tell you?" Dad shakes his head, smiling. "While you are inside the gates of Placid Meadows, you are safe. Totally and completely safe."

He presses another button on the dashboard. The garage door rumbles again, and behind us, the mouth on this safe, safe house slides shut.

Chapter 3

When Dad opens the kitchen door, French disco music bursts out to meet us. Mirielle is twirling around the room barefoot in a long flowered skirt and lemon-yellow tank top. Remi is six months old now and swaddled in a big, every-colored scarf slung around Mirielle's neck like she is part of the outfit.

Mirielle presses a button to send the potatoes down for peeling and—"Oh!"—almost twirls into me on her way back for the carrots. "Jaden, you're here!" She leans in to kiss my cheek. I smell Remi's head—soap and baby. Mirielle turns to Dad. "Did you get caught in the storm? I hate when you have to go out there." She says it as if "out there" and "in here" are totally different planets.

"I know, love." Dad steps up to the biometric panel on the refrigerator. He presses a finger to the reflective glass and taps impatiently, waiting for it to identify him by his print. "We spent about ten minutes in a safety lot. No problem." For some reason, relief cools my face when the fridge sends Dad out a glass of iced tea. He still drinks it with lemon, and at this point, anything that hasn't changed is welcome.

"You want something to drink?" Dad asks.

"No thanks." I look past him and wonder where my room is.

Mirielle catches me peering into the living room. "Would you like to see the rest of the house?"

"Go ahead." Dad steps up and rests his finger on another biometric panel just outside a steel door on the wall opposite the kitchen appliances. "I'm going to check in with headquarters before dinner."

I stand by the door for a second and see a bank of computers inside before I realize Dad's office won't be part of my tour. Then I follow Mirielle out of the kitchen and up a spiral staircase to a sleeping loft. It's bigger than mine at home, but it has a bedspread of the same bright blue. I wonder if they did this on purpose, tried to make my room look like home so I wouldn't miss Mom so much.

But then Mirielle pulls open the little drawer on my nightstand, and what I see inside makes me miss Mom even more.

It's a book. The hardcover kind with pages you turn by catching the corner with your fingertip. We have this one at home, but I didn't bring any paper books; Dad says reading paper books is like driving on square, stone wheels. He's been reading exclusively on his DataSlate since before I was born.

This book is by Rita Dove, an American poet who loves math as much as she loves words. In the photograph on the book jacket, she's beautiful and maybe around Mom's age, but she must be in her nineties now. I sit down on the bed and flip through the pages to find my favorite, "Geometry." It's about what she feels like when she proves a mathematical theorem.

. . . the house expands:
the windows jerk free to hover near the ceiling,
the ceiling floats away with a sigh.

When I first read this poem, the ceiling part freaked me out a little. Then Mom told me it was written way back in 1980, before most people knew what it was like to have the roof blow off your house for real.

I run my hand over the raised letters on the book's cover. "Did my mom send this?"

Mirielle smiles and sits next to me. "She thought you might miss your books, so she had your great-aunt Linda pick up a copy at the antique shop and drop it off when your father wasn't home." Mirielle glances toward the door. "She suggested I tuck it away for you."

"Aunt Linda? Really?" Even though she's technically my great-aunt, I've always known her as Aunt Linda. I haven't seen her in years, though. She paints and gardens, and I'm not surprised she likes poetry, too. She took care of Dad when he was little, pretty much raised him. I put the book down next to me. "How close does she live?"

"About twenty miles. But she and your father don't really talk."

"How come? Won't I get to see her? It's been a long time."

Mirielle's pretty green eyes cloud over. "Your father thought Linda should move to Placid Meadows, but she'd have no part of it. He was furious, and so no . . . she doesn't drop in for dinner."

My disappointment must show on my face. Mirielle reaches out and touches my arm. "But she is your relative, too, no? Maybe we will have a visit one day while your father is at work." She stands up, tucks the book back in the nightstand, and gently closes the drawer. She smiles like we're sharing a secret, and I realize we are. We both know Dad wouldn't want paper books cluttering up his house.

Besides, it's poetry. Dad always says a world like ours needs science to save it, that pretty words never protected anybody from a storm.

Which reminds me. "How do I get to the safe room from here?"

"There is no one safe room," Mirielle says. "Everywhere is safe."

The ugly concrete designs make perfect sense now, and so does Dad's promise to Mom. The whole *house* must be a giant safe room.

"I will show you the living room instead, yes?"

On the way downstairs, we pass the bathroom, and I peek inside. It's enormous, and there's no liter-meter on the wall, like at home. Could the Placid Meadows water rations be so much higher that we don't even have to keep track? I add longer showers to the list of good things about living here for the summer.

"Here we are." Mirielle steps into the living room. One whole wall is an entertainment window. There are plush black chairs, an antique rocker, a leather sofa, and bookcases like ours at home. But no books. Here, the shelves are full of digital frames. Most are storm shots, black-gray blurs of tornadoes from Dad's research trips all over the world, but the two frames on the end have a slide-show of family photos.

I stand next to Mirielle and watch the images change.

Mirielle and Dad at their wedding in Russia two years ago.

Eating cake.

Dancing.

Photos of Remi as a newborn.

Then pictures of me.

There are a bunch of photos taken in the first house Mom and Dad owned. I'm three years old, pushing a toy lawn mower in the yard. It's the old-fashioned kind that needed a person to steer it. There's me in a high chair with jam smeared all over my face.

Then I am four. Dressed for my first day of school. The tornadoes were spreading north then. I'd been so excited for school but so scared that a storm would sweep away the house while I was gone.

There are school photos for the next three years. I am five, then six, then seven. My backpack goes from purple, to pink, to red with blue stripes, to bright orange.

When the picture changes again, I am eight. The counter is torn up behind me—they must have been installing the SmartKitchen—and books are spread out on the table. That was the year before they built the StormSafe schools and shelters, and we all homeschooled with classes streamed to our computers. Mom created most of her own lessons, though, and I loved staying home. It was just before Dad left for Russia, too, the last year we were whole.

The frame flashes again, and suddenly, my face looks older—last year's school picture. Mom must have beamed it here.

"We need a new photograph of you," Mirielle says. "Your hair is longer now."

"Yeah, a little."

I step closer to the shelves to look at the other frame with family photos, the smaller one. One of the pictures looks like an old-fashioned portrait of my father.

"Is that Dad?"

Mirielle has been humming softly to Remi. "Hmm?" She stops and leans toward the frame. "Oh, no, that's your *grand-père*; these are your father's parents, Enam and Athena, when they were young. You have seen photos of them before, yes?"

I have, but never one that looks so real. There is something fierce in my grandmother's eyes. An intensity that looks like it should have burned out the camera's lens. "She reminds me a little of Dad," I say, and wonder how much Mirielle knows about the woman who would have been her mother-in-law.

I never met Grandma Athena. She died way before I was born, and it was Mom, not Dad, who told me about her. Like Dad, she had an amazing mind. She studied with a ferocity that made people afraid of her. She met Grandpa in graduate school, married him four months later, and had Dad right after they graduated. When the September 11th terrorist attacks happened in 2001 and the United States went to war with Afghanistan, Grandpa enlisted in the military and Grandma went to work for some secret government science program. It was all classified—like the scientists who developed the atomic bomb during World War II—so nobody knew exactly what she was doing.

When Dad was twelve, Grandpa was killed in Afghanistan, Grandma died in a car accident, and Dad had to go live with Aunt Linda, all within a few weeks. Mom says that's everything she knows; Dad never talked about it and still doesn't. I've always known not to ask.

Before today, I'd only seen one picture of Grandma Athena, faded on paper. It made her look old and brittle, too. But this photo feels alive, as if I might catch her blinking, and I have trouble looking away until Mirielle breaks the spell. "You must be hungry."

"Kind of." I follow her back to the kitchen. "Want me to hold the baby?"

Mirielle unsnuggles Remi from the scarf. She fusses for a minute but then gets a handful of my brown hair wrapped around her fist and curls up against me.

I turn back to the living room for one more look at Grandma Athena, but the picture has already changed.

Chapter 4

"Did you try the broccoli?" Dad raises his eyebrows at the perfectly formed trees piled on one side of my plate. "It's DNA-ture's bestselling vegetable for a reason, you know."

"I know." I've seen the pop-up ad on my DataSlate so many times I can quote it. *"DNA-ture: Vegetables Even Kids Will Love. Our foods have the undesirable qualities bioengineered right out of them."*

"It's true." Dad picks up a stalk from my plate. "No bitterness. No mushiness."

"Still the same old broccoli." I stand to take my plate to the auto-clean bin.

"Still the same old Jaden. Stubborn as usual." He frowns and pops the broccoli into his mouth.

I should have known better than to knock DNA-ture, the bio-botanicals company he runs along with StormSafe—but as I open my mouth to apologize, I see him smiling. "I'm going back to my office. There are still some storms around to deal with." I'm about to ask Dad how he'll "deal with" them when the doorbell rings.

"Would you answer that for me?" Mirielle asks, leaning down to pick up Remi.

The air-drumming girl with the green-streaked hair, Risha, is about to push the doorbell again when I answer. "Oh!" she says, jumping back a little. She brushes hair from her eyes, and two gold bangles, patterned with zeros and ones, clang together on her wrist. "You're here! Yay! I mean, hi!"

"Hi to you, too! I'm Jaden."

"I know." She bounces on the toes of her pink high tops. ". . . and my mom told me you're almost thirteen like me and you're going to Eye on Tomorrow, too. I'm Risha. Want to go for a bike ride?"

"What a good idea!" Mirielle joins us at the door. "Risha can show you around."

"Okay." The clouds are dark, but they're still a ways off, and Mirielle doesn't seem worried. "Let me get my bike."

I head for the garage, thinking how weird it feels to say that again.

My bike.

Riding a bicycle was something I thought was gone forever. Something future kids would hear about in stories from the old times, before the earth's average temperature grew so warm, before the atmosphere became so unstable, so friendly to huge storms. I thought bikes were gone, like hikes in the woods and picnics that aren't in the backyard. Somehow, Dad's company has found a way to give those things back to people.

"Come on!" Risha coasts by me, pedaling backward as fast as

she can, her sneakers a hot-pink blur. "We'll go by my house and then campus."

We ride around a corner, and Risha waves to two girls jogging on the sidewalk. "Hey, Tess! Ava!"

They wave back as we zip past them.

"Will they be at camp?" I ask, pumping harder to catch up with Risha.

"The Beekman twins? Of course." She lets out a snort that sounds more like a rhinoceros than a skinny girl with a delicate nose. "They moved into Placid Meadows a couple years ago, so they were in all my classes at school. Their father owns the British company that produced the first successful HV model. The storms in Britain have gotten bad, too, so he brought the family here and *paid* their way in."

Her tone of voice makes me glad I insisted on taking the test, even though Dad was ready to enroll me without it. "Is the camp mostly Placid Meadows kids?" I ask.

"It depends." Risha pedals up a small hill. "A few really high scorers moved here with their families, all expenses paid. Some guys who live around here like Alex and Tomas—I'll introduce you, but I have dibs on Tomas—come for free, too. My mom says it was part of the tax deal your dad's company got. They have to provide opportunities for local kids." She crests the top of the hill and starts coasting. I follow her down and over a bridge that crosses a little creek. Just on the other side, she squeezes her hand brakes and stops so abruptly I almost bump her rear tire.

"Here's my house," she says.

It looks like Dad's, right down to the gobble-up-your-car garage door, only this one is pale blue instead of adobe colored. "It's pretty," I say.

"Not really." She laughs. "But it's bigger than our apartment in New York, and safer. Plus it's close to school." She points to a concrete and steel building halfway down the block. It looks brand new. "And not far from the Entertainment Dome."

"Do you go there a lot?"

Risha shrugs. "Not really. Once you know when the T-Rex is going to pop out, it's not that exciting. And the American History show just makes me mad. Can you believe they spent so long arguing before the courts decided that people can marry whoever they want? Maybe if they'd worried more about carbon emissions back then and less about bossing everybody around, we'd still have real museums with real stuff in them, you know?"

Risha lets out a huff and starts pedaling straight ahead, but the clouds off to our left catch my attention. They're closer. And darker.

"Hey, Risha, do you want to head home?"

"Why? Don't you want to see the campus?" She keeps riding.

The wind whips up dirt from the empty lot, and it stings my cheeks. "Risha, shouldn't we go? It looks bad over there."

She hollers something over her shoulder but I can't hear what, and then she turns—an abrupt right down a driveway I would have missed—and stops. Looming ahead of us is a building twenty times the size of the houses. It's behind a fancy, locked wrought-iron gate.

"Whoa!" I pull my bike up next to her. "What's this?"

"Eye on Tomorrow." Risha leans on her handlebars and rests

her chin on her hands, grinning at the building. "Where the brightest minds of today prepare to lead us into the future. And that's just the reception building. You'll see the rest in the morning."

The reception building gleams, all steel and windows. There are another half dozen shining buildings behind it, built around a grassy quad. The largest has a huge white dome—five times the size of the Entertainment Dome—growing out of the center. Dad told me this place was impressive, but I thought he was exaggerating. This summer camp for schoolkids looks more high-tech than Mom's university.

It makes sense, though. StormSafe created Eye on Tomorrow four years ago as a model for the government's new Surge Ahead program to create leaders in math and science. The United States had been behind other countries in those areas when the storms intensified. Now, it's like everybody suddenly figured out science is important, so they're building facilities for gifted students around the country. Eye on Tomorrow was the first—and is apparently still the best.

"Were you here last summer?" I ask Risha.

She nods. "Once you test in, you get to come every summer. The idea is for campers to keep coming back and then work for StormSafe and its sister companies once they get out of school. Doesn't your dad tell you anything?" She looks at her watch. "Come on, it's almost eight o'clock, and I want to show you one more thing if you can keep a secret because my parents would kill me if they found out, and yours probably would, too. You can keep a secret, right?" She looks at me over her shoulder.

"Sure, I guess."

She leads the way down another hidden path through some brush. A branch tugs at my hair, and I have a pang of missing Amelia. She'd love this bike ride, with real trees and trails that aren't just in her imagination.

"Well, look who made it," a deep, older-than-us boy voice calls out, and again, I almost bump Risha's back tire because she stops so fast. In front of her, a chain-link fence rises up from the dusty ground to way over our heads. This must be the edge of Placid Meadows; the fence stretches out in both directions. The only opening is where the barrier is interrupted by a big old oak tree whose trunk and branches apparently ignored the fence and kept right on growing, twisting the wires and pulling open a gap that looks just big enough to squeeze through.

On the other side of the fence, two boys stand back a few steps, straddling bicycles of their own. Theirs are older and rusted, like they've been out in a storm or two.

"Sorry I'm late." Risha shrugs at the taller of the two boys. She jumps off her bike, climbs through the gap in the fence, and motions for me to come, too.

"We thought you stood us up."

"Never." She gestures toward me as I'm pulling a twig out of my hair. "This is my friend Jaden."

"Hey." The tall boy smiles one of those lazy, movie-star smiles with his eyes half closed. He must be the one she has dibs on.

"Jaden Meggs, meet Tomas Hazen and Alex Carillo."

"Hi." I nod to Tomas and wave past him to Alex, who's shorter, about my height, with dark skin like Risha's and black hair that curls around his ears.

"Hey." His brown eyes are asking questions, and he tips his head. "Meggs?"

"Jaden," I say. "I just moved in—"

"With your dad? *The* Stephen Meggs?" He looks at Risha and raises his eyebrows.

"Yes, her dad is Dr. Meggs, Alex. Get over it." Risha glares at him. "She's visiting for the summer because she qualified for Eye on Tomorrow." She turns to me. "*Somebody*'s a little touchy about DNA-ture because his parents don't believe in factory-made foods. They're part of the organic farming collective that still grows stuff in fields."

"Yeah, well, somebody else can't seem to take no for an answer when a piece of property's *not* for sale." Alex folds his arms in front of him.

"Well, maybe *somebody* shouldn't have accepted the camp scholarship if he thought Jaden's dad was so horrible. But I bet you'll be there tomorrow." Risha walks off toward the riverbank with Tomas.

I'm left here with Alex. "I don't know much about my dad's work," I squeak out.

"Sorry," Alex says, looking down. Risha's argument seems to have taken the wind out of him. "I'm kind of defensive about the farm." He scuffs his work boots in the dust. "You must know your dad wants to build more houses, right?"

I wish I didn't. But I remember his conversation with Lou about Phase Two. "I kind of heard about it. He's offered to buy your farm?"

"Yeah . . . about ten times." Alex puts down the kickstand, climbs off his bike, and stands looking out over the field. "Most everybody's selling. Mom keeps telling Dad we should take the money, but he won't. Every time your dad sends somebody with another offer, they fight. Selling this place would kill my dad. I know it would." He shrugs. "This is what we do."

"Well, it's not like you *have* to sell. He's just asking," I say. But I remember the frustration in my father's voice when he talked about the land. I bet he's been pushing hard.

"I know. And she's right, too." Alex nods reluctantly toward Risha, who's tossing stones into the river with Tomas. "What I said before was dumb. You're not your dad."

"I don't even know if my dad is my dad anymore." The words slip out before I can filter what I'm saying to this boy I just met. They hang in the air like dust, and Alex looks at me. I bend down to pluck a blade of grass and arrange it between my thumbs to make a whistle. Amelia used to do it all the time and finally taught me how. I lift my hands to my mouth and blow. It sounds like a crow.

"You have some impressive skills there," Alex says, smiling a little.

"Thanks." I try to do it again, but the grass slips from my hands and flutters back to the ground. "Unfortunately, it's not a very useful skill. Do you think they have grass-whistling at Eye on Tomorrow?"

Alex frowns. "Hmm . . . you could study how the force of your breath and the width of the grass affect the rate of vibration. . . ."

"I think I'll stick to meteorology."

"Yeah?" Alex says. "That's what I studied last summer. What's your focus going to be?"

"Honestly?" I haven't told anyone this yet, not even Dad. "What I've always wanted to do is work on storm dissipation. You know . . . the theory that you can actually stop a tornado from forming if you change the conditions in the storm so—"

"I know what storm dissipation is." Alex looks at me as if he's seeing me for the first time, as if we just arrived at the fence. "How'd you get interested in that?"

"I don't know." I lean against the fence next to him, watching Risha and Tomas trying to balance on a log at the edge of the river. They're laughing, and it makes me think of Mom's tree house in the woods from when she was young. She took me there once, on a day when that seemed safe. I climbed up and watched the sun peeking in and out of the leaves. I never wanted to leave. "My mom tells stories about when she was little, before it got like this. I always kind of wish I could have lived back then. Without the storms being part of everybody's lives."

A gust of wind whips the tree branches back and forth over our heads, and a few leaves fly past. One gets stuck in a diamond in the fence. I reach out for it, just as Alex does the same. But he pulls his hand back and looks up at the swirling gray sky. The dark wall cloud in the west is looming closer.

"Hey, Tomas!" he calls. "We gotta get going."

"But we just got here." Risha pouts for a second, but then she's smiling again. "See you in the morning, bright and early!"

"Too early." Tomas grins. "See ya."

Alex waves, and they get on their bikes and ride away.

"Risha, we should go, too. It's getting bad."

We climb back through the fence and head for our bikes. Risha looks back and sighs. "He is so cute."

For a second, Alex's dark eyes flash in my mind, but I know she's talking about Tomas. I climb on my bike and put up the kickstand. "He seems nice. Kind of quiet, huh?"

"He's usually more fun. His mom's been sick, having all these tests, and they just figured out it's pancreatic cancer."

"They can get her treatment, can't they?" Pancreatic cancer was one of the last kinds to be totally cured, but there've been treatment centers around for at least five years now.

"Yeah, but not here. Probably New York—Tomas's brother is in college there—but his dad's worried about the farm and where they'll stay and money and everything. They'll figure it out; it's just on his mind is all."

Wind shakes the trees, and suddenly the weather's on my mind. It's getting darker. "Risha, come on. We need to go."

She looks at me as if I've suggested she bring an umbrella out on a perfectly sunny day. She's not even on her bike yet. "We're fine, Jaden. It's not like it's coming *here*."

But then thunder rumbles, and I don't wait to find out. I start pedaling, and once we're back on the main road, I see the storm *is* closer—way closer. The sky has turned a gray-green color that makes my stomach churn. I don't know if Risha's following, and I don't look up. I remember the turns, back over the bridge, past Risha's house, and back to Dad and Mirielle's place.

I stop in the driveway, gasping for breath.

Risha skids up next to me. "Now what?"

I turn to her, ready to tell her how crazy she is, but over her shoulder, I see the wall cloud, the heart of the storm, moving away from us.

I can only stare.

"It's going the other way," I say finally.

"They always do." Risha tips her head and looks at me. "Let me get this right, Jay-girl. Your father runs the company that built this place. And he didn't bother to let you know you're safe from the tornadoes here?"

"Well, he did, but . . ." I remember his words in the car. His promise to Mom. To me.

Inside the gate, you are completely, one hundred percent safe.

"I figured it just had safer . . . safe rooms or something." I can't stop staring at the cloud that seemed to bounce off our neighborhood as if the chain-link fence extended all the way to the heavens. As if steel wires could keep out the weather.

Risha rolls her eyes. "It's not only the houses. It's *all* of Placid Meadows. That's the whole deal with a StormSafe community; technology keeps the entire property safe."

"How?"

"Well, I don't know exactly." Risha frowns a little. "I always assumed the storms got . . . like . . . zapped at the perimeter somehow. But whatever it is, it works. They *never* hit us. It's even in the contracts."

"In the contracts?" Since when did nature make contracts with anybody?

"When you buy a house. Right there with the number of bed-rooms and deeded rights to the playground and whatever. That's why people are willing to pay so much to live in such ugly houses, I guess." She laughs a little and looks at her watch. "I'm going to head home. Grandma's making chicken tandoori." She rides off in the direction of the storm clouds that are barreling off toward someone else's home.

Not ours.

Never ours.

It's in the contract.

Chapter 5

"You won't need that," Dad says as I'm sliding my DataSlate into my backpack Monday morning. "Eye on Tomorrow supplies everything except the brainpower."

"Seriously?" Back home, nobody leaves the house without a DataSlate; how else would you get an alert when a storm's coming? But Dad reminds me.

"You're in Placid Meadows now. You don't need the storm alert." He smiles. "We don't allow DataSlates at camp anyway, until everyone's settled and understands the rules about keeping research confidential."

"Okay." I pull my DataSlate out of my backpack and run my finger around the cool, smooth edge.

"See you this afternoon." Dad goes to his office. A few notes of Mozart drift out before the door slides shut behind him.

I put my DataSlate back in my bag—I'll feel too weird without it—toss the whole thing over my shoulder on the way to the garage, and take off on my bike.

When I get to camp, the wrought-iron gate is wide open, and

Risha's inside, riding her bike around the drop-off driveway with some other kids. There's a boy with a brush cut pacing back and forth on the sidewalk. Maybe he's new, like me. Tess and Ava Beekman, those twins from Britain, are sitting on the grass talking with a couple of boys.

"Hey, Jaden!" Risha waves and almost swerves into a dented green pickup idling by the reception building.

I gasp, first because I think Risha's going to crash, and second, because somebody's driving a gas-powered vehicle. They've been illegal for ten years. How could somebody still be driving one around? Are the rules here that different?

"Easy, genius!" Alex climbs out of the truck, waves to the woman driving, and brushes dried grass from his faded jeans. "Don't run me over on the first day."

Risha doesn't let a second go by. "Where's Tomas?"

"He had to help his mom; I guess she's been feeling pretty crummy. He'll be here later." Alex turns to me and smiles. "You up for this?"

"Of course." But looking up at the tower beyond the reception building, the billowing white dome next to it, the sprawling campus, I wonder if I really am.

Alex turns to say hi to another boy getting dropped off, and Risha and I start toward the reception building. I lean close to her as we walk. "What's up with the truck?"

She makes a scared face. "Oh my gosh, you're not a spy with the International Climate Commission, are you?"

"No, but—"

Risha laughs. "I'm kidding. You didn't really think it was gas-powered, did you? Nobody's that dumb. A bunch of the farmers around here have rigged up old trucks to run on vegetable oil. Kind of messy, but it's cheaper than a new HV." She pulls open the door to the lobby.

"Welcome, welcome." The man waving us inside has a reddish-brown ponytail and a face full of freckles that run together in splotches over his nose. He looks young enough to be a camper, but his badge says VAN GARDNER, EYE ON TOMORROW STAFF.

He steps up to me and smiles. "First summer here?"

I nod.

"I'm Van, camp director." He shakes my hand, then turns to Alex. "Good to have you back, my man." He nods at Risha. "Planning more work in bio-botanicals?"

She shakes her head. "I'd rather be in the cloning lab this summer if I can. Tomas was telling me about it, and it sounds interesting."

While Risha talks with Van, I reach over my shoulder to get my DataSlate from my backpack. I want to see if Mom answered the message I sent after dinner last night. Reception in the jungle's probably too spotty for videophone to work, but she should at least have text messaging.

"They're going to take that," Alex says. "No outside technology in the beginning."

"Really?" I pretend to be surprised.

"Got a drive you can put your stuff on so you don't lose too much when they destroy it?"

· · 36 · ·

"Destroy it?"

Alex raises his eyebrows. "Last kid who brought a DataSlate had to watch while they took it out back and ran over it with the Eye on Tomorrow field trip vehicle. They tried to run him over, too, but he was fast." A smile creeps onto his face.

"Very funny."

"I'm just messing with you. They *will* take it for now, though. You can get it at the end of the day."

Sure enough, Van steps up and holds out his hand. "Sorry, Alex speaks the truth."

I give it to him, and he points us toward the auditorium. "Let's head into orientation and get this show on the road."

I end up sitting between Alex and Risha, but all her attention turns toward Tomas when he arrives. "You're doing cloning again, right? Because that's what I'm requesting."

"So, Jaden," Alex says. "You and I kind of have the same area of interest."

"Yeah, I've always liked weather," is all I can think to say. My fingers are itching for the DataSlate Van took away. Even if I can't connect with Mom, having it makes me feel like she's not so far away.

"All right, campers! Good morning!" Van bounds down the wide steps to the podium at the front of the auditorium. "I'm going to help you get your bearings. These first few days, we'll walk through the facilities and review rules and regulations."

Van presses a button on the podium, and legs grow up from out of the floor in front of us, materializing from the shiny black shoes on up. I know it's only a holo-sim, but it still startles me. Within a few seconds, the figure has a torso, arms, a neck. And finally, a face.

My father's face.

And my father's voice.

"Good morning, Eye on Tomorrow campers."

Dad's American StormSafe employees opened Eye on Tomorrow four years ago, right after he left for Russia, but it doesn't surprise me that it's his face and voice greeting the campers. Even from overseas, Dad would have made sure his vision played out the way he wanted.

"We are so very glad that you're here," the holo-sim says.

It's just a computer-generated projection, but it makes my hands go cold, as if this picture made of light has Dad's real eyes and mind. Does it know I brought my DataSlate even though he said not to? That it was confiscated?

I look up, but the eyes on the holo-sim look like they're focused on something in the back of the auditorium. No one else seems fazed by Dad's appearance. Tomas is watching Risha doodle on her notebook, zeros and ones like those on her bracelets. I watch, too, for a second, until Dad's voice starts up again.

"As you know, Eye on Tomorrow is a special place. Here, you'll be provided with the most exclusive data sets, the most advanced technology, the most elite instructors . . ."

I glance over at Van and catch him mouthing the words that holo-Dad must deliver to every new summer crew.

"Along with that privilege comes responsibility. Here at Eye on Tomorrow, we expect campers to arrive on time each morning. Bring nothing but yourselves for now; we supply everything except the brainpower. And leave with nothing. No equipment, data files, or documents may be taken from the campus at the end of the day, and photography is prohibited, to protect the unique learning environment we've worked so hard to build."

"Now let's all keep an Eye on Tomorrow." The holo-sim winks. "And always do your best, because we'll have our eye on you." Then it vanishes from the top of Dad's head down to the last shiny black toe of his shoe, as if someone took an eraser to the air and rubbed him out, atom by atom.

Van steps forward. "Ready to take a walk?"

Alex taps my shoulder. "So are you requesting meteorology for a focus area? Some people work in teams."

Is he asking if I want to work with him? This is the same kid who didn't like my last name yesterday. "Haven't really thought about it yet."

"Well sure, there's no rush," he says, and looks down at his hands resting on the seat in front of us.

"You coming?" Risha calls from the door, and I realize we're holding up the line.

I leave Alex's not-quite-an-invitation alone for now and hurry to the door. When we step outside, sunlight burns my eyes, and warm, wet outdoor air wraps around me. Risha and Tomas have gone ahead, so I walk with Alex.

"This way." Van points us toward the next building over, the one with the white dome, a giant golf ball perched on top of a short, thick column of glass. "Might as well start with the best we have to offer."

The best the camp has to offer? I look over, and Alex answers the question before I even ask it out loud.

"Storm Sim Dome."

"What's in there?"

"Computers," he says as we step up to the huge building, waiting for Van to scan his fingerprint and open the door. "Turbo-fans. Storm simulators. Storm pool and plumbing."

I stare up at the dome, processing what he's just said. "Are you telling me there's real wind and rain and everything in there?" It's shiny, almost too big and bright to look at up close.

Van holds the door open. "File in." The air inside is cold and clean, and the main chamber of the dome is cavernous. It reminds me of the story Aunt Linda told me once about her family's trip to that old amusement park, Epcot Center, when she was little. It's gone now, wiped out years ago in one of the first inland hurricanes like the rest of Disney's Florida empire, but Aunt Linda said it was magical, like being inside a giant globe, the heart of the whole world.

My eyes drift down from the dome's ceiling, and I see what looks like the heart of this building—an enclosed safety-glass box housing the mainframe computer system that must control everything.

A model city surrounds the console. It looks like Oklahoma City used to look forty years ago, full of offices and shopping areas, parks and schools, homes, and barns on the outskirts, all built to scale. About half the city is in perfect condition; the rest of the buildings are as battered as the ones *outside* Placid Meadows are now.

The cement floor is still damp. Van gestures down at it. "Watch the puddles; we had a test run earlier."

I look around, wondering how it all works. The precipitation must come from the water heads mounted on the ceiling and the hoses that snake out from the walls every few meters. It even smells like a storm in here. Does that rain-ruined smell just happen, or is it pumped in with the wind, through the enormous fans that hang from the ceiling and walls?

"Why do they do all this?" I whisper to Alex. "Wouldn't computer simulations be easier?"

"They used to do that, but there were too many variables. Van says you need real buildings, real towns, to see what a real storm can do."

The last few campers file in. It's quiet, but then a motor clicks on, and the fans begin to hum quietly, almost as if they're whispering promises about what they can do.

Tomas is the first to speak up. "You gonna run this thing for us?"

Van shakes his head. "Later in the week, maybe. It doesn't mean much if you don't understand what you're seeing, but this is where our meteorology program is based. It's all exclusive, patented technology—one of a kind. Well, three of a kind, actually. There's one up at the StormSafe complex and one at the company's property in Russia. Just wanted you to have a look at it for today."

He walks us out of the dome, back into the bright light and sunshine air.

The rest of the morning is a parade of in and outs, more rooms filled with elaborate equipment. This is what I imagined Dad's

StormSafe headquarters might look like. If they provide this stuff at a camp for teenagers, what must he have at work?

After lunch, we're back in the orientation center to talk about areas of study.

This time, there's no holo-sim of Dad. Instead, a three-dimensional globe of light drops from the ceiling as classical music starts to play.

Alex leans over. "Mozart," he whispers. "They did some study that shows classical music helps to develop synapses between the hemispheres of the brain and makes us better problem solvers."

It's also Dad's favorite, but I don't mention that. Alex probably wouldn't like Mozart anymore.

Dad's voice rises over the violins. "Welcome back, Eye on Tomorrow campers. This afternoon, we'll take a look at the problems our world is facing today . . . and tomorrow. And we'll ask you to make a commitment to one of those challenges for the summer."

The globe at the center of the room spins and then explodes into a million bits of light that shoot out toward the walls, and in its place now is a spinning cloud. It's just light, just a holo-image, but somehow the air feels wetter, heavier than it did a few seconds ago. Dad's voice describes the first challenge, the one we all know about already—the storms.

"Warmer global temperatures have led to increased instances of tornadic storms, not only in the traditional storm belt, but worldwide. Through the careful planning and vigilance of the

International Climate Committee, we've managed to reverse the planetary warming trend. However, as you know, campers, it will be two more years before greenhouse gases are reduced to a level that will have a positive impact on weather patterns. Our goal at StormSafe and here at Eye on Tomorrow is to bridge the gap—to find solutions that will keep people safe until then."

It's not only the tornadoes, Dad says, but also hurricanes of greater intensity and size, tropical cyclones around the globe, droughts and heat waves, that need to be controlled. "When we master our climate," Dad's voice promises, "we'll be the masters of our planet."

He goes on to describe three more challenges: the bio-botanicals program that he promises will revolutionize the world's food supply and end hunger through an expansion of DNA-ture bioengineering and factory-grown food practices; the robotics research that will automate the world's industries and services, from motorcycles to medicine, within thirty years; and the cellular generation and human cloning center, where scholars have already begun developing successful technology to create, through DNA-based cloning, any part of the human body for transplant or other use.

When the human figure representing the last area of study fades and sinks into the floor, the lights come on and Van is back in front of us, bouncing on his sneakers. "Ready to solve the world's problems? We'll see you back here, first thing in the morning, to get started."

Chapter 6

The rest of the week flies past in a blur of computer screens, robotics, radar and satellite panels, stainless steel counters, test tubes, and greenhouses with more monitoring equipment than I could have imagined. Each day, Van leads us through a different research center on campus. Sometimes we do lab experiments and try out equipment. Van asks us questions along the way to see who might be best suited to each area of study.

I figured kids who have spent two and three summers here would be way ahead of me, but I can actually answer most of Van's questions. Especially when it comes to meteorology.

"You're doing great," Risha whispers to me as we walk between buildings.

"Thanks. I'm surprised I'm not further behind everybody who's been here before."

"You're not behind at all," Risha says, pulling open the door to the bio-botanicals building. "The program this year is way more intense than what we did last summer."

Even so, Risha knows the answer to almost every question in the bio-botanicals lab, where she spent last summer.

"Are you sure you want to switch to cloning?" I whisper.

She glances sideways at Tomas, smiles and shrugs at me, and answers another question. Her bracelets clink together whenever she raises her hand, and finally, when Van turns to explain some new kind of lower-carb sweet corn, I reach for her wrist. "What are the numbers supposed to be?"

She slips a bracelet off her hand and passes it to me. "It's binary code, the sequence of ones and zeros they used to represent processing instructions for a computer."

I run my finger along waves of numbers etched in the gold. "So what will this tell a computer to do?"

"Nothing." She wiggles the other two off her wrist. "This is just regular text." She points to the first line of numbers on one bracelet. "See this sequence?"

I read it aloud. "01011001."

"That's *y*."

"That's all one letter?"

"And then here . . ." She points to the second set of eight numbers, 01101111. ". . . is an *o*. It spells out, 'You must be the change you wish to see in the world.' It's a saying from some old Indian guy, Gandhi. My grandmother's always quoting him and trying to get me to read about him." She waves at the air with her green-and-black-striped fingernails. "She figured if she translated it into in a language I like, I might actually pay attention, so she had these made for me."

"Your grandmother sounds awesome." I try to imagine what Grandma Athena would be like if she were alive. What would she talk to me about? Risha slides the bracelets back onto her wrist as Van leads us down a hall toward the next lab.

"Is the code on your notebook a quote from the same guy?" I ask Risha.

"No . . ." She pulls me off to the side, tips her head toward Tomas, and whispers, "It's his name. In binary code."

That makes me laugh. I should have guessed. "Now I understand why you like it, even if it isn't really used anymore."

She shrugs. "Not everything has to be useful."

I think about the book of poems in my nightstand. "Don't let my dad hear you say that. You'll be tossed out of this place faster than you can blink."

She laughs and pulls me along to catch up with the boys.

On our second visit to the Storm Sim Dome, Van skips the quiz and sits us down on a row of long benches along one wall. "Instead of asking you questions here to check on your knowledge, we're going to try something else."

He pulls a box of DataSlates from under the bench and starts passing them out. "These are preloaded with the same software we have on the core system in the dome. You've all been asking me when you'll get to see the Sim Dome in action, and the answer is now. Show me what you'd do if I turned this entire dome over to you for one simulation." He hands the last DataSlate to Tomas.

"What are we doing with these?" Risha asks.

"You're formulating a theory about the effect that a given variable has on storm formation. Then I'd like you to design a simulation to test it."

Tess Beekman squints at him. "I don't get it."

Van sighs. "There's a simulation program loaded on each of these DataSlates. It will ask you for a theory. You need an if-then statement. For example, if you think that raising the temperature in the atmosphere will cause a storm to move more quickly, you select that theory. *If* the temperature is raised x degrees, *then* this will happen. Then you design a simulation. Don't worry—the software will walk you through the steps. Essentially, you'll be telling the Sim Dome what conditions to create in the atmosphere above our model town, and then you'll see what effect that has on the storms." He looks around. "At least some of you will. We're only going to run the most promising simulations in the dome." He looks back at Tess. "Understand now?"

She shrugs. "Kind of."

"Okay then. Get to it." He looks at his watch. "You have one hour." He heads for the staff computer in the corner of the room.

The DataSlate suddenly feels heavy in my hands. This isn't a quick question I can raise my hand to answer or a click-the-right-response exam. It's an actual problem with no solution in sight, and I'm supposed to come up with one.

Risha sits next to me on the bench, her fingers already flying over her DataSlate, words pouring onto her screen. I look down the row of DataSlates in laps. Everyone else is inputting text.

My heart feels like it's thumping out that frantic stream of numbers from Risha's bracelets, but I open the Sim Dome software and stare at the blank text box with "Theory" written at the top.

The only sound is the hum of fans and the tapping of fingers, reminding me that Eye on Tomorrow is in a different league. This is a place for people with theories.

I stare at the empty box and panic. I may have a head full of ideas, but none of them are my own. My parents are the scientists; I'm the kid who loves to read, who can always get a hundred on the test when the answers are supplied ahead of time. But here, we are starting from nothing.

I look down the row. The anxious boy with the brush cut types a few words. Looks at his watch. Types a few more. Rubs his finger under his lower lip. Looks at his watch again. Just being near him makes me nervous.

There must be something. Some theory I can test.

If. Then.

If. Then.

If something, then . . . what?

I close my eyes and imagine the storm from my first night here. The one that never touched Placid Meadows.

If a housing contract promises storm-free living, then the tornadoes stay away.

If a company builds a magic fence around a neighborhood, then the residents live happily ever after.

None of it makes sense. What's keeping the storms at bay? Where do they go when they turn away from the fence?

If. Then.

Where could the storms go that wouldn't hurt anyone?

Not away. But up.

Back into the sky.

If. Then.

What makes a tornado go away?

I close my eyes. The DataSlate is still cool in my hands, but the rest of me breathes in the memory of hot, humid air. An August night, five, maybe six years ago, watching a storm in the distance with Dad. It loomed, big and dark, over the Adirondacks, heading east across the lake to Vermont. We creaked back and forth on the porch swing as the thunder grew louder.

We watched that storm swell bigger, watched it uncurl a long, dark arm that wrapped around the sky and started spinning. It dropped down from the cloud, then stretched into a longer, skinnier funnel as if some potter's hands were shaping it, all the while spinning the wheel faster and faster.

"Dad, should we go downstairs?" I felt like we should. The storm was getting closer, and tree branches were starting to scratch against the porch roof in the wind.

"Soon." Dad stared at the storm, mesmerized. Then he squinted off to the west. "Or maybe not."

Another cloud was approaching, a big brother to the first, taller, with broader shoulders. When they met, it was like the younger brother flinched. The tornado lifted up from the ground and never caught its breath again. We watched, creaking back and forth as it rose slowly back up into the cloud.

Then we sat and listened to the rain.

Later, when Dad tucked me into bed, I asked where the tornado had gone. Most fathers would have made up a story for a kid my age, maybe something about God pulling on the rope, tugging it back to the heavens, away from us. A cozy-under-the-sheets, sleep-tight story. Mine gave a meteorology lesson.

"Sometimes, Jaden, a cold outflow of wind from a storm system can cause a tornado to dissipate."

"You mean go away?"

"Yes. And in this case, it was that second thunderstorm that came and wrapped up the first one in its outflow." He tucked the cool sheets around me. "Bet you can't spin around now either."

I wiggled, and giggled, and Dad kissed me on the head. "Night, WeatherGirl."

"Twenty-five minutes left." Van's voice snaps me back to now. I open my eyes and stare at the blank box on my screen.

I have an idea. It's an old one from a hot summer night that feels like a lifetime ago, but it's all I have, so I start typing.

IF a tornado-producing storm collides with a second, larger storm . . .

That's a good start. There will be data from different-size storms loaded in the simulator. I can choose two that should work.

THEN . . . Then what?

I fly through the procedural steps, and I'm thinking how to state the outcome when Van calls time, so I simply type:

PROJECTED OUTCOME: Tornado dies.

—just as he steps down the row, takes the DataSlate from my hands, and adds it to the stack teetering in his arms.

"Well, now," he says, lining them up on the counter outside the safety box that encloses the real control panel. "This is an interesting collection of theories." He picks up the first few and sets them back down without saying anything. "I can see we'll need to work on experiment design. Some of these aren't even in a format that could be entered into our dome software."

He moves on to the next DataSlate, which he reads and tucks under his arm, nodding. He goes through the rest of the slates and picks up the last one, too.

He holds those up and turns to us. "We have two theories that are developed enough—not perfect, mind you—but developed *enough* to run on the simulator. Mr. Carillo?"

Alex stands up.

"Come on into the control chamber with me. Miss Meggs? You, too. The rest of you head over to the observation area behind the glass. We'll explain each simulation on the microphone so you know what you're seeing. Let's find out if either theory holds up in the Dome."

Chapter 7

"Can everyone hear me?" Van's voice booms out of the speakers, and on the other side of the room, behind the safety glass, the rest of the campers nod. He turns back to Alex and me. "Who's first?"

I look at Alex. Is his stomach churning like mine?

"I'll go first," he says. Van stands up, and Alex slides into the chair in front of the control panels. "Do you want me to explain what I wrote?"

"Of course." Van adjusts the microphone.

"My theory involves storm dissipation," Alex says. His voice echoes through the dome.

Van leans in toward the microphone, glancing back at me. "Actually, both theories do. That's why this is a particularly interesting pairing."

"Okay." Alex takes a breath. "Current theory holds that tornadoes form when the hot updraft within a supercell meets a cold rainy downdraft. So here's my idea." Alex reads from his DataSlate. His fingers have dirt and grass stains as if he came right from working on the farm this morning, but his hands aren't shaking like mine.

"*If* the cold downdraft of a tornado-forming supercell is heated with microwave energy from an orbiting satellite, *then* an essential ingredient for tornado formation will be absent, and the storm will dissipate."

He looks at Van, who nods. "Similar to the research you were doing last summer, no?"

"It is, but I've been tweaking it," Alex says. "Should I just . . . run it now?"

"Go for it. The Dome has simulated satellites built into the ceiling. Adjust the level for how much energy they'll be giving off. Choose one of the preloaded historical tornado models—any one of those should work—give it a few seconds to form, and then run your simulation. We'll see if it dissipates." He almost sounds bored, but my heart is pumping, and it's not even my turn yet.

Some of the confidence has drained out of Alex's face, but his hands are steady as he connects his DataSlate to the main system, transfers his data, and presses the button to start the Sim Dome recreation.

The lights go down, and immediately, water vapor hisses out of ducts in the ceiling and on the upper walls. Like magic, clouds form over the model city. The synthetic fabric that makes up the tree foliage rustles and then whips in the wind generated by the fans that surround the community on all sides. When the cloud darkens and gives birth to the beginning of a swirling, charcoal-colored funnel, Van nudges Alex. "Go ahead."

Alex's finger hovers over the INTRODUCE VARIABLE button. He takes a breath and then taps it lightly.

A panel slides open on the ceiling, exposing a model satellite that lowers slowly, a foot or so. Under the clouds, the tornado stretches lower, lower, until it touches down inches from the first building—a small red barn next to a white farmhouse outside the city.

A sharp ray of light streaks down from the satellite. I can't look away from the light, the storm, the clouds, the funnel, to see how Alex is reacting, but I feel his body tensing next to me. Will this blast of energy warm the tornado away?

The tornado licks at the edges of the barn. "Come on," Alex whispers, and I tear my eyes from the storm to look at his face.

His eyes travel down the beam from the satellite, as if he could strengthen it by pure will, all the way to the heart of the cloud, where that blast of energy *should* be warming the downdraft, *should* be stopping the storm's rotation.

"Come on, come on!"

The storm explodes then, with a sharp burst of lightning, and even Van jumps in surprise. Blinding light fills the dome and seems to feed the tornado. It swells up bigger, darker. It devours the barn, the house, and then races from the farm to the first simulated neighborhood. Houses. A school. In pieces. A church steeple flies off into the vortex. The rest of the building follows. A playground. Slides. Swings. A tumbling jumble of monkey bars all sucked into the storm.

Alex's fist pounds down on the counter, and Van reaches forward to press a red button on the control panel.

The lights flicker, then come on overhead.

The rain stops pounding. Leftover drips from the ceiling plunk down onto the rubble as the clouds are sucked into the ventilation system in the walls.

When they clear, I stare out at half a town, perfect and painted with trees still standing, plastic people still posed on porches.

The other half is flattened.

Alex's jaw is tense, his fist still clenched on the counter where it landed.

"That's why we have the Sim Dome, my friend." Van puts a hand on Alex's shoulder. "Sometimes, things work on paper; they work fine in your mind, but the real deal turns out very different. That's why we don't do this all digitally anymore. Until you're dealing with real wind, meeting real buildings, you don't know what'll happen." He turns to me. "You're next, Miss Meggs. Let's see what you do with the half a city that survived your colleague's experiment."

Alex stands and steps back so I can sit down, and I feel his eyes on me as I'm opening my file. I glance over my shoulder, expecting . . . I don't know. Maybe that he'll want me to fail, too, not to show him up. But even though his eyes are still intense, frustrated, he gives me the smallest nod. Encouragement?

I make the connection and feed my data to the mainframe computer.

"Which storm's going to be your subject?" Van leans over my shoulder and taps the screen, and a list of model storms appears. I choose an NF-3 that hit Germany eight years ago. And then I'll need to introduce a larger supercell to serve as the second storm in my experiment. My hands shake so much I can barely control my finger to point to the right model. Some of the shaking is nerves—Van standing over me, Alex's eyes on me, the wall of faces behind the glass, all staring from the other side of the room—but some of it is excitement, too. Could this actually work?

"Go ahead." Van flicks his hand toward the button that will dim the lights and start the clouds building.

I swallow hard and tap the command: BEGIN SIMULATION.

Clouds swirl out of the walls and down from the ceiling, like they did with Alex's storm, and this time, I'm ready when the wind starts to whip the trees and the rain pounds down on the roofs that are left in the model city. I watch the bottom edge of the wall cloud, holding my breath, until the funnel cloud takes shape and touches down.

The ground explodes in a whirl of dust, and Van points to the words INTRODUCE VARIABLE on the screen. "Do it now."

I press the button and hold my breath.

The tornado is already on the ground as the second storm begins to form off to the left. The vapor is still gathering when the first storm hits the model town's business district. It's not as strong as Alex's tornado, so the buildings aren't flattened, but roofs tear away from shops, and debris flies.

"Come on," I whisper, and I hear the echo of Alex's hopes as I watch the new funnel finish forming, watch it darken and advance toward the first. "Come on. Go. *Go.*"

The first tornado strengthens. It tosses cars that were parked on Main Street, hurls them through store windows, and the sound of shattering sim-glass—how do they make it so loud?—crashes over the wind.

My second storm closes in on the first. "Come on," I whisper. "Knock it down. Do it."

And I hear Alex's voice, quiet behind me. "Come on, work."

For a second, the tornado stops in its path, churning up dirt, frozen in time as the two storms finally touch.

Then it goes wild.

The big brother cloud, the one that was supposed to wrap around the first storm and settle it down, does something else. It opens up its arms, sucks the first storm inside, and squeezes, until the whole thing turns into a darker, angrier, super-charged monster.

"No!" I scream. I can't help it. Because a second tornado drops down from the cloud like an angry whip. And a third. Both stronger than the first. They barrel down streets, through downtown, and the office buildings implode and feed the storm until the whole city is gone.

Van's arm blurs in front of me and presses the button to shut down the dome. Only then do I feel my face is wet with tears. I swipe at them with my sleeve.

Van smirks. "Well, scholars. We have some rebuilding to do, don't we?"

I feel a hand on my shoulder. Alex.

I brush it away, stand up, and head for the door, but Van puts up a hand to stop me. "Those were good efforts from both of you. But you've got a long road of research ahead before you can produce something that works in this world as well as that one." He nods down at the DataSlate in my hand. I'd forgotten it wasn't mine.

Mine's at home in the drawer with my poetry book. I haven't brought it back since that first day.

I set the DataSlate on the counter, but Van shakes his head. "Keep that one over the weekend. Play with some new ideas. Bring it back on Monday. I'm going to recommend you two for the meteorology team." He opens the door, and we head out into the humid air of the Dome to meet up with the others, filing out of the observation room.

"All right, campers, let's call it a day. I've seen what I need to see. On Monday, I'd like you to tell me what you'd like to study and whether you'll work alone or with a partner."

We leave the Dome and start back toward the welcome building, but there's none of the usual in-between-buildings banter. I get the feeling that even the campers who were around last summer have never seen anything in the Sim Dome quite like this.

"Whatcha doing for lunch?" Risha finally asks when we get back to our bikes.

I shrug. "I'm not too hungry. That was just so . . . intense."

"I think we need a picnic!" Risha stands up on the pedals of her bike and pulls the front wheel off the ground to spin around.

It's such a crazy idea, I laugh, which I'm sure was her whole goal. Picnics are like bike riding back home. But it figures there'd be a StormSafe picnic shelter, too. "Where do you have picnics?"

"I know a place," she says, "but I'll have to blindfold you to take you there; it's top-secret-super-classified."

I laugh again, and my stomach grumbles.

"You guys have to come, too, okay?" She makes her top-secret-super-classified picnic eyes at Alex and Tomas.

"I guess." Tomas gives her the lazy smile. "As long as Alex and geek girl put their killer DataSlates away."

Risha laughs, but Alex doesn't. "I'll come," he says, and puts the DataSlate into his backpack.

I reach over my shoulder to unzip mine, and a warm hand catches my fingers.

"Got it." Alex lets go of my hand and unzips the bag so I can slip the DataSlate inside. He gives the strap a light tug, and I turn around. "Sounds like we're going to be in the met program together." He takes a deep breath. "Maybe we can talk about being partners?"

I can't help smiling a little. I wasn't crazy that day in the auditorium. It was an invitation after all.

I nod and get on my bike. "Sure. We can talk."

Chapter 8

"Your top-secret picnic location looks kind of familiar, Rish." Tomas weaves through trees to the fence, holding a cooler full of food from Risha's house out in front of him.

I scan the horizon for clouds, but the sky's all blue. My DataSlate in my backpack is quiet—no weather alerts for now—and the afternoon sun feels good after a morning of air-conditioned camp.

We climb through the gap in the fence, balance beam our way across a fallen tree stretching over the river, and follow Risha, who's run ahead through the trees, bracelets clinking on her wrist.

"Here we go." Tomas steps into a field with neatly planted rows of grain, and we head for the gazebo on the other side. Its white paint is peeling, but Risha flies up the steps and perches herself on the fence as if it's her fairy-tale castle, and she's been waiting all day for the prince to get home.

"It's beautiful." It's like I've fallen into one of the olden-days books Mom used to read to me.

"Yeah," Tomas says. He looks a little sad.

"How long have you lived around here?"

"Since I was born. It's getting hard to take care of the farm, though, with my brother gone. My dad's not sure . . ."

"You can't sell, man," Alex says. "No way."

"Yeah, I know. Dad's all talk. I don't think he'll ever leave this place." He lifts the cooler onto the picnic table.

"Jaden, sit by me!" Risha pats a spot next to her on the splintery bench.

I sit down and get a sandwich from the cooler. I'm starving, and for the first time since we left Eye on Tomorrow, I feel relaxed enough to talk about the Sim Dome. "Sure is nice to see blue sky after this morning."

"I know!" Risha takes a big bite of her sandwich and goes on talking through the lettuce. "That sim was crazy-real."

Alex sits down across from me. "Have you ever . . ." He pauses. "Never mind."

I take a bite of my DNA-ture apple and look up at Alex. "Have I ever what?"

"Well . . . have you seen the equipment your dad has at work? I mean, you probably can't talk about it if it's classified and stuff, but I wonder if it's the same."

I shake my head. "Never even been there."

"It feels like . . ." Alex unwraps his sandwich but doesn't eat. He turns it over and over in his hands, as if the bread and turkey and cheese layers hold the answer to some puzzle. "We have so much equipment at Eye on Tomorrow—and I'm sure your dad has even better stuff up there." He nods toward the StormSafe compound in the distance. The sun is reflecting off its steel and safety-glass walls, making it glow. "It feels like we should be able to figure this out."

I nod and look to the west, where the sky's clouding up. I know exactly what he means. How could we know everything we know, have everything we have, and not be able to live in a world where you can go for a walk without watching the clouds?

"I'm going to pick flowers." Risha tips her head off toward the meadow. Before she goes, she bends down by the picnic table and plucks a dandelion that's gone to seed. "Make a wish!" She blows on it, and silver stars swirl all around our heads as she runs off. Tomas picks up the bag of *nankhatai*, the Indian tea cookies Risha's grandmother made, and follows her.

Alex looks toward the clouds on the horizon. "They better not go far. This isn't Placid Meadows."

His voice has an edge.

"What's wrong with Placid Meadows?"

He shakes his head. "Nothing. I'd imagine it's great if you can afford to live there. But you must know what those places cost."

I shrug, rather than admit that I don't. I wonder if our picnic spot is part of the land Dad's trying to buy for his Phase Two.

There's a rustling in the weeds then, and a golden retriever bounds out of the brush and up the steps to our table. It puts a paw up on Alex's lap and tips its head.

"Hey, Newton." Alex scratches the dog behind an ear, then carefully untangles a burr stuck in its long reddish fur.

"Sorry," he says, looking up. "I didn't mean to make you feel crummy. It's just hard to take sometimes. But what Risha said before is right. If it weren't for your dad, I'd be right here—and only here—this summer, pulling weeds and picking worms off tomato plants and running for the storm shelter every other day instead of spending half of it in a huge science complex."

We sit for a long time, watching the clouds. Alex feeds Newton scraps of turkey from his sandwich, and I listen to Risha laughing with Tomas.

When Alex finally speaks, it's so quiet I barely hear him. "I'm frustrated, I guess. I thought I'd figured out how to stop them all together."

"The storms?"

He nods and starts picking at the weathered wood of the picnic table.

"I'm starting to think it's impossible. My dad's been working on this forever. He's got some exclusive agreement with the government for his weather manipulation research. Anyway, Mom told me they were sure they had the formulas this winter, but when they did the simulation, it failed."

"Did you see the formulas?" He leans forward.

"No. I probably wouldn't have understood them anyway. This stuff is out of our league."

"No, it's not. Last summer at Eye on Tomorrow, I had a formula drawn up, based on the same theory, and it *worked*. At least on paper."

"Did you run it through the Sim Dome?"

He sighs. "That didn't work, and I don't know why. It should have." He jerks his hand back from the table. "Ow! Splinter."

He pulls it out, and blood seeps out from under his thumbnail. He stands and shoves his hand into his pocket. "Look, I just . . . I feel like I'm out of ideas. That's why I was kind of hoping we could work together." He doesn't look at me and doesn't wait for an answer. He starts gathering sandwich wrappers and picks up the rest of my apple. "Are you going to finish this?"

I shake my head. He looks down at the DNA-ture sticker and grimaces. "Is this stuff all you ever eat?"

"It's not bad. I'm not in the mood for fruit right now."

"Oh no?" His dark eyes smile a little. "Come with me." He takes off across the field with Newton at his side.

I look over my shoulder for Risha, who's plopped down in the weeds, showing Tomas how to weave daisies together into a chain. Behind them, the clouds are growing, but they're still a long way off.

There's time before our weather alerts go off, so I catch up with Alex as he reaches the barn. It smells like old paint and hay. A twisted copper weathervane with a rooster on top leans against the side.

"That's an old one, huh?" I run my finger along the W for West.

"It was already here when my grandpa bought this place way back," Alex says. He looks up at the barn's sloped roof. "Came flying off in the wind Friday night."

"That storm we saw coming from the fence?"

He nods. "Just missed us. We were lucky. Tomas says their

neighbors two places down lost their barn and almost their whole herd of Scottish Highland cattle."

"That you, Alex?" a deep voice calls from the barn, and a man in a faded blue shirt steps out, brushing dust off his hands. His face looks like he's spent a lot of time working in the sun, and he has warm brown eyes surrounded by the kind of wrinkles you get from laughing. "You take care of the chickens yet?" he asks Alex. Then he sees me.

"Dad, this is my friend Jaden I told you about. From camp."

His father nods at me and reaches out to shake my hand. His is warm and rough with calluses. "Very nice to meet you," he says. But he doesn't smile. He looks back at Alex and raises his eyebrows. "Don't forget we have a farm to run." And heads back into the barn.

"Sorry," Alex says, turning to me. "He's . . . not thrilled with us being friends."

"Oh."

Goats or sheep bleat from inside the barn, and there's the sound of feed pouring into a trough. Alex looks at the barn door as if he can see through it. "He's really not cold like that. He's just—I made the mistake of telling him who your dad is, so . . ."

"So he figures I'm here to make another offer on your farm?" My face flushes hot, and I turn away from the barn. "I . . . I should be getting home anyway. It's—"

"Jaden, wait." He puts a hand on my shoulder. It's tentative, barely there, but it keeps me from walking away. "I want to show you something." He steps onto a low stone wall that runs along the barn. "Follow me."

I hesitate.

"Please?"

I climb up and follow him to a patch of garden on the south side of the barn. Mounds of green grow out of straw-covered soil, and ripening red spots peek out from each plant.

"You *grow* strawberries?" I've never seen strawberries growing outside, as far as I can remember. They were one of the first DNAture products. Dad used to bring home cartons full of fat, smooth, seedless berries. "These are so much smaller than real ones."

Alex laughs. "These *are* real ones." He squats down, gently brushes aside some leaves with one hand, reaches deep into the heart of the plant with the other, and pulls out a perfect red berry.

No. It's not perfect.

The berry is asymmetrical. One ripe, red side bulges higher than the other, and raggedy green leaves stick out the top in every direction, like some crazy puppet hat. The dimple at the base of the fruit looks a little like the one on Alex's chin.

He holds it up. "*This* is a *real* strawberry. Look."

"It looks great," I say.

"No. *Really* look." He rests one hand on my shoulder and with the other, holds the strawberry out about a foot in front of my face. "Tell me what you see." I try to ignore the warmth spreading down my arm and look, really look.

"It's red." But even as I say it, I know it's more than that. It's not red like the strawberries in Mirielle's refrigerator at the house. Not the perfect, crayon-box red, the same on every side. This one is a million shades of red, from the deep rich color of new blood to the blush that must be creeping up my cheeks. "It's a lot of different promises of red."

"What else?" He turns the strawberry slowly, but doesn't move his hand from my shoulder.

"The seeds are different colors, too." I can't compare them to the seeds on DNA-ture strawberries because they've been engineered out—people who took the "build-a-better-fruit" surveys complained they got stuck in their teeth—so they're gone now. The skin is perfectly soft and smooth. But this strawberry has tiny hairs that catch the sun and raindrop-shaped seeds spilling down the sides, around all of its uneven curves. "Gold and pink and brownish."

"Now." Alex smiles a little. "Close your eyes."

I look at him.

"Don't worry." He laughs a little and takes his hand off my shoulder. "I want you to taste this. *Really* taste it."

I close my eyes. I can still feel the warmth of his hand on my shoulder, or maybe it's the sun getting warmer.

"Ready? Open your mouth."

I do.

The soft-rough seeds brush my lips first. Then that same surface—alive, I think—settles on my tongue, along with the warmth. It feels like this berry still holds the heat of the sun inside it.

I am almost afraid to bite down, but Alex's hand rests on my shoulder again, and I am painfully self-conscious of what I must look like standing here with my mouth around a strawberry, so I take a bite.

And I taste the sun.

All of the warmth, the sweetness, this imperfect outdoor berry has collected explodes in my mouth. And eyes still closed, suddenly, I am three years old, sitting cross-legged in a garden or field—I don't know where exactly—but I am picking berries with Aunt Linda. Dropping them into a big wicker basket in the dirt between us, and my hands are stained red, and my chin is sticky with sweet red juice, and Aunt Linda is laughing in the sun.

I had forgotten what strawberries felt like until now.

I open my eyes. Alex has dropped his hand from my shoulder again, and the one that held the strawberry hangs at his side, still pinching a clump of leaves and a bit of berry with my teeth marks.

"Now are you in mood for fruit?" he asks.

I would answer, but I'm afraid it would come out a million kinds of stupid. So I nod, and bend down to pick another berry. It's rough and imperfect, and perfectly warm, in my hand.

Chapter 9

You *have* to partner with him at camp. You guys look so cute together!" Risha's cheeks are flushed as we hurry back to the fence, and I'm not sure if it's because we're rushing now that the clouds are rumbling closer or because she was having her own picnic moment with Tomas and the daisy chain.

"Aw, cut it out." I climb through the gap in the silver wires. "He did ask if I wanted to work together, though. And we're interested in the same theories of weather manipulation, so maybe . . ."

Risha strikes a professor pose, with serious eyes and hands pressed together. "We're interested in the same theories," she mimics, and laughs. "I think you're interested in more than his theories, Jaden."

When we reach the end of the dirt path, she looks up and down the street, hands on her hips. "What do you want to do? They're running Animals of Yesterday at the Entertainment Dome. You get to walk along a trail with a bunch of extinct wildlife—woolly mammoths and polar bears and stuff."

"No, I think I want to go home." I wonder how Mom's doing in

Costa Rica. I hope her endangered frogs don't become part of the Animals of Yesterday show anytime soon. I wish she'd get in touch.

Our DataSlate weather alerts go off, and I jump about a mile. Risha laughs.

The storm is close enough now that people outside Placid Meadows will be heading for safe rooms. Even here, the high-pitched alert makes me want to walk faster, but Risha veers off toward the park. "Relax, we're inside now. Let's hang at the playground a while."

I follow her toward the slide. "Has it been like this since you moved in?"

"Like what?" She climbs the ladder and slides down.

I wait at the bottom. "Like this . . . where you just *know* the tornadoes won't touch down here?"

Risha dusts off her shorts and heads for the monkey bars. "Yeah, I told you, it was in the contracts."

"But how can they promise that? Did the contract say *how* they do it?"

"Nope." She shrugs. "Most people moved here from places where it's gotten so bad that no one cares *why* they're safe. I mean, people ask, sure, but your dad obviously can't be giving away all his company's secrets, and really everybody's just happy to be able to go outside again, you know?" Two little kids are on the swings, daring each other to go higher, while their moms sit on a bench by the carousel talking.

"But my dad's storm dissipation project failed—that's what

Mom said. It can't be that technology. And if it's not that, then what is it? Some kind of force field around the neighborhood?" I climb up to the top of the jungle gym and sit down on one of the crossbars, dangling my feet down through the middle.

"I guess." Risha scampers up after me and hangs upside down from her knees a few bars over. "Does it matter what it is, as long as it works?" Thunder rumbles in the distance, and tree branches rustle as the wind picks up. The moms on the bench don't even miss a beat in their conversation.

"S'cuse me, lady!" One of the kids from the swing set climbs up the other side of the jungle gym and runs into our Jaden-and-Risha roadblock here at the top.

"Sorry." I lower myself to the ground, and Risha climbs down the other side.

"Let's go swing!" She takes off and is swinging six feet off the ground by the time I even get started, but pretty soon I'm flying beside her. I can't remember the last time I was on a swing outside. Our underground play centers at home have great swing sets—huge ones—but the air on your face is still indoor air. Stale and safe. Here, it's real wind, carrying the smell of the storm.

"You know," Risha says, her hair flying around her face, "if you swing back and forth a hundred times with your eyes closed and then open them at the very top, then the first boy you see from up there will be the one you marry. Think I can see Tomas from up here?"

"Doubt it." I swing forward, so high that the chain goes slack and for a second I feel like I'm hanging there, attached to nothing. Then the chain catches, and I swing back with Risha at my side. "Besides, they must be in a safe room by now. That storm's growing. Hey, how's his mom?"

Risha stops pumping her legs and just swings. "She needs to get into a treatment center, but Tomas says there's a waiting list for most of the good ones. We didn't talk about it much—and don't you dare tell Alex because he doesn't know this yet, but Tomas said they might even move."

"*Move*? What about the farm?"

Risha smiles a sad smile. "Well, they know they won't have trouble selling it." She waves her hand through the air as if that idea is a bug she can swat away. "But they've talked about other things, too, like his mom staying with his brother in New York if she can get into that clinic. I'm sure it'll be okay."

"Mama, look! Look! It's almost to the fence. Let's do the rhyme!" The two kids from the jungle gym run toward the bench, pointing to the cloud. I stop swinging and listen.

Twister, twister, go away,
Don't you bother us today.
Take your rain and winds that blow,
Turn around now, I say, GO!

They point and giggle, and make shooing motions with their hands.

I stare at them, these kids who have no memories of a place

where storms come into the neighborhood. Here, it is nothing but a game. It's like that "Ring Around the Rosy" chant Mom told me about. The rhyme was all about symptoms of the plague—rosy cheeks, sweet-smelling breath, falling down dead—and kids chanted it, laughing while they jumped rope, without ever realizing where it came from.

I look up at the monster cloud and try to imagine what it would be like never to have been afraid of it. A funnel is creeping down from it, but the storm doesn't seem to be getting any closer. It looks like the system is stalling on the other side of the fence.

Just like Dad's contracts promise.

"Better do it one more time," one of the moms says, smiling.

"I'm standing up on the bench this time," the little girl says, climbing up. "So it'll hear me better."

Twister, twister, go away,
Don't you bother us today.
Take your rain and winds that blow,
Turn around now, I say, GO!

She points fiercely toward the storm cloud, which is indeed moving away from the fence now, still churning, still blowing, but most definitely going.

"Yay!" The little girl jumps down and cheers again. "I made it go away!"

"Good job." Her mother pulls her in and kisses her above her ponytail. "Now get your jacket, and let's go make Daddy some supper."

I scuff my sneakers in the dirt under my swing and watch them leave. The mothers, the kids, the storm. All leaving.

Risha's been swinging this whole time. She jumps off and flies into the brown grass in front of me, tumbling into a somersault and laughing like the kids. "Clearly, I am the champion of the swing set," she says. "How come you stopped?"

I shake my head. "No reason. You ready to head home now?"

She shrugs. "Sure."

We make small talk on the way home, but I can't stop watching the storm as it moves away. It isn't dissipating. If anything, it looks like it's still growing.

And leaving.

As if someone steered it away, with a magic chant.

Or maybe with a bank of computers, in a home office, behind a shiny steel door?

Chapter 10

Jaden, what would you like? More oatmeal?" Mirielle is dancing around the kitchen clearing breakfast dishes and cooing to Remi, cradled in a blue and green scarf this time. She must feel like she's riding around on an ocean wave, the way Mirielle swoops and turns.

Mirielle's DataSlate reader is open next to her empty cup of tea; she must have been reading at breakfast. I'm surprised when I lean over to read the title on the screen: *Quantum Reality: The Physics of Consciousness in a Post-Romantic World*. Mirielle was one of Dad's interns in Russia; she was studying physics when they met, but she's so busy with Remi it didn't occur to me she'd still have time for science.

She sees me looking at the reader. "Would you like me to send you a copy?"

"That's okay." I look at her, spinning away with the orange juice glasses. "I didn't know you were still interested in stuff like this."

"Oh, I am interested in many things. Too busy to read about them all sometimes. Just like I'm too busy to dance anywhere but in my own kitchen these days." She tickles Remi's chin.

"Where did you used to dance?"

"In Paris, of course!" She stops spinning and smiles. "And Moscow after I moved there. I danced professionally for six years. Your father never told you?"

"No. Why'd you stop?"

"Busy with my studies at first, and then as the storms spread, there just weren't opportunities." She looks up at the kitchen lights as if she's remembering brighter lights on a stage. "And of course here in the U.S., there's only the National Ballet performed for cameras. It wouldn't be the same without a real audience." She pushes my bowl of fruit closer. "You can't be full. At least have more fruit."

"I'm fine, thanks." I poke at a strawberry with my fork and puncture two little holes in its perfectness. I can't help but think of Alex and his father, and their farm. "Do you ever get organic fruit?" I ask Mirielle.

"Oh, *mon dieu*, no!" She glances quickly at Dad's office door as if it might slide open and eat us at the very suggestion. "We eat only DNA-ture. Always. The deliveries are so convenient; I never have to go out to the market," she says as if she's in a DNA-ture advertisement. She looks at the door again, then leans in closer to me. "But your aunt Linda?" She lowers her voice. "She grows berries the old way, and vegetables, too. She gave me some raspberries when she dropped off your book. They were a bit overripe, some of them, but oh, they were so sweet!"

That makes me smile. And it makes me like Aunt Linda even more. "Can we go see her soon?"

Mirielle nods. "I think we can figure something out. Maybe later this—"

She stops at the sound of Dad's office door humming open. He's just inside the room, holding something small and round—is it a compass?—in one hand and his DataSlate in the other. He's on a video call. "No, Mom. I'm certainly not going to—" He sees us standing there and turns away, lowering his voice. All I hear after that is the word "later."

Did I hear right? He almost always called Mom by her first name, Rebekah, but sometimes he'd call her Mom if I was around. Was that Mom on the phone in Costa Rica? And if it was, why didn't he let me talk?

He steps out and presses his thumb to the fridge panel.

"Who was that?" I blurt out.

"What?" He squints at me.

"On the phone? Was that Mom in Costa Rica?"

"Oh, no. No. It was . . ." He looks at Mirielle. "Your mother. She wants you to call her later." She nods, and Dad reaches for the Bio-Wake Cola the refrigerator sent out. He's still holding the compass thing. It's made of wood and looks old.

"What's that?" I ask.

"This?" He looks down as if he'd forgotten it was in his hand. "It's an antique barometer I keep in the office. I use it as a paperweight, picked it up while I was talking, I guess." He slips it into his pocket. "Listen, I need to head into work. I've called a meeting for noon at headquarters. We have to reevaluate the perimeter because some debris blew up against the fence. There was never any danger, but we had a few complaints."

"Was that the storm from dinnertime last night?" I take my fruit salad to the counter. "I . . . saw it turn away from Placid Meadows," I say quietly.

"Of course it turned away, and in plenty of time, too. Nothing's hit since the fence went up, and if that's not—"

"How does it work?" I'd stayed up until midnight waiting for him to come out of his office so I could ask about the storms, where they went, and what made them go. But he must have worked all night.

He takes a gulp of soda, then holds in a belch. "What do you mean? You know about my research."

"But Mom told me your project didn't work. And that was about dissipating tornadoes, anyway, wasn't it? The storm last night didn't stop rotating. It looked like it was getting bigger. If you're not destroying the storms, then what . . . what *are* you doing?"

Mirielle's DataSlate chirps on the counter. "Oh! It's my sister." She jostles Remi, who's starting to fuss a little.

"Here, I'll take her," Dad says, and carefully lifts her from the scarf. The baby wiggles a little, as if she can't quite get comfortable against Dad's bony shoulder. Dad strokes her soft fluff of hair until she settles. Then he takes a deep breath and looks at me. "You're right, Jaden. I'm not dissipating the storms." The muscles around his eyes tighten. "That was my research, and that was my intent, but as I'm sure Mom told you, after all our years of research, the simulation failed. I've been over it a thousand times. It works on paper, but not in real life."

"Have you *tried* it in real life? Maybe it does work."

He shakes his head. "We can't. What if something went wrong and we made a storm more powerful? You can't test theories with people's lives. That's why StormSafe is so far out ahead with weather modification research. We have the patent on the Sim Dome, so we can actually test our theories."

"And this one always fails when you try it as a simulation?"

He nods. "We have the very best Sim Dome money can buy up at headquarters. More advanced than yours at camp, and that's nothing to laugh at. It's failed every time." He chugs down the rest of his soda, feeds the can into the recycler, and settles into a counter chair with Remi snuggled against him. "But I had already made a promise to all these people." He nods to the hallway, where Mirielle is chatting into her DataSlate. "We *will* get it right one of these days. We will. But for the moment, the best I can do is keep my family, and a handful of other families like ours, safe another way."

"Which is?"

"An electromagnetic storm shield that we *were* able to test successfully."

"What's that do? Send the tornadoes away?"

Dad nods. "Deflects them, yes." I watch him stroking Remi's hair as she sleeps. His hands are soft, but his face is hard, eyebrows furrowed.

"So the field sends the storm . . . ?"

"Away from the most populated areas. Away from her." Dad kisses the top of Remi's head. "Away from you. Away from here, and that's the best I can do for now. At least it's something."

He says it like it's a success but still looks like someone who thinks he's a failure, and it makes me sad for him, after all his work.

"Well, it's a start anyway, right?"

He doesn't smile, but he nods.

I stand up and take a banana from the counter. "Do you think I could see StormSafe soon? Like a tour?"

"Sure. How come?"

"We're getting assignments at camp, and I may work with this other kid in weather manipulation. I . . . uh . . ." I decide to say it. "I'm interested in the dissipation technology."

"Hold on a minute then; I have something you might like to see." He disappears into his office, comes back out with his DataSlate. "Got yours?" I hand it to him, and he starts copying his file called "Effects of Microwave Radiation on Supercell Downdrafts and Vortex Formation."

"Is this your research?"

"It's the summary." The file finishes transferring. Mirielle's done talking with her sister, so Dad hands Remi over, heads for his office, and holds his thumb to the panel. "Read it," he tells me. "You'll see in the last section how the simulation failed, sent us back to square one. But maybe you'll have better luck." He steps inside, and the door slides shut.

Chapter 11

Alex is in his usual seat at camp Monday morning. He looks up from his DataSlate when I sit down next to him. "Hey."

I gasp. "What happened to you?" Even in the dim light, I can see the angry red scrape on his forehead.

"Aw, nothing." He shrugs. "It was dumb. Newton went chasing after a groundhog when you guys left. It was right as that storm turned and started heading up our way. I went after him and caught a tree branch in the head. Stupid." He touches it as if to show me it's no big deal, but he winces.

"All right, scholars!" Van jogs down the aisle holding a remote, aiming it toward the front of the room as if it's a laser gun. "Today, we face down the problems of the future." He presses a button on the remote, and Dad's holo-sim appears.

"Welcome back, campers. Today, you'll learn the concentration for your studies at Eye on Tomorrow. Please look at the screen behind me for your assignments."

A map of the campus appears on screen, with the different

buildings labeled by specialty. Then, campers' photographs start appearing next to buildings, while Dad announces who will be where. "Risha Patel, cellular generation and human cloning center." Risha's face breaks into a smile when Tomas is assigned to cloning as well.

The Beekman twins high-five one another when they both end up in robotics and artificial intelligence. The two boys they hang around with are assigned to bio-botanicals.

I already know from what Van said that I'll be in meteorology, but still, a shiver of excitement runs through me when my face appears on screen next to the Sim Dome. Alex is there, too.

Finally, the last camper's photograph appears. The brush-cut boy, whose name is Randall Harrington, is headed to cloning, and I can't help imagining an army of anxious brush-cut kids checking their watches. Then the screen goes black and it's just Dad looking out at us. "Today is the start of your life as a scientist," he says. "Make us proud. And always keep your eye on tomorrow."

Alex turns to face me when the lights come up. "So, will you work with me? Two brains are better than one."

"Depends on who the brains belong to." I smile as the door opens, and sunlight streams in. "But in this case, yeah. I think two are better."

Alex grins. "Want to start in the library? We can go over what we already know and build on that. Hopefully, Van will give us another shot at the Sim Dome soon."

"Sure." I turn to Risha. "Want to work in the library with us?"

"Not now, thanks. I'm off to the cloning lab."

"With *Tomas*?" I tease her. "I can't believe you switched from bio-botanicals just to hang out with him."

"I'm interested in *all* of it." She laughs. "So I might as well be interested *and* work with him." She gives me a shove toward the door. "Go on, weather geek. Get studying. I'll catch up with you later."

I walk with Alex across the grassy quad. "Ready to get to work?" He pulls open the library door. "Hey, Ms. Walpole." The librarian, a tall, slender woman with brown-gray dreadlocks, red-framed glasses, and dangling turquoise earrings, is twisted around a computer, apparently trying to fix something. She looks up, smiles, and waves as we step inside.

"Wow." The smell of paper books surprises me. "I thought it would be all computers."

"Over my dead body." The librarian stands there with a data cable dangling from one hand. "People ought to be able to get their information however they like best." She nods and goes back to wrestling with the computer.

"You tell 'em, Ms. Walpole." Alex laughs and heads for one of the tables. "She's awesome." He nods back over his shoulder as we sit down. "She's been here since the place started, from what I hear. She was one of the people whose property they needed to make room for the campus, but she wouldn't sell unless she got to be in charge of Eye on Tomorrow's library and education program for the little kids. Then she drafted up this list of conditions: it has to be open to the whole community—she was big on that since the town library shut down—and it has to have books in paper, too. I guess your dad agreed." Alex grins and gestures around a room full of floor-to-ceiling bookshelves, in addition to the row of computers up front. "Besides that, she brings us oatmeal raisin cookies sometimes when we're working. That's my kind of librarian."

"Me too," I say. I wonder if Ms. Walpole has paper poetry books at home, too. I bet she does. "Should we get some books?"

"There's a lot on supercell formation over in the five hundreds if you want to go look. I'll find my notes from last year."

"Okay." I head for the stacks, running my hands along the bumps of book spines as I go. A ton's been written about our topic. *Supercell, Superstorm* and *Planet Earth: The New Storm Belt* chronicle the shift from climate norms to the new weather patterns that have developed over the past fifty years, since the climate's warmed and grown so conducive to storms. *Seeds of Disaster: Foundations of Tornadogenesis* is probably the best-known text on the actual structure of tornadoes and why some supercells give rise to funnel clouds while others don't. *In the Eye of the Storm: Five Researchers on the Cutting Edge of Weather Modification* looks at the wave of scientists who worked on weather modification in the years before Dad and his colleagues.

I'm surprised to see a copy of *Playing God: The Case Against Meteorological Manipulation*; it flies in the face of everything Dad believes in, but I pull the book and add it to the teetering pile in my arms.

"You call that a few books?" Alex meets me on my way to the table, in time to keep the pile from toppling. We spread the books on the big table.

"Where should we start?" I ask.

"We're not exactly starting. I did a lot last summer." He pulls out his DataSlate. Van gave us clearance to bring them, now that we're settled in our concentrations of study. When Alex turns his on, there's a photograph of his family on the screen. There's Alex smiling at the camera in a white shirt and jeans. His mom, looking neater and less frazzled than she does when she's dropping him off. His dad, actually smiling. And a little girl hugging Newton.

"You have a little sister?"

"Julia just turned seven." He touches the DataSlate screen, and a document opens. "Here's the formula I came up with last year. It's based on some stuff from the Sim Dome computer. You know the basic premise, right? The one I tried in the dome? It's the same thing your dad is working from."

I nod. "Heat the downdraft." Dad used to talk about it all the time at dinner, back when there were still Meggs family dinners. He believed you could find the spot where a storm is beginning to rotate and stop a tornado from forming. It was like any recipe, he told me one night in between bites of chocolate cake. If you didn't have flour and cocoa and butter and all the other ingredients, you couldn't make cake. Tornadoes have ingredients, too—the rotation begins when a warmer updraft comes up against a cold, rainy downdraft. So what if you heated the air to get rid of that cold rainy downdraft? No ingredients—no tornado.

Alex turns to a sketch screen on his DataSlate, and there's a diagram like the one Dad used to draw on his napkins. He taps the center of the partially formed funnel cloud. "Right here is the spot we'd need to blast."

"Microwaves?"

"Yep. From satellites."

"Powered how?"

"Solar." He swipes the screen with his finger, and the next page appears—a sketch of a satellite with solar panels mounted on top. Yellow sketch lines representing microwave energy beam down to the bottom of the screen. "This is all in place already. They've had satellites collecting solar energy and beaming it down to storage facilities for almost ten years. It would just be a matter of amping it up and redirecting it into the heart of the storm."

"But that's what nobody can quite figure out, right? How much do you amp it up?"

"Right. Last summer, I played around with a formula for the amount of microwave energy you'd need, depending on the size and energy of the storm." He swipes to another page. "And every time I ran the numbers, it made perfect sense. But when I got time in the Sim Dome, I couldn't get it to work. It always . . . well, you saw what happened when I tried last week."

"That's what happened to my dad." I turn on my DataSlate and find the file he copied for me. "He gave me the summary."

Alex leans in, and his dark eyes scan line after line of numbers, explanations of what should have happened, but didn't.

Alex nods slowly. "Where did he do the simulation, do you know?"

"Up at StormSafe."

"Shoot." Alex sighs and tips back in his chair. "I was hoping it might have been a glitch with the Sim Dome here at Eye on Tomorrow, but if he used StormSafe equipment, that stuff's gotta be right. That means the data must be off." He stares off into a corner of the library, then nods toward my DataSlate.

"Did he use data from a real storm for the simulation?"

"I'm not sure." I skim through the document again. There's a link at the end. I click on it, and video from an online archive fills the screen. "This must be it." It's amateur storm footage from 2008, the kind people used to get when they went driving around in trucks, chasing tornadoes, back when you had to go looking for them to see one.

"Man," Alex says, breathing out. "It's a big one for back then."

Shaky video, shot through a car windshield, shows a funnel cloud forming and then touching down. It's nothing I haven't seen before, but the reaction to it—the way the guys in the car are acting—makes my stomach clench.

"We got debris! We got debris!" one of them shouts, as if he's won a new HV.

"Look at that thing!" the other one screams. "Dude, look! Can we get closer?"

They drive closer.

"Idiots," Alex whispers under his breath. But he doesn't turn away. There is something mesmerizing about watching these people sitting in the line of a tornado as if it's some kind of old-fashioned video game.

"Come on, baby," the camera guy's voice says. "Come on. Keep going." Like he's coaxing an animal out of a cave.

"Oh my God!" one of the guys yells. "Reverse! Put it in reverse!"

The tornado comes straight at them, and they're cursing and the video is shaking everywhere as they fly backward down the long stretch of road until the tornado gains on them and gains on them and they stop driving.

"Duck down! Get down!" one of them screams, and wind whips the car, pelts it with branches and dirt and rain until finally, the storm passes.

A few seconds of quiet. Then whooping, cheering. "Man, we were all over that thing! That was awesome! That was just—"

Alex presses the STOP button, and there is silence.

I realize I've been holding my breath. I breathe out and turn to him. He is shaking his head.

"It's surreal, isn't it?" he says. "That they'd put themselves in the path? That anyone could think this was entertaining?"

I stare at the frozen images, the men in their baseball caps, laughing, high-fiving each other. They must be in their twenties in this video. They're old men now. If they've survived. "They didn't know," I say. "It was fun for them. Exciting and fun. They didn't know what was about to happen with the climate, the storms."

"Stupid," Alex mutters, opening a book.

But I can't stop looking at their frozen faces amid the dust. They had no idea what was coming. Are we like that today? Is there something worse on the way that will make our storms seem like nothing at all?

"Come on," Alex says. "Let's work."

I turn the pages of the *Seeds of Disaster* book. The theories about tornado formation here are the best and latest, but there's still a big mystery about why the storms form some times and not others, when almost the exact same conditions are present.

I flip through the weather text, but in my mind, I'm turning pages in the poetry book on my nightstand, and I remember that one, "Geometry."

> *. . . the house expands:*
> *the windows jerk free to hover near the ceiling,*
> *the ceiling floats away with a sigh.*

I stare up at the library ceiling, gleaming golden wood with dark brown knots, and I imagine it lifting up, up over our heads and drifting off. The idea of solving a problem, feeling everything open up with possibility and with more problems to solve, too, fills me like a kite filling with wind.

Alex's shoulder brushes mine, and I jump.

"Sorry, I was looking at what you were reading." He nods down at the book. "You finding anything good?"

"Not yet. Just thinking."

"Me, too."

He lowers his head, and I watch him swiping through pages and pages of numbers, numbers that should have been the magic formula to make the winds stop blowing, to keep the weathervane on his family's barn where it belongs, to let Newton chase groundhogs in the afternoon. But the deeper his frown gets, the more I start to believe there will never be a magic formula to make every-thing okay.

"It's about time to call it a day, kids." Ms. Walpole steps up to our table, a stack of books in her arms. She smells like the vanilla candles my mom likes. "Did you find everything?"

"Not exactly." Alex tips back in his chair and sighs.

"Put your chair down. You'll crack your head open," she says. When his chair legs are back on the ground, she nods. "Now, what is it that you need?"

"Data," Alex and I say together, and that makes us laugh a little, even though it's been a frustrating afternoon.

"Solid tornado formation data that will work in a simulation," Alex adds. "Nothing you can help with, unfortunately."

Ms. Walpole frowns and puts down her pile of books. "The data you have isn't working?" she asks.

Alex shakes his head. "Nope. Even though it should."

"You've checked it and rechecked it?" She clicks her tongue against the roof of her mouth.

"Yep."

Ms. Walpole raises her eyebrows. "Then that's an easy one. Collect new data."

Alex lets out half a laugh. "Sure. Do you happen to know where there's a high-tech weather balloon or something we can borrow?"

She crosses her arms in front of her and looks over her glasses at us. "As a matter of fact, I do."

Chapter 12

This wasn't on our orientation tour," I say as Ms. Walpole unlocks the warehouse tucked behind the Sim Dome. It's such an unremarkable building—dull aluminum paneling, nestled among all the shiny steel and glass—that I didn't even notice when we walked past it before.

"Hmph." She presses her finger to a biometric panel alongside a garage door, and it slides open. "That's because Van Gardner's so caught up in his shiny new toys that he forgets everything else."

We step inside a room that's bigger than any airplane hangar—huge and basic.

"This place is simply to hold equipment—acres and acres of equipment that somebody thought was too old to keep using," Ms. Walpole says as we start down one of the long rows of floor-to-ceiling storage racks, and right away, I can see that people here have strange ideas about what's old.

There's a whole fleet of four-wheel-drive vehicles that look like they've been converted from gasoline to hydrogen, each one outfitted with some fancy gizmo on top. "What's sticking up from the trucks?" I ask.

"That's a mobile meso-net unit—a multipurpose measuring machine made up of steel rods and twirling computer weather sensors that record things like barometric pressure and wind speed," Ms. Walpole says.

I nod; I read about them in one of Dad's old journals. In the early days of tornado research, scientists used to drive these things close to the storms and drop off probes in the path, hoping for a direct hit. They wanted to see inside the heart of the tornado. That's how they learned a lot about storm formation, how vertical wind shear can turn an ordinary thunderstorm into something stronger.

"And they don't use these anymore?"

"Oh, they still use them. They just have better ones now." Ms. Walpole leads us around a corner and down another long row of shelves. These are loaded with computers that can't be more than a year or two old—not state of the art like the ones in the Sim Dome, but still plenty powerful.

"Hey," Alex says. "Aren't these the ones from the camp lab last summer?"

Ms. Walpole nods. "They've been replaced. They may bring these out for the Tomorrow Kids program we run during school vacations."

"Is that for younger kids?" I ask.

Alex nods. "It's open to anybody, and really, they just do fun stuff, but they're always looking for future campers. That's how I got in; two weeks after my first vacation camp, they invited my folks to get me tested. Tomas, too."

"If they'd only known what they were getting into." Ms. Walpole smiles. "How's Mrs. Hazen doing, have you heard?"

"Not that good. Tomas doesn't like to talk about it." Alex shrugs. "She needs to go to New York or somewhere for treatment."

Ms. Walpole nods. "I thought I heard him say something like that to Van this week. I hope they're not thinking of giving up the farm."

"They're not," Alex says quickly, and I bite my lip to keep from telling him what Risha said.

"Right down here," Ms. Walpole says. At the far end of the warehouse there's a tall rack filled with bins of rain gear, and one of the old National Weather Service trucks is parked behind it. In the back of the pickup is a sleek model airplane with a five- or six-foot wingspan.

Alex's eyes get huge. I step closer and see this is no toy; it's one of the original DataDrones—the indestructible, remote-operated planes that helped scientists make some of their first real breakthroughs in figuring out how tornadoes are born.

Alex runs his hand along one of the wings. "Graphene, right?"

Ms. Walpole nods. "It was the strongest substance in the world when this was developed."

And it wasn't that long ago. Five or six years, maybe? I remember Dad talking about how amazing the drones were. "They're not using it anymore?" I ask.

"This showed up a few weeks ago," Ms. Walpole says. "I guess the new ones have more efficient radar built in."

Alex reaches into the back of the truck and picks up the

remote-control device that must run the plane. It has regular remote buttons and levers with some kind of computer screen below them. "So . . ." He sounds like he's trying not to get too excited, but his eyes give him away. "This still works?"

Ms. Walpole gives a sharp nod. "I'm sure it does. Contrary to popular opinion around this place, just because something is a little older doesn't mean it's not useful." She pushes her glasses up on her nose.

Alex looks down at the control panel in his hands. "Can we . . . uh . . . borrow it?"

"Well, it's not doing anyone any good sitting in the back of a van, is it?" Behind the glasses, Ms. Walpole's green eyes have a glint of mischief in them, and I smile, imagining Dad trying to negotiate with her. "I'm certainly not going to stop you from making use of the tools you need to carry out your research. I'm here to help, after all."

"Should we check with Van or something?" I ask.

She purses her lips. "I'm not sure I would recommend that. It's often easier to be forgiven than it is to get permission in situations such as this." She pauses. "But of course, I never said that." She looks at her watch, silver and obviously antique. "I'd better get back to the library. I'm afraid I often forget to lock up when I leave a building, so you two will need to do that on your way out, all right?"

Alex grins. "You got it. And thanks."

She walks briskly back down the aisle, then turns back to us. "You'll want to leave promptly, and use the main entrance. The other staff members are all in a meeting in the auditorium for another hour. I'd best join them now."

I can't quite believe what we're about to do, so I just stand, listening to her footsteps fade all the way to the door. It thunks closed, and Alex turns to me. "Ready to borrow an airplane?"

Chapter 13

"How long can you stay?" Alex leans against the bottom of the playground slide at the park near campus, frowning down at his DataSlate. A storm is forming west of us, but there's no way to tell yet if it will spawn tornadoes. Just in case, we set up the drone so it's ready to take off from the open space where kids play kickball.

"I can stay a while, I guess." Dad never mentioned a curfew, and Mirielle usually makes dinner pretty late. "So . . . if we do get a storm, the idea here is to fly the plane into it and gather data so . . ." I was so bowled over by the very idea of "borrowing" a weather drone, so nervous as we carried it silently out the Eye on Tomorrow gate and lugged it here, that I never actually processed what we're trying to do. Gather data about a storm, sure. Then what?

"Well, I figure the numbers I'm using in my project must be off. I tried the simulation with two different storms last summer and got the same results, which means maybe all the storm data in the system at camp is wrong."

"So if we have a brand new storm . . . and collect our own brand new data . . ." This kind of problem-solving is so different from the

Eye on Tomorrow entrance exam, this starting-from-scratch thinking, but I'm getting it. "Then the simulation should work?"

"Well, hopefully," Alex says. "Or if not, we'll know the data wasn't
the problem and the whole theory's a bust." He sighs and looks
down at the DataSlate. "Oh!" He jumps up and climbs the ladder to
the top of the slide, facing west. "I think we're in business. Come up
and see!"

There's not much room on the platform at the top of the slide,
so we crowd together, and Alex points to the horizon. "See that
rotation?"

The rotation I notice first is in my stomach, which is kind of
flipping out being so close to him up here, but I force myself to focus
on the clouds. "Yeah. That looks like it's going to produce a funnel
cloud."

Before I've finished my sentence, he's climbing down the ladder
and heading for the remote control we left by the kickball field. The
storm is moving fast; the sky is darkening, and the wind is already
picking up. I can't believe we're actually going to fly this thing. It
feels too adult-scientist, too serious, too *real* to be happening to a
couple of kids at science camp. But Alex hands me the remote.

"Hold this while I check the sensors, okay?"

My hands shake, even though Alex swears he's flown remote
control planes before and this is no different. All we have to do is fly
it into the storm; once we punch through the wall, the drone will
be swept up into the tornado and sensors can gather data. The wireless system is set up to send information directly to my DataSlate,
so we'll get readings right away. Then we'll recover the full set of

data from the hard drive when the drone lands. Or crashes. I'm picturing us returning the plane to the storage building in pieces, explaining to Van or, worse, my father, what we were thinking, when Alex shouts, "Press the red button! Now!"

I press it, and the drone's engine hums to life. "I thought you were going to fly it!"

"I want to make sure the sensors are working," he says, waving over his shoulder at me as he squints down at the plane. "You'll be fine—just start it going forward and then throttle up to lift off, and I'll take over from there!"

Throttle up? The controls feel like some kids' video game in my hand, but I know this is real, with real consequences. If something happens to this plane and we have to—

"Jaden, start it! The storm's coming and if it turns away before we get there, we're not going to make it!"

I force my thumb to push the lever, and the plane jerks forward on the ground.

"Good!" Alex yells. "Good! Now speed up! Go!"

I push the lever all the way forward, and the plane bounces along, speeding up, bumping over the dusty kickball field where second base would be.

"Now throttle up! Now!" Alex shouts as he grabs the DataSlate from the grass and runs to my side.

I press the button to throttle up, and the plane rises off the ground, just missing a shrub at the edge of the park. It wavers, headed for the fence, and I can't imagine how we're going to keep it steady in the wind. "Here!" I shove the controls into Alex's hands, take my DataSlate, and call up the program that will receive the drone's data.

The page comes up blank but immediately starts filling with numbers. Columns and columns of numbers. Wind speeds. Temperatures. Barometric pressures. They're mostly the same numbers, over and over, as Alex maneuvers the plane over the fence, outside Placid Meadows and closer to the storm.

The rotation we spotted from the top of the slide is swirling faster, and already a thick, dark rope is forming, stretching down from the cloud. Alex takes his eyes off the plane to watch the storm and lets out a whoop. "We got it!" He sounds like one of those storm chasers on the video, and I wonder if we're as stupid as they were, playing with fire, with something we don't understand.

"Here we go . . . getting close now . . . Watch!" He means to watch the plane or the storm, or maybe the data, but I watch Alex, his eyes as intense as anyone's I've ever seen. He bites his lip in concentration, and the tendons in his hands tense as he clutches the remote and drives the plane full throttle—faster, faster, faster—until it surges through the gray wall of wind into the heart of the storm.

"It's in! Watch the data, Jaden! What are we getting?"

I look down at the numbers flying over the screen in my hands. Flying faster than the wind, but my eyes start to see patterns. Changes. Wind speeds rising. Temperatures rising. Barometric pressure dropping like mad. This is what it's like to be inside a storm.

"Okay, it's turning. The storm's turning. I'm going to try to keep the drone inside. Tell me what you see!" I sneak another glance at

Alex, but his eyes don't move from the handheld controls. The computer screen below the control panel shows a blinking blue dot, swirling, flying, inside the storm.

The numbers on the DataSlate hold steady. Soon, I should see . . . what? If there's a field at the edge of Placid Meadows that dissipates storms or deflects them, the numbers should start to show it weakening.

But they don't.

"I'm not sure how long before it's thrown clear. Are you getting stuff?" Alex's voice is tense with concentration. "Jaden, talk to me! We've got maybe another ten seconds. I'm losing the signal. What are you seeing?"

I can't answer. Because I can't begin to process the numbers flying past my eyes.

"I . . . It's going too fast for me to see." But that's a lie. I can see the numbers, and I know what they mean. As the storm pulls away from Placid Meadows, the wind speeds are increasing. The temperatures are getting higher. And the barometric pressure has plunged to a level I've never even seen before.

I understand, but I can't make myself say it out loud.

This storm didn't weaken when it hit the Placid Meadows perimeter. It turned away, toward someone else's home. And got stronger.

Chapter 14

The brave thing would be to ask Dad more about his failed project tonight. Ask him why he thinks his simulation went wrong, why all the number crunching wasn't enough, and what he's doing about it now. Ask him what really happens to storms when they leave Placid Meadows. And maybe that would start to answer the questions swirling in my head since Alex and I flew the drone this afternoon, since I lied to Alex. I told Alex it all went by too quickly, that my DataSlate's battery died before I could process the numbers. I told him we'd need to recover data from the hard drive to see what really happened. I couldn't tell him the truth. Not without asking my father some questions first.

But Dad's eyes are angrier than the clouds as he bursts into the kitchen, and Mirielle's delicate spinach salad just about wilts when he slams his briefcase on the table.

"Stephen, what is it?" She sets down her wineglass and rushes over to press a hand to his cheek.

He brushes it away, pops open his briefcase, pulls out his

DataSlate, and drops it onto the granite counter with a clatter. "We're losing support for Phase Two. Look!"

He turns on the DataSlate—I'm surprised the screen doesn't shatter under his glare—and jabs at it until the document appears. "This is from our investors' group. Sixty days to acquire the rest of the property we need, or we lose our funding. And I've got two hold-outs who *will not* sell."

My stomach twists. I'm pretty sure I'm working with one of the holdouts' kids. And Risha's in love with the other one.

"Can you not offer more money for the farmland?" Mirielle asks, setting a place for Dad at dinner. "It seems to me that—"

"Do you have any idea what we've offered? Ten *times* the market value of their property, but *noooo* . . . these are *family farms*. Well, they can take their worm-bitten apples and their lumpy, seedy strawberries and kiss my—"

"Stephen!" Mirielle is back in her seat at the table, but her eyes shoot lasers over the roast chicken and gravy, and Dad stops. Mirielle puts a gentle hand on Remi's head and looks my way, too. "You are scaring the children."

As much as I don't like being called a child, her words take the electricity out of Dad's anger at the farmers, and I'm thankful. No wonder Mirielle keeps Aunt Linda's berries a secret.

"Sit down." Mirielle motions to the chair next to her, and Dad sinks into it like a scarecrow that's lost its straw. She pours him a glass of Scotch.

Dad presses his hands against his eyes. "How am I going to pull this off in sixty days?"

"Isn't there somewhere else you could build? I mean, you can't very well make somebody sell land if they don't want to, right?" When Dad turns to look at me, I wish I could pull the words back, but like Risha's dandelion fluff, blown into the wind at our picnic, they're swirling all around our heads, impossible to catch.

The voice that follows his glare isn't angry; it's measured and calm, like Dad sounds in his holo-talks. "The planned expansion of Placid Meadows will allow another fifty families to live within the secure environment of a StormSafe community. This is about people's lives, Jaden—not about some silly family tradition."

"I know." I nod. But I think of Alex and the strawberries his family grows in the sun. A wad of spinach sticks in my throat. "What are you going to do?"

"I'll tell you what I'm not going to do." Dad takes a drink, then thumps his glass down, hard, on the wood table. "I am *not* losing this project."

As soon as Mirielle leaves to put Remi to bed, the storm clouds settle back in Dad's eyes, and he doesn't say another word to me. I sink into the old wooden rocking chair in the living room—perfect except that Grandma Athena's creepy photo always stares at it—and read through the files that Alex beamed to my DataSlate. I can't help keeping one eye on Dad, though, pacing back and forth from his office to the kitchen. He's in and out all night. A few times, he blusters out to the porch and stands there, muttering and looking off to the west. The last time the screen door slams, he comes back smiling.

"Jaden, you're still up?"

"I'm reading through some data my camp partner shared with me from last summer." I hesitate, afraid that talking to him at all will somehow give away what I did this afternoon at the park, who I'm working with, what I saw. "We're working together on the storm dissipation project."

Dad nods. "Good challenge, that one. You read that abstract I gave you?"

"Yeah. My partner had the same problem when he ran the simulation on his data last summer." This is where I should ask him more. Instead, I wait to see if he'll offer up details without my having to ask.

"Well, some things aren't meant to be." He yawns.

"I guess not." His office door is open, so I expect him to go back there like he usually does, to lift a tired hand to the sensor and make the steel door slide shut so he can work into the night.

But he doesn't. He stretches his arms up so high that his fingertips brush the ceiling and then heads for his bedroom. "Don't stay up too late."

I say good night.

I listen to the lock click, hear the water in the bathroom, the toilet flushing.

I hear the snap of the white noise machine turning on, the smooth, soothing whoosh that he says clears his mind of all the numbers and formulas so he can rest.

I page through Alex's files one more time, until I'm sure Dad must be asleep.

I start to stand, and the rocking chair creaks.

I freeze.

But no one's watching except Grandma Athena, trapped in her frame.

I turn away from her and head for the open office door.

Chapter 15

The room is dark.

Only the tiniest bit of kitchen light creeps in, and even with the door open, all the sounds from outside get swallowed up by this space.

I set my DataSlate on the edge of the huge mahogany desk and look out to the kitchen clock. It's midnight, and I don't know when Remi usually wakes to nurse. Will Mirielle bring her to the kitchen? Just in case, I press a button—no need for a fingerprint scan on the inside—and watch the cold steel door slide closed. The kitchen light snuffs out, but a power switch glows next to the door.

I flick it on. Overhead lights glimmer, and flat screens flicker to life on every wall.

The screen to my left shows real-time images of a row of satellites. Eight of them. I step closer. Are those solar panels attached? Underneath each image is a display panel with numbers, all gradually climbing. They are labeled in kilowatts. I reach out to touch one of the panels, and a new window emerges from the center of the screen.

It's full of constantly changing numbers. Some look like the data that whizzed past on my DataSlate while the drone was flying in the storm. Wind speeds, barometric pressure readings, and temperatures. Some look like kilowatt levels, measures of energy. Others appear to be geographic coordinates, latitude and longitude. What do they all mean?

What does any of it mean? Maybe I read the data wrong this afternoon. Maybe it's not what it looks like and I'll never have to talk to Alex about what I think I saw.

I cross the room to Dad's desk and turn on the computer.

It hums to life, flashing a blue background at me while the system loads. Over the desk is a screen showing live radar images of the region, from north of the airport, all along the river. A second big storm looks like it just missed us around the time Dad went to bed. It was close to Alex's house, from the look of this track.

I hope Newton was in for the night.

I hope they're safe.

The computer login screen appears. Dad's username, SMeggs, is already in the login box, but it's asking for a fingerprint scan or password.

I have the wrong prints, so I ignore the biometric panel and set my fingers on the keys, hoping for inspiration.

I try the obvious first. What he loves most.

stormsafe. dna-ture. I try it with the hyphen and without. No.

Then I try mirielle. And remi. jaden.

The message flashes again: incorrect password.

I sink back in the chair. I should have known I wouldn't be able to just pop onto his computer. The desk has a single drawer, and I slide it open looking for a list or scrap of paper, even though deep down I know Dad's too smart to leave his passwords lying around. Of course he is. The only thing in the drawer is a jumble of computer and DataSlate wires, a couple of storage drives, a bottle of BioWake pills, and the barometer he had in his hand the other day.

It fills my palm when I pick it up, a perfect ring of dark, polished wood with the barometer mechanism showing through a quarter-size glass window. Around the window is a yellowed ring of barometric pressure markings and five weather patterns written in fancy old script.

Stormy.
Rain.
Change.
Fair.
Very Dry.

Why would Dad, with his walls of satellite maps and live radar screens, keep something like this around? Dad, whose motto is "Science will save us," who won't even read a paper book anymore, is hanging on to an old weather instrument that has words like *fair* instead of data? It's not even in great shape for an antique. It doesn't seem to work at all, and the wood finish is worn away at the bottom and on the sides, as if it's spent a lot of time being held in someone's hand.

I put it back in the drawer and look back at the log-in box on the computer screen.

barometer.

Incorrect password.

I try combinations of all the words that have already failed. remijaden. placidstorm. I even try Mom's name, rebekah, in case his password is left over from a long time ago. Nothing works.

And then as if the walls suddenly dissolved, I sense Grandma's eyes staring out from her photo in the living room. Grandma, who loved science as much as Dad does.

I type athena.

The desktop appears.

I pull up a search box and type in latitude and longitude coordinates from the screen across the room.

35° 24' N 97° 36' W

A map appears on the screen with a marker pointing to the center. I click to zoom in on the satellite image of that spot, but I already recognize enough of the streets and the bend of the river to know what I will see.

The fence. The river and the trees. The daisy and dandelion meadows, and the field with the gazebo.

The barn with the battered weathervane. And the strawberries.

The Carillo farm, where Alex's family works and lives. Why is Dad's satellite focused here?

My breathing quickens, though I still don't know what it all means. I swivel Dad's chair around—I feel too small in it, swallowed up by black leather and his smell of work, sweat, and Scotch—and face the satellite wall again.

Current output: 00:00

PowerBank: 327.9 MW

35° 24' N 97° 36' W

I stare at the numbers and wait for them to arrange themselves into something that makes sense. I wait for the windows to jerk free and hover near the ceiling, like in the poem.

They don't.

But the more I stare, the more two letters stand out.

MW. The abbreviation for megawatts. Energy.

Energy mixed with geographic coordinates.

Is someone blasting energy—microwave energy—down from the satellites?

Is this the technology that didn't work in the simulations? It didn't work in Alex's trial, and it didn't work in Dad's. The whole concept of blasting energy at a tornado to stop the rotation was deemed too risky, too dangerous for the real world. So what's going on here?

Is Dad testing it anyway? Without government approval? Do the other scientists at StormSafe even know what he's doing?

My brain is churning. I swing the chair back around to face the radar screen. The storm is getting smaller now. What happened before? Did something go wrong when Dad tried to dissipate the storms today? Did he make them bigger by accident? Is that why the numbers from the drone's data readings looked the way they did?

I look down at the computer screen and start scanning the file names. Most of them have only project numbers: RL7421, 139Q, SS451.

Meaningless. And the more I stare at the numbers, the more I want to scream. I take a deep breath and look up at the ceiling that will never float away with a sigh.

When I look back at the computer, a file called Family Photos catches my eye. I click on it and find the same collection of photos running on the Data Frame in the living room. I'm about to close the folder and go back to the numbers when I notice that one of the files in that folder isn't an image. It's text, and it's labeled AGM.

Those are Grandma's initials.

Athena Grace Meggs.

As I click to open the folder, there's a faint sound from the other side of the door. Footsteps on the kitchen floor.

I freeze.

My father's voice drifts in, muffled. "No, honey, I'm fine. Go back to bed. Couldn't sleep, so I'm going to get some work done."

My heart freezes, and my hands are shaking so much it's all I can do to close out the folder and log out.

The fingerprint sensor beeps.

The lock mechanism clicks.

The door will slide open in seconds, and no matter how wildly I look around the room, there is nowhere to hide in this sparse electronic workspace.

I race to the power switch, hit it, and the room goes dark. In the blackness, I dive under Dad's desk just before the door hums open and he turns the lights back on.

He's wearing dress shoes with his pajama bottoms. They click on the floor and echo off the walls and make my heart pound harder.

He steps right up to the desk and pauses in front of his computer. If he sits down, will he notice that his chair is warm?

The dust under here tickles my throat. I swallow a cough, eyes watering.

What am I doing? Why am I hiding from my own father in the house that's supposed to be my home?

I should come out; he'd probably laugh. But something in the click of his shoes, something in the faces I've already seen him wear this week, tells me to stay still. And quiet.

Dad doesn't sit. He walks to the satellite wall and touches the panel under the screen. He's facing away from me, and I let my eyes move around the room again. At least I got logged out of his computer. At least there's nothing to—

My heart bolts up into my throat, and I almost choke on it. Because right there, its corner hanging over the edge of Dad's desk above me, is my DataSlate.

I can't let him see it.

I take a deep breath and inch forward on the floor.

Dad turns, and I freeze. He stands still for a second—is he looking at the radar screen above the desk?—and then turns back to the satellite wall.

I stretch my arm up slowly, silently.

I can't reach it.

I slide one knee forward, then the other, and reach again. My fingers close around the edge of the DataSlate just as Dad's Data-Slate chimes.

I startle, and it falls from the edge of the desk and almost through my fingers, but I make a last mad grab and catch it.

"There you are! It's about time," Dad says quietly.

"That's a fine way to say hello, Stephen." A woman's voice. I lean out the tiniest bit, but the screen is facing away from me, so I can't see her face.

"Shh . . . hold on, let me plug in my earpiece so we don't wake the whole house."

Under the desk, I pull my DataSlate back into the shadows and try to slow my breathing while Dad talks. I can hear only his side of the conversation now.

"I know," he says into the DataSlate's camera. His shiny black shoes click back and forth, louder and fainter, over and over. When he walks away, I breathe.

"Yes, good timing." He laughs a little. "It was a monster. They won't be able to find their roof in the morning. And maybe they'll decide they don't love that farmland as much as they thought. We'll have the bulldozers here before you know it."

Dad walks away again, but I keep holding my breath. My father is *laughing* at the storm that just came through.

"Yep. Listen, I need to get some work done, but I'll see you tomorrow. . . . Love you, too. Good night."

I gasp, then hold my breath, afraid he's heard. His shoes click closer again, and I tense as he sinks into the leather office chair.

Above, there are clicks on the keyboard. I calm my breathing, but my brain feels like it's about to explode.

Love you, too? Who *was* that? He was talking like she knew all about the storm and the lawsuit. It must be someone he works with. *Love you, too.* No wonder he spends so much time at StormSafe. My heart sinks, thinking of Mirielle, so understanding while Dad's at work all the time.

"Hm." Dad's heel lifts off the floor and he starts bouncing his knee, something he's always done when he's thinking hard.

More clicks.

A sigh.

Then the chair pushes back from the desk. Shoes click all the way to the entrance, then out and through the kitchen until the door slides shut and I am alone in the office again.

I don't come out.

Not yet.

I wait with my itchy nose in the dust for what must be another ten minutes until I'm sure he won't be back until morning.

Finally, I unfold my cramped legs, climb out, and slide into the leather chair.

I log in, go straight to the AGM folder, and start reading data files.

The numbers look almost exactly like what Alex shared with me, right down to the formulas, the projected kilowatts necessary to warm a downdraft enough to stop rotation within a storm.

I read through file after file, willing my eyes to stay open.

This data should work. It all makes sense, just the way Alex explained it. The simulation should have worked, too.

I go back to the beginning and start reading again. There must be something here I'm missing. Something that will give me that understanding, that vision of how it all fits together.

But the numbers blur.

They start to spin and mix with dust and broken glass and tree limbs. I look harder. There has to be a pattern, but everything is moving so fast it's blurry.

Then the whole screen swells and darkens, and there is a monster tornado coming. I'm riding my bike, and someone is behind me—sometimes it's Risha, sometimes Alex, and sometimes Amelia from home. The voice keeps changing but it always shouts the same thing, "Go! Faster! Hurry!" But no matter how fast I try to go, how hard I push down on the pedals, they just spin effortlessly, and I go nowhere. I can see the house—not Dad's concrete block but our house back in Vermont—and I keep pedaling, pedaling, as the storm gets closer and closer. The drone flies back and forth, back and forth. Roof tiles start flying off the house. Windows shatter, and in one of the gaping empty windowpanes, I see Mom's face for a split second before the blackness swallows her up.

"NO!!"

I wake up with a jerk. My hands are sweating, despite the air-conditioning in Dad's office. And the computer clock says 4:30 AM.

How could I have let myself fall asleep? What if Dad had come back?

I take a last look at the computer screen, the folder full of swirling file names, and this time, one file stands out. Not numbers, but initials and words.

AGM-FAKEABSTRACT

Was it even here before? How could I have missed it? I shiver and click on the file.

I have read this document before. Dad put a copy on my DataSlate. It is the file that summarized his research on storm dissipation and its failure. That's what he told me.

With my heart racing, I search the folder, looking for another document, but there is nothing else labeled abstract or summary or AGM.

Nothing.

I open up each of the remaining documents. Only more data.

Now the computer clock reads 4:52. And I know that no matter how late Dad stays up, his alarm goes off at 5.

I need to get out of here.

But I can't.

I have to know.

I run a full hard-drive search.

Find: AGM

The list that scrolls down must be a hundred documents long, and it looks like all of them are in the folder I just finished reading through.

I scroll to the bottom.

All but one.

A file named AGM-AB buried five folders deep in a file called 2048 TAXES.

The digital clock reads 4:57.

I double click the file and realize I've been holding my breath.

It starts out like the other summary. I suck in words as if they're oxygen until I get to the spot in the document where it diverges from the one I've already read.

The rest of this summary is nothing like the one on my DataSlate.

The simulation did not fail.

Dad's experiment worked.

The computer clock turns to 4:58, and there is no time for questions. No time to ask why he gave me a phony summary, why he wanted the world to think he failed. I grab my DataSlate, click out the data-transfer stick, plug it into the back of Dad's drive, and drag the file over. I go back to the original folder with the data and copy that, too.

4:59.

The progress bar can't move quickly enough, and it makes me want to pound the computer. *Faster! Transfer! Go!*

The last file copies as the clock turns.

Forcing myself to keep breathing, I unplug from Dad's computer, log out, and press the button to make the steel door slide open.

Dad's alarm is beeping in the bedroom.

The SmartKitchen is brewing his coffee.

As the office door begins to slide closed behind me, I look back at the wall of satellites, the wall of radar images, of storms, and dissipation data and secrets, wondering . . . what really goes on in this room?

Chapter 16

Alex isn't at camp. When we left the park yesterday, his plan was to recover the drone and then head home. Did he find it? Has he seen the data it collected? What if that second storm hit before he made it home?

I sit through Van's morning directions with my DataSlate in my hands, half expecting him to snatch it away, even though I have permission to have it. It's off, but I can feel its weight, its danger, practically burning my hands with what I learned last night. Part of me is dying to talk to Alex about our results from the drone flight now, to show him this new data and see what he makes of it. But there's also a knot in my stomach. What if he sees something awful?

The holo-sim turns on, and Dad rises out of the floor. In today's lecture, he's talking about responsibility, integrity of data, and cooperation. My chest feels tighter with every word.

Responsibility? Integrity?

He lied. He lied about everything. Why?

I need to talk to Alex, but at the same time, I'm terrified. I've started the conversation with him in my head a thousand times, and I've thought about never telling him at all. But he needs to know that his research was solid. I want to give him that.

"Hey." I know it's Alex behind me from his whisper as he leans forward.

"You're here!" I turn in my seat to see him. "I need to—"

Even in the dim light, the sight of his face steals my words. He's hurt again. And the scrape on his temple from the other night is nothing compared to this. There's a gash across his right cheek, butterflied together with a steri-strip. Another over his left eye still bleeds under its bandage. His chin is scraped raw.

"What happened?" I whisper.

But even as the words leave my mouth, I know it was the storm I saw on the radar.

The storm that made my father smile before he went to bed.

The one he laughed about in his office with his *love-you-too* woman on the video call.

"I'm okay. And I got the drone."

"But you're not okay. Where—"

"Shhh . . . we'll talk later. Turn around now, or Van's going to get on your case," Alex whispers, so I turn back to face my father. His holo-image talks over my head, smiles at the back of the auditorium. How can he do this? How can he *laugh* at someone's farm being hit, someone's body being beaten like this? How can he have the power to stop these storms and not use it? I want to throw myself at him, pound him with my fists.

But he's untouchable.

I'd fly right through him to the floor.

"Now that you have your partners and your focus, we'll skip the lectures and go straight to morning research. This is the last day you'll see me for a while," holo-Dad says.

Unless you happen to live in my house, I think.

Dad's image disappears, and I shiver. Knowing what I know about Dad's research, what he found and isn't telling anyone, makes me wonder about camp.

The high-tech equipment. The library. The top-of-the-line computers. Why is education such a big part of his company's mission? Why spend so much money on—

"You coming?" The lights are back on, and Alex is standing halfway down the row of seats, waiting for me.

I tuck my DataSlate in my backpack as Van comes walking up the aisle. "What happened to you?" Van pauses next to Alex and raises his eyebrows. "Get in a fight with your girlfriend here?"

Alex laughs a little. "Got caught out during the storm last night."

"Be more careful, my man. We're counting on you here." Van frowns at the bandage on Alex's forehead. "Stop by the first aid station before you get to work today. Marcy'll fix you up."

"I'll come, too," I say. "I need to talk to you . . . about stuff."

Van tips his head in a question, but I don't answer. He shrugs, says "You go easy on him today," and heads out the back door.

Alex and I walk down a long hall to the first aid station, tucked into a bright room near the entrance. Every time I turn to say something, the bandages on his face feel like accusations. Dad knew how to stop the storm that did this. He chose not to.

I finally find words. "So that weather hit while you were out looking for the drone?"

Alex shakes his head. "Not really." He turns toward me and says quietly, "I got the drone, and it's fine; it's back at the house, but I haven't downloaded the data yet because that storm . . ." He shakes his head. "It came out of nowhere."

"Why weren't you in a safe room?"

"Never got the alert."

My face falls. "Was your DataSlate out of power, or—"

"There *was* no alert. You didn't get an alarm on yours last night, did you?"

I shake my head. I'd had it right in my lap, going over and over that data. The alarm that should have sounded on every data device within a ten-mile radius never went off.

"We had no clue until the wind kicked up. Thought we had time to get the chickens in, but debris started flying before I got back to the barn."

Alex pulls open the door to the first aid station, and we step inside. The room is full of sunlight, and the white walls are so bright they make me squint. A bouncy young woman in scrubs—she must be Marcy—is scrolling through records on a DataSlate. She lifts her head, takes one look at Alex, and says, "Well, I don't need to guess which one of you is my customer, do I?" She starts rummaging in a drawer full of bandages and ointment.

Alex hops onto one of the stools near the window and motions me closer. "What'd you want to talk about?"

"I . . . can talk to you later." I glance over at Marcy, who seems nice enough, but I'm not ready to tell anyone else about this. I'm not even sure I'm ready to tell Alex. But I have to.

"Here we go." Marcy swoops over Alex and eases off his old bandage. "Ooh, that's a good one. Let's clean it and get you patched up." She raises a UV wand, gives the wound a quick zap to sterilize it, and is reaching for a new bandage when the door opens.

It's Tomas. "Oh, hey, guys." He waits until Marcy looks up. "Van sent me to get him something for a headache?"

"In the meds kit right there on the counter." She starts unwrapping a bandage, but the door bangs open again, and one of the Beekman twins—I can't tell them apart—is holding her arm.

"I tripped on Ava's robot. I think I sprained something," she whines.

Marcy sighs, hands me the bandage—"Can you finish up here?"— and reaches into the freezer for an ice pack.

While she's having Tess try to move her arm in different ways, I finish unwrapping the bandage. "When you were flying the drone yesterday," I whisper, leaning in toward Alex, "I . . . I did see some of the numbers." I cover his cut gently with the clean gauze and take a deep breath. "I wasn't sure I was reading them right, but . . . I think I was."

His eyes light up. "And?"

"I'll be right back; I'm going to take her to the main office to file an accident report." Marcy hustles out of the room with Tess, and we're alone with Tomas, still shuffling through the bottles of pain reliever.

He looks over at us, then picks up one of the bottles and grins. "Better get these to Van before he gets grumpy." He leaves, and I turn back to Alex.

I have to force myself to say the words. He'll see for himself when we download the data anyway. "The storm wasn't dissipating at the fence."

"But it turned away at the perimeter."

"And kept going, remember? Whatever happened at the fence didn't weaken it, Alex. Wait until you see the numbers."

"You saw the numbers?"

I nod. "I saw enough."

He stares up at me from the stool, and I watch his eyes shift from a look of confusion to shocked understanding. "It left . . . and got stronger?"

I nod. "And then last night, my dad left his office open." I take my DataSlate from my backpack on the floor and pull up another stool next to him. "I went onto his computer and looked up his results from his dissipation research, from the simulation he did that was like yours."

"And? It failed, right? You told me that before."

"That's what I thought." I click into the folder I copied and turn the screen so he can see the full list of files. "Remember the abstract he printed up for me? The one that summarized his failed simulation?"

"Yeah."

"This is it." I point to the document.

AGM-FAKEABSTRACT

His eyebrows knit together, and the new bandage tugs at his skin. He raises a slow hand to it. "It . . . wasn't real?"

"This is the real one." I click the other document open, hand him the DataSlate, and hold my breath.

Alex reads. His eyes grow wider with every word. Finally, he shakes his head. "Why?" He turns to me, as if I'm a stranger. "Why would he hide this? This information . . ." He taps the DataSlate screen, and his voice gets louder. "This is gold. This is going to solve everything. With proof of the simulation's success, they could have gotten government clearance to do an actual storm-trial using the satellites that are already up." He's talking faster now. "I mean, I don't know if they're totally equipped to send down the right amounts of energy or if the accuracy is what it would need to be yet, given it's not the reason they were originally built, but still . . ." He shakes his head again and looks at me, angry. "What's your dad thinking?"

My mouth goes dry. "I don't know." I'm afraid to tell him more. About the wall of satellites, about the digital kilowatt readings fluctuating during last night's storm.

And I cannot bring myself to tell him the detail that haunts me, that makes my stomach hurt the most. That when the whirling cloud of dust and debris swept across the river last night, my father was happy. As happy as he had been all day.

Without warning, Alex springs up. His stool clatters against the counter and almost tips over. "We need to rerun this simulation." He waves the DataSlate at me. "We can use your dad's original numbers . . . and then try our new data from the drone, too. Let's see if there's availability this morning. It's early in the project, so most people haven't had time to get their sims set up yet."

I follow him to the door, and when he pushes it open, Tomas jumps back to avoid being smacked in the face.

"Oh!" He holds up the bottle of headache meds—"Got the wrong kind. See you guys later on"—and hurries past us back into the first aid room.

Alex walks down the hallway, out the door, and across campus so fast I can barely keep up.

Van's working on the main computer when we get to the Sim Dome. "Hey, champ," he says to Alex.

"Do you think we could run that simulation once more?" Alex blurts out, waving his DataSlate.

"Seriously, my friend?" Van folds his arms in front of him.

"I know it failed before, but I'm positive I have the numbers right now." He turns to me. "We know that—"

"That sometimes a minor input error can throw off a whole experiment," I interrupt. Was he actually going to *tell* Van that I *stole* my father's data? My eyes flash a warning at Alex before I turn back to Van. "We have two sets of numbers we want to double-check."

Van chuckles and shakes his head, but he walks to the access panel and slips in the key card that provides access to the simulation computer. "You found a kindred spirit, Alex. She's as stubborn as you are." He winks at Alex as the door slides open. "Go for it, but this is the last time I can let you run this one. It's a waste of resources."

"Okay, thanks." We step into the control room, just as Tomas arrives, hopefully with the right meds this time. We need Van in a good mood.

Alex plugs his DataSlate into the mainframe and feeds in the numbers. The same numbers my father used for the successful simulation he ran up at StormSafe. The one that worked.

The computer beeps, and a red button appears with the words BEGIN SIMULATION. Alex looks over at Van, who's huddled close to Tomas, talking. Finally, he glances up and gives us a sharp nod. Alex takes a deep breath, clicks the button, and leans back in his chair to watch.

A new button appears on the computer screen—INITIATE VARIABLE—but Alex's eyes are on the charcoal clouds forming high up in the dome to his left. They darken and swirl as they cross the river, and right before they reach the model city laid out on the grid in front of us, a funnel cloud drops down.

"Okay," Alex whispers. "Here we go." He watches, intent as the funnel widens and stretches toward the field of faux grass and synthetic trees, and just as it looks ready to touch down, he triggers the variable, presses the button that tells the computer-generated tornado that three hundred virtual kilowatts of microwave energy are blasting into its heart, heating the air in the downdraft. He's told the tornado to imagine the exact circumstances that would lead to its death.

I hold my breath and watch.

There is a spark from the vortex of the storm, and it seems to pause as if it's considering the new variable. Then the funnel cloud swells and pushes forward into the model city. It devours the library, the fire station, the school, four-five-six-seven houses, and grows fat with debris, heading for the business district.

Then the computer screen goes blank. The wind stops blowing, the clouds disappear, and the swirling-whirling-flying debris clatters to the floor. The lights in the dome flicker and go out.

When they come back on, Van and Tomas are stepping out of the observation room. Tomas leaves the dome without waving or even looking at us. "Sorry," Van radios into our cube, "I don't see the point in continuing. You're done."

Alex slides open the door, steps into the main dome, and throws his hands up in the air. "I don't understand how—"

"What you don't seem to understand is that it's time to give up on this one." Van ushers us toward the door.

"Van, wait. We have another set of numbers, different data." Alex doesn't say where the new data came from, thank God, and Van doesn't ask.

Alex starts to turn back to the control panel. "Couldn't we—"

"No," Van snaps. "At some point, you need to accept when a theory isn't working." He opens the door for us to leave, and a rush of warm air flows in. "Go back to the drawing board and consider some other ideas. You've tried the heat-the-downdraft approach, and it failed. Look into wind shear or another theory. But it's time to let this one go."

Alex's hands are clenched into fists. "But I know this should work." He looks back into the dome as if there might be someone else who will give him permission to run the other numbers. But there's just Van blocking the way.

"Has the Sim Dome been checked over since last year?" Alex asks. "Has it been recalibrated to make sure the storms react in line with the data? And the software's up to date and everything?"

Van's face relaxes into a little smile. "It stinks to be wrong, doesn't it? I wish I could tell you it wasn't you, my friend, but this Sim Dome is as up-to-date and fine-tuned as they come. It was checked over, top to bottom, and recalibrated over the weekend."

Alex sighs. "Well, couldn't the guy have made a mistake?"

"I doubt that very much." Van walks us to the door, smirking. "The guy was Dr. Meggs himself."

Chapter 17

Alex doesn't say a word as we walk across the quad. He doesn't hold open the library door.

"So now what are we going to do?" I ask Alex.

He wheels around, eyes burning. "*We?*" He looks at me hard, then lets out an incredulous little laugh. "*We* aren't going to do anything because *we* just got completely shut down. I'd say this one's in *your* court now."

"Alex, why are you mad at *me*? What's wrong?"

"What's wrong? Your father did the maintenance on the Sim Dome himself. He could calibrate that system in his sleep. Do you think for one second it's an accident our simulation didn't work?"

"Well, maybe . . . ," I begin. The thought had already crept into my brain—no, into my gut, in an awful twisting way—before we even left the observation cube. But part of me needs to believe that the dad who used to sing to me at night might still have something good inside.

Alex doesn't wait for me to finish my sentence. He plows into the library and stomps toward the table where we were working.

"I know what it looks like," I whisper, "but maybe we could talk to him about this. There might be a reason. Maybe he has, I don't know, some other information that . . ."

Alex's eyes burn the rest of my words into ashes. "Listen to you." He leans back against a bookshelf and stares at me as if I'm someone he's never met before, someone he wouldn't want to know. "This isn't a computer game." His voice trembles, and his hand shakes as he raises his arm and gestures back in the direction of the Sim Dome. "This is about people's lives. About my family. What your father is doing here is—"

"You don't *know* what he's doing."

"Yes I do, and so do you. It doesn't take a genius, Jaden. And unless you do something about it—"

"Unless *I do something about it?*"

Ms. Walpole pokes her head around the corner. "Is everything okay?"

"Fine, yeah." Alex pulls a book from the shelf and starts flipping through it.

She frowns and steps up beside us. "Shall I ask about the 'library materials' I loaned you yesterday? Or shall I presume you've returned them already?"

Alex looks up at her. "The plane is fine, but it's—"

"Mr. Carillo, the book that I loaned you is a rare volume, and I trust it will be returned in good shape when you're finished." Ms. Walpole raises her eyebrows at him and raises a finger to her lips.

I look around, but we're the only ones in the library that I can see. Is she suggesting that the place is bugged? That someone's listening in? What kind of camp *is* this?

Alex nods slowly. "The book has been very useful. Thanks. It's at my house, and I'll return it soon."

"Perfect." She walks back to her desk, picks up her book, and starts reading.

Alex goes back to flipping pages in the book he's holding, but I put out a hand to stop him. "You say you want me to *do something?* What am I supposed to do?" I whisper, and my thoughts are swirling so much I hardly care who's listening.

He looks up from the book, and says in a voice too low for anyone listening in to hear, so quiet I can barely make out the words myself, "Get yourself into the dome at his company somehow," he whispers. "Run the numbers there." His eyes are urgent, pleading. But I'm already shaking my head.

"I can't." I remember the feeling of hiding under his desk. What would he have done if he'd caught me? "It's too much of a risk. I can't."

The light in Alex's eyes clicks off. "Then you're not the person I thought you were." He looks more sad than angry as he pushes the book back onto the shelf and walks out the door.

In the morning, I sit in my usual auditorium seat and wait for a hand on my arm or a whisper in my ear. When Van finishes a quick morning update, Risha runs to meet Tomas, and I walk to the library alone.

I upload four new meteorology and climatology texts to my DataSlate and spend the next three days reading, bookmarking, and trying to get used to being a team of one.

Ms. Walpole drops a little paper bag on my table as she walks by on one of her book-shelving missions. Oatmeal raisin cookies.

"Thanks," I whisper when she comes by again.

She stops next to my chair. "Where's our boy?"

"He's . . . not happy with me," is all I can muster.

"Well, he'll get over it. Have a cookie," she says, as if it's some ordinary boy-girl thing like him having a crush on somebody else. If only. "And tell him he needs to return that rare book before people start asking questions." She raises her eyebrows at the ceiling, and I wonder again who's listening.

I keep watching the library door after she leaves, but Alex never walks through it.

He won't even look at me the rest of the week.

Saturday's too hot to go outside, so I spend the afternoon in my room, reading.

I try writing to Mom, but it bounces back again, so I call Amelia for a video-chat instead. It's good to see her face and great to hear what everyone's doing at home, but when she asks how things are going here, I don't have much to offer. I try to explain the projects at camp, but she makes a face, and I feel like I've moved away to another planet where the language isn't even the same as it is on Earth.

Sunday morning, Dad leaves for StormSafe before it's light, and when I come downstairs, Mirielle is packing the diaper bag. "Good morning!" She winks at me. "I thought we girls might go on a little adventure today."

"What kind of adventure?"

"Your aunt Linda invited us to visit." She hums a light, breezy song that seems to match the lilacs on her sleeveless blouse. I watch her tickling Remi in her bouncy chair, setting the timer to make sure Dad's dinner will be ready later, and my chest tightens.

Who was that woman on the phone? Does Mirielle have any idea what Dad's whispering to somebody else in his office late at night?

Mirielle pauses with a bottle of juice in her hand and tips her head at me. "Are you all right? I thought you'd be pleased."

I realize my whole face is clenched up, and I force myself to relax. "Yes, it's great. Thanks."

As we drive out of town, past the beat-up trailer parks, past the Corrections Department energy farm and an underground play center that's seen better days, I lower my window. The country roads are lined with big old maple and pine trees that have somehow survived the storms. The fields are strewn with wildflowers. I take a deep breath and sigh. "I know it's not as safe out here, but it feels . . . I don't know . . . fresher. Cleaner, somehow."

"It's safe enough for right now. We have two DataSlates. We'll get alerts if anything changes." Mirielle glances over at me and smiles a little. "And I know what you mean about the air. Sometimes, Remi and I go for drives when your father is at work." She glances in the rearview mirror. "Only when the weather's quiet, of course."

We drive through a long stretch of woods—even the trees smell different out here—and then out into a more open stretch where the trees are smaller, planted in rows.

"Are these fruit trees?" I ask.

"Mmm-hmm." Mirielle reaches behind her to tickle Remi's foot. "Peaches mostly. Linda grows them, too."

Around a curve, the orchards end, and finally, there's a white farmhouse. It's old, the kind you'd expect to have lots of long hallways and closets. There's a porch with big pillars and rocking chairs out front. Behind the house is an old red barn, half falling down, and a brown horse wandering around outside a stable. Next to the barn, there's a tiny farm stand that looks like someone might have nailed it together out of old barn pieces this morning. A hand-painted sign leaning against it reads:

SWEET RASPBERRIES: $12/PINT
FRESH PEACHES: $2 EACH
COMPLIMENTS: FREE

Mirielle pulls into the driveway, and I smile. This place feels like everything I remember about Aunt Linda. She comes running from the house in a flowered blouse and blue jeans and pulls me into a hug the second I'm out of the car.

"My great stars, Jaden! It's been years." She holds me back so she can look at me. "You are your mother's daughter, aren't you?"

"Most people say I look like Dad."

Aunt Linda's smile flickers like a lightbulb with a loose wire, but then it's back. "Well, I suppose you look like Jaden," she says.

The horse whinnies outside the barn, and I turn.

"That Nutmeg . . . always looking for a treat." She digs into her pocket and pulls out a few sugar cubes. "Do you want to go say hello to her before we go inside?"

"Sure."

Aunt Linda leans in to talk quietly to Remi as I clunk down the wooden porch steps and across the grass. It's hard to imagine a person as gentle and relaxed as Aunt Linda raising someone as intense as my father. But I guess part of who you are is genetics, and when I think of Grandma Athena's fiery eyes staring out from her frame, it's easy to see her spirit alive in Dad.

The sugar cubes are rough and sticky in my palm as I step up to the split-rail fence. Nutmeg ambles over, and I climb onto the first rung to pet her on the nose.

"Hold the sugar flat on your palm," Aunt Linda calls to me, "so she doesn't get your fingers."

I do, and Nutmeg's warm, snuffly lips scarf it up.

I feed her my last three cubes. She sniffs my pocket, decides I'm of no more use to her, and wanders away.

"She's beautiful," I say, joining Aunt Linda and Mirielle back on the porch.

"She's been with me a long time." Aunt Linda holds open the door to the kitchen, and we walk into a bright yellow room with a wooden chopping block in the middle and, above it, a rack of copper pots and pans. The wall over the sink has old wallpaper with tiny apples all in rows.

Aunt Linda serves up lemonade and peach pie, and we sit at the big wooden table, talking about camp and Mom's trip and Remi sitting up all by herself. When I finish my pie, I get up to look at the dishes displayed over the sink, all painted in bright colors.

"That's my wall of fame," Aunt Linda says, laughing. She pulls down a coffee mug with an old guy's face painted on it. On the other side there's a short poem called "Fire and Ice."

"Robert Frost." She nods up at the shelf. "And there's Emily Dickinson and Walt Whitman. All my favorite poets. I paint their portraits on one side and a poem on the other."

Rita Dove's not there, but the poet mugs remind me of her. "Thank you for the book."

"You are most welcome." Aunt Linda pulls me into a hug and looks at Mirielle. "Can you stay a while?"

Way in the distance, thunder rumbles, as if it's answering for Mirielle. *No, time to head home.*

Mirielle smiles but shakes her head. "We'd better go. But we'll find time for another visit soon. I'll get Remi changed, and then we'll be off." She picks up the diaper bag and carries Remi into the living room.

"Thanks for today," I tell Aunt Linda, and she has no idea how much I mean it, how much I needed some plain old family love. "I wish you lived closer."

She grins and raises her mug. "Placid Meadows is not my cup of tea, my dear. But I would love for you to visit often."

"Me too," I say, "but there's Dad . . ."

"Oh, I know. He's not too fond of me these days."

"He's not too fond of anybody. Except Mirielle and Remi some-times." I hadn't said it before, but that's how I feel. "It's kind of like he's not *my* dad anymore."

Aunt Linda puts a warm arm around my shoulders. "Oh, sweet Jaden," she says. "He loves you. But you can't count on him showing it in any of the usual ways, I'm afraid. Lord knows I loved that boy when he was growing up—still do—but he wanted his mother all those years and could never have her. Not even before she died, which is the saddest thing of all. She loved her work so much, and it was always urgent-urgent-urgent. She thought she'd have plenty of time for your dad later." She shakes her head.

In the other room, Mirielle sings to Remi, something soft in French.

"So now Dad does the same thing," I say, "to me."

Aunt Linda looks like she wants to argue, but she can't. She gives me a squeeze.

"All set?" Mirielle carries Remi back into the kitchen. "We'll be back soon, I promise." I hug Aunt Linda one more time and hope Mirielle means it.

Nutmeg is at the fence when we step off the porch, probably hoping for more sugar. "Bye, girl," I tell her, and I pat her nose. It feels like velvet in the sun, soft and warm and good.

The clouds are already closer when we pull out of the drive-way. Mirielle catches me sneaking glances out the rear window.

"Not to worry," she says. "We will be home soon. Safe and sound."

We will be, I think. But what about Aunt Linda? What about Nutmeg, who's not protected by anything other than weathered timber once she's in the barn? How long will it be before one of these storms makes a direct hit?

Chapter 18

The storm comes just as we're pulling into Placid Meadows and passes quickly. It's small, so I don't worry about Aunt Linda—this time.

With the sun blazing again, it's steaming hot, so after lunch we collapse on the couch with iced tea while Remi naps in her bouncy seat.

Mirielle turns on the entertainment window. "Oh good! There's ballet streaming from the National Arts Center." Two men and two women twirl and leap through a routine in the underground theater hundreds of miles away.

Mirielle watches the dancers. And I watch Mirielle. Her face flickers between happy and sad, and I wonder if she's remembering performances of her own, back when there were real audiences all over the world.

"Do other countries do this now, too?" I ask.

She startles as if she'd been far away. With the dancers, maybe. "Do they do what?"

"Have a national arts feed instead of live performances."

She nods sadly. "Most do. My sister in Paris says they're building a new theater there, with a safe room directly underneath. Around here, there are only tiny local dance groups. They perform in church basements mostly, community safe rooms. Your father has never wanted to go, but I'd love to see them." Her eyes drift back to the entertainment window, where one of the men is lifting the woman high over his head. In her gleaming white dress, she looks like a seagull soaring. Mirielle sighs. "They aren't professionals, of course, but it would be lovely to see real live people dancing again."

Watching Mirielle's eyes mist makes me clench my jaw. Dad was probably too busy at work, too busy with whoever he was talking to on the videophone, for some stupid ballet. "I'd go with you some time," I blurt out.

She smiles. "I'd love that. I'll see what I can find."

"Maybe Aunt Linda could come," I say. Somehow, I miss her already. I bet she'd like the dancing, too.

She nods slowly. "On some night when your father is busy." Her green eyes dart over to his office door for a second. "We will tell him we are doing some shopping, perhaps."

The doorbell rings then. "I'll get it." I step carefully around Remi in her bouncy chair and go to the door, where Risha's lifting her hand to ring again.

"Where've you been all weekend?" She pulls her BeatBuds out of her ears, steps past me into the kitchen, and paws through the fruit bowl on the counter. Her hair is tied back in a gauzy purple scarf that flows down her back. "You have to come on a bike ride with me or I'm going to die of boredom." She polishes an apple on her purple-and-red-striped T-shirt and takes a big bite.

"It's too hot."

"Jaden, pleeease? Just to the park for a while."

If I say no, Risha will want to know what's wrong, and I don't want to talk about Alex, so I call good-bye to Mirielle and get my bike.

The air is heavy as soup-steam, but it still feels good to pedal.

"Hey," I say as Risha takes a turn toward the fence. "Aren't we going to the park?"

"Change of plans." She glances back at me, eyes twinkling. She's made plans with the boys, I can tell, and my stomach twists at the thought of seeing Alex now.

"Not today, Risha." Besides, the clouds are starting to build again, and just because the first storm today was mild doesn't mean the next one will be. "You said you wanted to go to the park for a while. I'm not going outside the fence. There's weather coming."

"Not even for a little while? Tomas has hardly talked to me all week. He's been acting all weird, and I know he's worried about his mom. I just want to see him."

She keeps riding toward the fence, and I follow her, thinking I'll stay back while she goes to see the boys.

But when Risha jumps off her bike and climbs through the gap without looking back, something in me can't let her go alone with the clouds swirling. "Fine," I say. "This better be fast."

"Yay!" She's already on the other side, and I have to scramble through to catch her.

Risha winds her way toward the gazebo where we had our picnic—it's empty—and then races to the Carillos' barn and pulls open the door. Two chocolate-brown goats nuzzle each other in one stall. In another, a fat black pig is sleeping. Some chickens are wandering around, too. One wall is lined with bales of hay or straw. Another has dozens of tools—pitchforks, shovels, and axes—hanging from cast-iron hooks. "Hellooo?" Risha looks around. "Shoot," she says, turning back to me. "They probably figured we weren't coming."

I try not to look too happy. "They probably figured they should head for a safe room." The sky looks grayer and greener, more menacing than it did a few minutes ago.

"Well, boo," she says. Then she grabs my hand. "That's okay. I still want to show you something." She ducks between two vintage tractors with steering wheels for actual people who'd drive them and ride around on them. Then she bends down and tugs at a big metal ring sticking up from the floor. "Help me with this, will you?"

I wrap my hand around the cool metal, too, and pull. A creaky panel of wood lifts up from the floor—a trapdoor.

"Check this out." Risha climbs down a metal-runged ladder and fades into the dark.

I wait for her to pop up again, but she doesn't.

"Are you coming back?" I call, squatting by the swung-open door. My voice sounds echoey and cold. The skies have opened up now, and rain is pelting the roof like a mad drummer. The wind blows a flurry of wet, battered leaves through the open door, and I shiver, even though the air is still warm. "Risha, I want to go home."

She doesn't answer.

I stand up, shake out my knees, and head for the barn door. I'm about to step out into the rain when a colossal bolt of lightning cracks through the sky, close enough that the tiny hairs on the back of my neck tingle. Thunder follows half a second later—a sharp, deep crack that shakes the whole barn.

Wind rattles the windows, and outside, tree branches are starting to snap. The sky is dark. Too dark.

Don't let this happen now. Not with us out here.

There's no way I can leave now. I turn away from the pounding rain and call again, "Risha?"

Something knocks on the barn roof. Again. And then two knocks turn into frantic pounding, beating on the roof, and outside, hailstones the size of my fist pummel the dirt.

The sky explodes in light and thunder again. Vibrations shake the barn.

And then there's another sound.

A growing roar that rumbles through my body.

I run for the trapdoor.

I don't know what's down there, but I know what's coming, and I can't be in this room full of sharp metal tools when it hits.

I step onto the ladder, cling to the cool metal rungs, and lower myself, step by trembling step. Above me, where the trapdoor is flopped open, the square of light flashes with lightning. The whole foundation of the building seems to shudder, and the wind blows through the door, through gaps in the beams, with a high-pitched whine that makes me shiver.

Without stopping to think, I climb back up the ladder rungs

into the barn and tug on the handle of the trapdoor. It's solid wood, and I can barely move it, but throwing all my weight against it, I'm able to lug it up from the barn floor, ease back down onto the ladder, and let the door thump shut over my head.

I know I am on the ladder with three, maybe four rungs to climb down, but the darkness feels too thick to move through. Even with the heavy wooden door closed over my head, I can hear the wind roar.

"Risha!" I call, but her name echoes back at me off the floor.

I take a shuddery breath and blink hard, but my eyes don't adjust, so still swallowed in the dark, I start climbing down again.

The rusty metal scratches my palms. I hold on tight, concentrating on that as I lower myself one rung at a time.

Down, down, down, until I see a sliver of light off to one side. I follow it down a long hallway with cool stone walls, and the roar of the wind grows muffled. The light brightens, and finally, I get to the source, a room at the end of the long hall. I push the heavy, half-shut door until it swings open.

"You came down!" Risha is lounging on a daybed. Rock music plays from speakers mounted on the walls. She pats the seat next to her. "Isn't this so perfect?"

I step into the room, and the door swings shut behind me with a thick, wooden thud that makes me jump. *Perfect?* She's bouncing lightly on the daybed, grinning, while the storm rages outside. I can't hear it way down here, but I know it's still there.

She reaches for a bottle of water—there are cases of them, rows of canned goods and packages of all kinds of food. Might as well be comfortable if you're stuck in a tiny room, pretending everything's all right.

"Jaden, we're fine here. What's wrong?"

What's wrong? I open my mouth to answer her, but nothing comes out. This. This is wrong, I think. This world where people have to run for shelter nearly every afternoon, where most people live in fear that this storm—this one—might be the one that destroys everything. This world, where a handful of people are so used to being safe, so used to living inside StormSafe's little bubble, that they never worry at all.

"What is this?" I finally ask. "It doesn't look like a regular safe room."

"It's an old bomb shelter from the 1960s. Isn't it the best? It's just like a safe room, really—concrete walls, reinforced with steel. I think this must be what the StormSafe houses were based on." She grabs a package of chocolate sandwich cookies from the shelf above her, tears it open, and shoves a whole one in her mouth.

"Want one?" She holds the package out to me. Cookies. In the middle of a storm that looks like it could devour us whole. My stomach twists, and I shake my head.

I strain my ears for the sounds of the storm, but I can't sort anything out anymore. The fluorescent light overhead flickers. What's going on up there?

"Sure you don't want one?" she asks.

"How can you sit there eating cookies?" I blurt out.

She swallows. "We hang out here all the time. It's fine. Tomas and Alex and I kind of took this place over, so we always—"

The music stops and the lights go out, and it feels like the blackness swallows up Risha, too, because she never finishes her sentence. The roar whooshes louder, and the wind isn't low, loud static anymore. It's growling, hissing, popping over our heads.

I reach out for Risha in the blackness, where I hope her hand might be. It's cool and damp. An edge of her fingernail scratches my palm.

"Has this ever happened when you were here before?" I whisper.

"No." She squeezes my hand. "But Alex told me he rode out a storm here once. We'll be okay." But her voice is quiet. Not so confident. Not so Risha.

I don't let go of her hand.

It sounds like the storm is chewing its way through the building over our heads, spitting out mouthfuls of metal, crunching wood into splinters.

I close my eyes and open them again. It looks exactly the same.

Black and terrifying and loud.

When I was little, afraid of the dark, Mom used to tell me that nothing could ever be as scary as the monsters in my imagination, that all my nightmares would vanish when she turned on the light. But this time, I already know that's not true. I am imagining a monster upstairs, and I'm afraid—so afraid—that reality will be a million times worse.

I squeeze Risha's hand and hear her ragged breath. I lean closer, and she rests her head against my shoulder, the smell of chocolate cookies on her breath mixing with something else. Sweat. Or fear.

The monster roars louder. How long can the barn hold out?

Glass shatters over our heads. Something splinters, crackle by sharp crackle by groan. Is it the support beam right above us? The barn roof? A wall? Whatever it is creaks, moans a long final moan, and then CRACKS.

Is it broken? Gone?

The wind doesn't answer; it only screams and roars.

Until finally, the sounds fade.

I don't know how long we sit. Long enough for chaos to turn to distant rumbling and then silence.

Long enough for our pounding hearts to sound like cannons in the dark.

We huddle together without moving, without speaking a word, and somewhere inside, I begin to understand what has happened. Even Risha, with all her StormSafe confidence, knows this was no everyday storm. It was bad. But we sit in the dark, still holding hands, both under the spell of the same fairy tale lie.

If you don't look, it won't hurt.

It you don't turn on the lights, you'll never see the monster.

If we stay here in the blackness, if we never go up to see what happened, then maybe it never happened at all.

But then come the sounds.

Quiet at first.

Uneven. Stopping and starting footsteps.

Creaking. Lifting. Wood-sliding-against-wood.

A voice so faint I can't tell whose it is or what it's saying. But the tone is unmistakable. The raw edge, the desperation. Someone needs help.

"Risha?" I start to pull my hand away from her, but she holds on. I wiggle my hand free and stand.

I still can't see, but I hear the daybed creak and know she's standing to follow me. I slide a hand against the cool dampness of the wall until I feel the doorframe and take a step out into the hall.

"I'm scared," Risha whispers, and admitting that is so not-Risha that a wave of cold terror races through me. What's waiting for us out there?

"Me, too." We feel our way down the still-night-black hallway, scuffing our feet all the way to the end. The toe of my sneaker bumps something that makes a dull metal clang.

The ladder.

"Ready to go up?"

I wait until I feel her closer to me, feel her shoulder brushing against mine. I take hold of a cold metal rung and start climbing.

Risha's right behind me; her hand brushes my ankle every couple of rungs.

At the top, I keep one hand clutched around a ladder rung. With the other, I reach over my head to push on the spot where the trapdoor should open.

It doesn't budge.

"Can you steady me?"

"Hold on." I feel one of Risha's arms wrap around my calves to help me stay balanced on the rung. I let go of the ladder and use both hands to push up as hard as I can, until I'm sure my face is bursting red.

There is nothing at first—as if the door's been sealed. I give it another big push, and then, a crack of light appears.

I bend my knees and push harder. Something slides off the tilting door onto the floor, and the crack grows wider, until the light opens up into a bright, narrow beam of sun. The trapdoor swings wide, thuds down on the barn floor, and there is light. Bright, blinding yellow-white light, like we've flopped open the door to heaven.

I step up another rung and see I am wrong. So wrong.

This is as far from heaven as a world can be.

The light is so bright because there is nothing between us and the sky.

The barn is gone.

Gone, except for half a wall whose skeleton teeters, creaking as if it's in pain. A splintered wooden rod sticks out from the middle of the wall—it wasn't there before—and somehow in the midst of this chaos, I am fixated on it.

I crawl up out of the hole in the floor, my knees scraping over splintered wood, and rise, shaking, to my feet.

I climb over twisted metal, boards, and beams, through wood splinters and feathers and dust—up to the wall where the wooden rod sticks straight out.

It is the pitchfork I'd seen hanging from a hook on the other wall, part of the tidy row of tools, all lined up before the storm.

I wrap my hands around the handle and pull. I hang on it with all my body weight.

It doesn't move.

I breathe, hoarse and deep, and rest my hand on a ragged beam. It feels as if it's the only thing holding me up. I hold on as if the winds might return any second and blow me away, and slowly, I turn away from this piece of wall.

Around it, beams lay scattered over one another like pickup sticks tossed by a giant.

An ax is embedded in what must have been one of the main support beams. Shreds of roofing litter the foundation like bits of paper torn to shreds.

The tractor is gone. Way down near the driveway, I make out a mass of twisted red metal wrapped around a tree.

Risha is frozen halfway up the ladder, clutching the trapdoor frame so hard I worry the metal edge will cut her hand.

"Rish?" I call. But she won't come up. She's in shock.

"Risha?"

She stares. Blinks hard. Squeezes her eyes closed. Opens them again.

I know what she is trying to do.

It doesn't work.

It's all still here.

And then the voice returns, clearer this time, but ragged and choked.

"Newton! Newton!"

I turn toward the farmhouse, or where the farmhouse would have been, and suck in my breath. The concrete safe room is all that's left, but I can breathe after I count the figures coming out of it. Alex's parents. His little sister, Julia. Tomas.

Alex climbs over the debris, and even from here, I see his tear-stained face.

"Newton! Newton, come on, boy!"

"Alex!" I call from the barn, and he whirls around as if I'm a ghost or another storm. I don't care; I start running, tripping over twisted metal tools and clambering over splintered boards until I reach him. I want to throw my arms around him.

But I don't.

"I . . . let me help you," I say.

"Where were you?"

"In that room under the barn. With Risha."

"Where is she?"

"She's okay." I turn to the barn where finally, Risha is rising up from the shelter, ladder rung by ladder rung.

When I turn back to Alex, his face is twisted in pain. "I could hear him barking," he whispers. "But we had to close the door." He turns and heads toward a high pile of debris that looks like it might have been the garage once. "Newton!"

He is flinging boards, and tears burn my eyes. If Newton is under there . . .

"Alex . . ." His father's quiet voice cuts through the clattering wood. He stands at the edge of the heap of house pieces, shakes his head, and holds out his arms. Alex collapses into them, sobbing.

"Is there anything we can do?" whispers Risha, who's made her way over to the safe room that still stands.

Alex's mom is leaning against the concrete wall, holding a first aid kit. It looks small and pathetic in her hand. She shakes her head. "Maybe . . . maybe tomorrow." She looks out over the farm, at debris that's scattered all the way out to the main road. What can we possibly do to help tomorrow? Or any day? What can anyone do?

Risha tugs my sleeve, then slides her hand down to hold mine again. Tight. "We should probably go," she says.

But I can't. I can't move from this place, watching Alex's shoulders heave under his father's arm. His dad waits until the sobs slow and finally stop. He doesn't say a word. What can he say? That everything will be all right? It won't.

"Hold on," I tell Risha. I make my way to Alex and put a hand tentatively on his back. I expect him to whirl around and push my hand away, but he doesn't. Alex's dad gives his shoulder one last squeeze and leaves us alone.

"I'm sorry," I whisper.

He doesn't answer. He stares at that one wall left of the barn with empty eyes.

The sky is so quiet now it's hard to believe what has happened. How can something vanish so quickly and leave so much brokenness behind?

"Alex, please just know that—"

"Shh!" He holds up both hands and squints his eyes shut tight, and I'm sure it's because he can't even stand the sound of my voice. But then I hear it, too.

A whimper.

"It's coming from over there!" Alex pushes past me back toward the one wall that's left of the barn. He steps over boards and twisted metal.

"Newton!"

He starts to step over another pile of rubble—did it used to be the goat pen?—but stops and collapses to the barn floor.

I run, tripping through the debris, until I reach him.

And then I stop.

Newton is splayed in the dust, panting with shallow breaths. His head is bleeding between his ears. A patch of fur is gone, and the rest is matted with blood and dust. One of his legs is twisted at a sick angle, bleeding, too. My breath catches, and my stomach twists, and I have to look away.

"Get some water," Alex's father says quietly behind me. I run back to the shelter because it's the one thing I can do instead of crumbling. I climb down the ladder, stumble down the hallway into the blackness. I crack my shin on the daybed frame, fall forward, and feel the shelf. I flail my arms around until they connect with cool smooth plastic. I take two water bottles and find my way back up into the light.

"Here." I kneel down next to Alex and unscrew the cap from one bottle. He takes it from me and pours it first over the open break in Newton's leg, then over the cut on his head. The bleeding has slowed, but Newton's breaths are coming fast and shallow.

"Shhh . . . it's okay, boy." I put a hand to Newton's shoulder and feel his heartbeat, rapid. Scared.

"We need . . ." Alex is choking back sobs. He squeezes his eyes shut, then opens them again. "I gotta have a bandage or . . . or something."

Risha slips the scarf from her hair and hands it to him. She walks off and sits down in the grass next to Tomas, still in shock.

"Wrap it around the leg just enough to secure it," Alex's father says, leaning over us. "We'll try to get him into town to the vet. Maybe . . ." But his voice trails off.

Alex wraps the scarf around Newton's leg, careful to avoid hurting him even more. He swipes at his eyes with his shirtsleeve and stands, staring over the debris of the barn. Not far from the trapdoor he finds a long piece of board and drags it back next to Newton. Together, we ease the dog onto it.

"Careful," Alex whispers. It must hurt, and I'm expecting Newton to snap at me, but he never does. He just keeps panting, looking up at Alex with big dog eyes that seem to say a million things at once. *How could you let this happen to me?* But also, *I trust you. Please help.*

"I'll get the truck," Alex's dad says quietly. Somehow, it survived the storm, parked at the edge of a field not fifty yards from the barn, as if the tornado couldn't be bothered with it. Alex's mom has already gone back to the safe room with Julia. She doesn't need to see all this.

Alex kneels next to Newton, rubbing behind his ear. His hand is caked with blood.

"I'm sorry," I whisper.

He doesn't look up.

"I am." The words are choked, but I force them out. "About Newton and the farm, and about not doing anything. This is awful, Alex, your family and Newton . . ." And Aunt Linda and Nutmeg, I think. Did this storm hit them, too?

"Alex, I was wrong. It *is* worth the risk. Stopping this is worth almost anything." Hot tears streak down my cheeks. "I'll do it. Okay? I'm going to go up there. I promise."

He turns to me and shrugs. The pickup rumbles up, and he stands to help his father lift Newton into the back.

I watch as Alex climbs in next to his dog, holding him close as the truck pulls away.

Chapter 19

It's a full week before I can make good on my promise.

A full week of watching and waiting. Of making weather small talk with Dad, chitchatting with Mirielle, and playing peek-a-boo with Remi.

A full week of camp, going through the motions without Alex.

A full week of wondering when he'll be back. Wondering if Newton is going to be okay.

Finally, on Monday morning, Dad finishes breakfast and heads to his office. Mirielle is out shopping, so there's no one to swoop in and clear the counter. I watch the door close, grab what I need, and call Risha. "I got it."

She's been amazing since the storm. I told her everything when we got back home that night, about Alex, our argument, and what I promised him I'd do. I confessed my plan to somehow get into my father's work office and access his computers. Instead of telling me how crazy I am, Risha asked about the security systems at Storm-Safe. When I told her it was probably a fingerprint scan, she smiled.

"That'll be the easy part then," she said. "You just need the right fingerprints."

And now I have them.

I meet Risha and we ride as fast as we can to camp; we get there half an hour before it starts.

Risha scans her print and ushers me into the Finger Factory, the nickname she and Tomas gave Eye on Tomorrow's cloning center.

We step into what amounts to a coatroom, with hooks on the walls and a row of lockers. Risha opens one and hands me a lab coat, hair cover, and latex gloves. "Put these on, okay? We don't want any cross contamination or it'll mess everything up."

Once we're outfitted, she scans her print again, and the door to the actual laboratory slides open. Humming with high-powered computer servers and packed with DNA extraction equipment, this is every bit as impressive as the Sim Dome.

The entire room shines with stainless steel. Every countertop gleams; most are covered with trays of test tubes in perfect lines. There are incubators—some quietly warming genetic stews, some turning in slow rotation.

Risha leads me to a workstation along the wall and nods toward a white petri dish on the counter. Something pinkish gray is floating in it. "We've been trying to grow an ear," she says. "It seems to be working, but Van says it'll be another couple weeks before we can find out if it has all the parts it'll need to hear."

"Well, good luck."

"What?" she says.

"Good luck."

"What?" She holds her hand up to her ear—her real ear—and I realize she's making a joke. I laugh a little, and it takes away some of the fear racing through me. It's not that we're not allowed to be here. Van gave Risha permission for early work sessions a while ago, and if anyone asks, she'll just say she's giving me a tour. But if anyone here found out what was in my bag—Dad's coffee mug from this morning, with his fingerprints on it—that would be another story.

"All right, let's get moving." Risha walks down the long counter to a larger, more high-tech workstation and climbs up onto a high stool.

"This is it," she says, and motions for me to take a seat next to her. In front of us is a device that looks like some combination of an electron microscope, an incubator, and a petri dish. Risha pulls clear goggles down over her eyes, picks up a pair of stainless steel forceps, and bends down over the dish, squinting. She holds her breath and pokes with steady hands at the fleshy something in the fluid.

"This turned out perfectly . . ." Slowly and smoothly, she lifts the tip of the forceps from the petri dish. Hanging from the end is a crumpled, yellowish clear membrane. "Here it is." She takes a second pair of forceps and uses it to grab the other edge so it hangs in a thin oval strip. "Got the cup?"

I pull the coffee mug from my bag and point to the clearest print.

"Perfect." Risha carefully maneuvers the tissue into place over the print and presses down on it with a gloved finger for a few seconds. She peels it back off the mug with the forceps and holds the tissue up to the light. "Beautiful." She lowers it back into the solution in the petri dish, and it floats delicately on top. "Let's give it the rest of the day for the pattern to grow. But I'd say you can stop back before you leave today to pick it up." She gestures to the dish with a flourish. "Your brand new fingerprint."

I spend the whole day in the library, half-hoping I'll look up and see Alex, but I know it's too soon. There's too much cleaning up to be done after the storm, too much debris and sadness to wade through.

Risha comes to get me at the end of the day, and we walk back to the Finger Factory while everyone else is heading for their bikes to go home.

The print is ready. I reach for it, but Risha pulls back the forceps. "Ah, ah, AH!" She shakes her head. "This isn't like a glove you can put on and take off all day. You're going to be able to wear it once for a few hours. That's it." She pulls out a shallow glass jar filled with fluid. It's shaped like the tiny container where Mom used to keep her contact lenses before she got her eyes fixed. Risha lowers the tissue into it. "Keep it in here until right before you need it."

She tightens the lid and holds it out to me but then pulls back. "Wait a second. I'm going to start another copy. It'll be easier than starting from scratch if you have a problem with this one." She takes out the tissue, presses it against some kind of glass plate, then puts it back in the jar and hands it over. "All set."

The whole bike ride home, the little jar in my pocket pokes into my hip, reminding me of the crazy thing I am about to try. I tell myself there's time; it may be days, weeks even, before Dad remembers that tour of StormSafe he promised me. There's plenty of time to think about this. Plenty of time to plan.

When I get home, the kitchen door slams closed behind me, and Dad's voice booms out, "Thank goodness!"

He rushes to the entryway, holding a BioWake Cola in one hand and bouncing Remi with the other arm. "Oh." His face falls. "You're not Mirielle."

He paces back toward the kitchen with Remi clinging to his shoulder. "She's out shopping, but she knows I need to be up at headquarters this afternoon." He taps his watch. "I'll have to take the baby with me, I suppose."

I put my backpack on the counter and take a deep breath. This is the opportunity I thought would take weeks to come. It may be my only chance. "I could come with you and help," I blurt out before I have time to think about it any more. "And maybe do that tour you promised?" My heart thuds while I wait for him to answer. The tiny jar in my pocket suddenly feels huge. How could he not see it?

"Well, that's a great idea. Thank you!" Before he even finishes the sentence, he's steering me toward the door. I grab my backpack with my DataSlate and head out to the HV.

Once Remi is strapped in her car seat, Dad pulls out of the garage and starts down the street so fast the tires actually squeal. I wonder what the big hurry is, but his brows are knit together so tightly, the line of his mouth so thin right now, that my question settles back inside me.

We're at the Placid Meadows gate when Dad's DataSlate chimes.

He presses the speaker button, and Mirielle's voice pours out in a recorded message.

"Honey, I am so, so sorry I am running late. We are about to have a storm at the mall, of all things, and I must wait until it passes." Her voice is thinner than usual, like she's scared. But I don't know if that's about the storm or about being late for Dad. "I will see you at home later."

Dad lets out a sharp sigh and veers to the side of the road.

"What are we doing?"

His face is lit by the blue glow of the DataSlate, and he either doesn't hear me or isn't answering. His eyes are trained on the screen, full of columns and numbers and symbols. Dad highlights two of the cells, types in new numbers, and pokes at the CALCU-LATE button.

A new page of numbers appears. He takes another deep breath, and I watch his eyes twitching as they move down the columns. He seems satisfied, and pokes at the APPLY button at the bottom of the screen. I catch a split-second look at the box that appears on the screen next, before Dad notices me reading over his arm and angles the screen away from me.

It was only a second, but it was long enough to read two words: "Satellites responding . . ."

Dad looks down at the DataSlate for another few seconds, then powers it down and puts the car back in drive.

"Did you . . . ?" The words are seared into my mind. *Satellites. Satellites responding.* Responding how? Responding to what? Or to whom? "Did you just . . . do something?"

"I checked on the storm path." He reaches over to turn on the music player. "Don't worry. Mirielle's fine; it took a turn to the east."

It took a turn to the east? All on its own? *Satellites responding.* Responding to commands he entered. He knows how to dissipate storms. Is that what he did? The pieces of this puzzle are popping faster and faster in my brain, like raindrops plunking into a puddle. First one, then two and three at a time, and then so many you forget the surface was ever calm at all.

I stare out the window at the retreating clouds as Dad turns into the long driveway that leads to StormSafe.

"I keep forgetting you haven't been here." He's in a better mood now. "I'll show you around a little before my meeting."

"Great," I say. But it's during his meeting that I expect to see the most. The container in my pocket presses into my hip as I shift in my seat. *Please let this work. Please let it work.*

When we round the final curve in the long driveway, I get my first glimpse of StormSafe headquarters up close.

When I look up from Placid Meadows, the buildings of this place seem to glow, and now I see why. Every wall is made of windows.

Windows like they used to have in houses when Mom and Dad were growing up. Glass ones that squeak if you lick your finger and run it down the pane, windows that smudge and streak and sparkle in the sun. Is it all safety glass?

Dad pulls into a parking space, and we get out of the HV. I balance Remi on my hip and follow Dad up a walkway lined with bright orange poppies. I don't need to check to see if they're symmetrical;

I'm sure every plant is DNA-ture. I wait while Dad presses a finger to the data panel. The door swings open, and there's a receptionist at a long chrome desk. "Hello, Nadia." Dad gives her a wave and heads for the elevator.

Nadia gives a fluttery-fingered wave and tucks a lock of black hair behind her ear. Was she the woman on Dad's DataSlate that night in his office? She doesn't say anything, so I can't compare the voices.

"Want a real quick tour?" He starts down a carpeted hallway. "We've got our conference room down here." He opens a door to a lush room with a long conference table and big leather chairs. "It's the brain center, where we have all our planning and problem-solving sessions."

I step up to the big window and see that this main office isn't all of StormSafe; there are smaller buildings around the parking lot and gardens. "What's in the other buildings?"

"More offices. Some research labs and data centers."

One of the buildings, set apart, looks less modern than the others—just a squat concrete structure, almost like an old storm shelter. There's only a steel door and one window. "What about that one?"

"Nothing exciting, just storage. Come on upstairs," he says, heading back down the hallway. "I'll show you my office."

"What about the Sim Dome?" I ask.

"That's in the basement, but it's in use right now, and I don't want to interrupt."

Dad pushes the elevator button for the eighth floor, and when the bio-scanner beeps, he presses his index finger to the panel. The elevator starts to rise.

Remi reaches for the buttons with chubby hands, too little to understand why her fingers won't get us where we need to go. It needs to be Dad's fingerprint. Or a perfect imitation.

The elevator leads directly to Dad's top-floor office and lab. It's a huge, open space, every wall made of windows with a view over the land. The mahogany desk in the center of the room is an exact copy of the one I hid under in Dad's office at home, and from his chair, he has a view of any weather system approaching.

"Not bad, huh?" Dad takes Remi from my arms and gestures toward the bank of computers. "Go ahead and have a look."

I walk over to the heart of the office—no, more like the brain. Plasma monitors taller than I am grow up out of the floor alongside each workstation. One spews out a constantly scrolling screen of computer-generated weather models. Another three are Doppler radar composites, and two more seem to be live cameras trained on the surrounding landscape. One of those shows the storm Mirielle called about, way off in the distance.

"Amazing, isn't it?" Dad says, bouncing Remi. "This place never sleeps."

"People work here all night?"

"Somebody's here around the clock, and the rest of us check in from home often. This is all tied into the wireless network so it can be controlled remotely." He motions for me to take Remi. "I have to get to that meeting."

I put Remi down on the soft rug by the couch with a couple of toys, and Dad heads for the elevator.

"Will you be long?" I call after him as the door opens. "I mean . . . I wondered if she'll need to take her nap here."

Dad shakes his head. "No, I should only be about twenty minutes." He steps into the shiny silver box, and the door closes.

"Twenty minutes," I whisper to Remi, who's chewing on her toy dolphin's tail. How could that be enough time when I don't even know what I need to do?

I arrange couch cushions around Remi to make a sort of play area, and then I head for one of the lab counters. I pull the jar from my pocket and unscrew the top slowly, as if something might jump out the minute it's open. When I lift the lid, the sharp, sour smell of preservative fluid invades my nose, but even with watering eyes, I can see it suspended in the chemical broth.

My new fingerprint.

I didn't think to bring forceps or tweezers, so I reach into the container, grasp the new tissue between the fingernails of my thumb and forefinger, and pull it out. It hangs like a wet scrap of cloud.

I take a quick glance at Remi—still playing with the dolphin, but her eyelids look heavy—and then as delicately as I possibly can, I spread the new skin over the tip of the index finger on my left hand. It's so thin and elastic that it wraps right around, and when I press the edges together, they stick.

I try bending my finger, pointing, wiggling it. The new print doesn't fall off, doesn't loosen at all. It feels like part of me. *Thank you, Risha.*

I cross the room, sink into the plush leather chair at Dad's desk, click the login button, and wait.

"Access restricted to Dr. Stephen Meggs," the screen reads. "Provide bio-verification."

I press my finger to the bio-reader and hold my breath.

The computer beeps, and Dad's desktop menu appears. I scan the icons—satellite feeds, data streams, radar from at least eight different sites in the county. Where is the latest data for his storm research?

The antique clock on the wall ticks loudly. Eight minutes have passed. Remi has fallen asleep and is drooling all over her dolphin. I need to find whatever's here and get off this thing.

The radar, satellite, and model applications seem to be the same ones running on the other computers. But in a corner of the screen, there's a folder I didn't see on any of the screens across the room.

STORMBANK

I click to open it and a box filled with dozens of sub-folders spills out on the screen. Each one is labeled with a set of numbers.

5-7-1840

6-12-1899

6-9-1953

No, not just numbers. Dates.

I scan the list.

5-27-1896

4-5-1936

3-18-1925

5-4-2007

6-17-2010

It goes on and on. Dated folder after dated folder inside the STORMBANK file. Does each folder have meteorological data for that particular date?

The clock ticks again. Ten minutes left.

There must be something here about the dissipation project. There has to be.

My eyes dart from file to file. Half the titles are simply project numbers. I can't begin to guess what Re-creation #129 means, so I keep looking, hoping that the right thing will catch my attention. I feel so certain the answer is here.

Remi murmurs in her sleep.

As I'm standing to check on her, the elevator rumbles to this floor and the door begins to slide open. I fly across the room and practically dive for the couch.

I sit next to Remi, my knees tucked up against me, heart pulsing in my throat.

My view of the elevator is blocked by the row of workstations, but I can still hear whoever it is stepping out into the reception area of the office.

"Stephen?" It's a woman's voice. Maybe the one from Dad's DataSlate that night, but I can't be sure.

I hold my breath. Should I answer? I haven't logged off the computer; the storm notes are there on the screen for anyone who approaches.

"Stephen!" The voice is sharper now, colder.

Is it the receptionist from downstairs? I can't just sit here and let her find me shaking. She'll wonder why I didn't answer.

"My dad's in a meeting right now," I call. I take a deep, shaky breath and get ready to face whoever it is when they come around the corner, but there's only quiet.

I wait, listening to my heart in my ears. Where did the woman go?

The clock on the wall ticks again, and I jerk my head to look. It's been sixteen minutes.

I need to log off that computer before Dad gets back.

I walk slowly around the bank of workstations, expecting the visitor woman to be waiting with more questions. But when I get to the elevator, there is no one. The door is closed and rumbling with a distant hum.

Whoever she was, she left without answering. Apparently, she was only interested in Dad.

The clock ticks. Dad could be back any second, but I can't walk away from this. Not now.

I go back to his desk and skim the pages on the screen. Most of it is over-my-head science, but in one file, the words I do under-stand jump out. They jump out and grab me by the throat, and shake.

Possibilities for Replication: In simulation exercises, researchers successfully recreated the atmospheric conditions that led to the June 17, 2010, EF4 tornado near Deer Creek, Minnesota, through the heating and cooling of particular features of supercell thunderstorms. In the Simulation Dome assessment, this resulted in the genesis of a tornado that would easily be classified NF4 or above.

In the first non-laboratory trial, certain atmospheric variables interfered, resulting in a smaller vortex forming and veering slightly off the intended track so that intervention was necessary to reroute. Still, damage was impressive, and with further development, more precision in both the scope of the storm and the track may be expected.

Damage was impressive?

I look at the date listed next to the words "first non-laboratory trial," and a throbbing pain shoots through my temple. 5-30-2050. That was our first day at camp. The day Risha and I had the picnic with Alex and Tomas. The day we watched from the jungle gym while the kids at the park "sang" the tornado away from the Placid Meadows fence.

When really, the magical storm songs were coming from this office.

My stomach churns with the poison of what I've learned. This makes it look like Dad isn't doing research to get rid of storms any-more. This research is focused on—no, that's impossible. Is it? I look back at the last paragraph, but my head hurts. Letters are swimming out of place, rearranging themselves, and I feel sick.

Bile rises in my throat, but I swallow it down and pull my DataSlate from my bag.

I don't wait for the clock to tick away my last minutes. I need this—all of it. I don't know yet what I can possibly do with it—I don't know yet what it all means or who I can possibly show—but I know I need it.

I jam my DataSlate connector into the port on Dad's computer.

"Transfer file command restricted to Stephen Meggs. Please provide bio-verification."

Come *on*, come *on*, I think, pressing my finger to the reader. After three failed reads, probably because I'm shaking too much to hold still, the computer beeps, my storage drive appears, and I'm able to drag the STORMBANK folder in to copy.

Remi stirs again.

The file transfer bar progresses slowly, and I curse under my breath because I can't make it zip to the end.

Remi's awake fussing, so I start across the room to pick her up, just as the elevator begins to hum.

No!

I fly back to the computer. Remi's crying, wiggling in my arms as I lean over the screen. The files are still copying.

Go. Go, GO.

Just a few more seconds.

But the elevator dings, and there are no more seconds. I pull the DataSlate from the port and ignore the error message that appears. Right now, it doesn't matter if any of the data actually transferred—I need to get off this thing before Dad comes. But it won't shut down.

I try the escape key.

The elevator dings again.

I yank the power cord from the back of the computer, and the screen puffs to black as the door slides open.

Dad steps out. "How are my girls doing?"

I stand up from the leather chair and bounce a little with Remi. I force my voice to sound calm. "We're fine. She's been fussy, so I thought she'd like spinning in your chair, but she wanted to grab everything." I glance at the black screen, praying it will reboot—and not return to the last screen I was on—when the power returns. "She unplugged your computer. Sorry."

"No problem." In four long steps, he's at the desk, putting the cord back where it goes.

The machine hums to life, and I hold my breath.

Dad turns back to me. "Ready to head home?"

I nod. Remi's quieting down in my arms, her head drooping onto my shoulder, and her rhythmic breathing helps my heart settle down, too. "Let me get my stuff."

I reach for my DataSlate and backpack to follow Dad to the elevator. Just before the door slides shut, I see Dad's computer monitor flash back to life on his desk. There is only a log-in screen.

No sign of the data I was never supposed to see.

No evidence at all that I logged in tonight as Stephen Meggs.

Chapter 20

"Jaden, do you have plans after camp tomorrow?" Mirielle passes me the fruit salad at dinner. "I'd love for us to have a girls' afternoon—maybe some shopping?" She winks at me, and for a second, I don't know why. Then I remember "shopping" is code, and she must have found a dance performance for us to go see. I wonder if Aunt Linda is coming, too, but I can't ask now.

"Sure." I should be excited, but mostly, I'm dying to finish dinner so I can be alone and think about everything I saw on Dad's computer. I spoon out a little heap of globe-perfect blueberries and seedless strawberries. Their plastic-smooth surface feels cold on my tongue. I swallow and try not to think of berries warmed by the sun. "Shopping sounds great."

"Terrific idea." Dad's in one of his good moods. He reaches over to Remi's high chair and gives her a grape that looks like it came out of a mold in a factory. "I have a late meeting tomorrow, but I'd love to see all my girls for an early dinner. Why don't you drop by the office after your shopping, and we'll get something in the cafeteria?"

"Wonderful." Mirielle takes the grape from Remi and cuts it into quarters so she can eat it without choking.

"Perfect," I say, but my brain has left the dinner table and gone upstairs, where my DataSlate is waiting.

On the way to my room, I pass Grandma Athena's picture, and somehow her eyes seem sharper than usual. I stop and pick up the frame.

What Alex and I have been trying to do—what we're so close to figuring out—has absolutely consumed me these past weeks. If Mirielle didn't call me to the table for meals, I don't know if I'd even feel hungry. What I've been starving for is information, and the more I get, the more ravenous I am for more.

Tonight, looking into those charcoal eyes that almost pierce the glass, I understand Grandma Athena's passion for science more than ever.

I sigh and put the digital frame back on the shelf. Grandma Athena probably had a whole team of secret government scientists working with her.

Without Alex, I'm completely on my own.

I'm in pajamas, teeth brushed and lasered, and in bed, but as I'm about to power on my DataSlate, there's a knock at the door.

"Come on in." I'm expecting Mirielle with clean laundry, but when the door swings open, it's Dad.

"Hi there."

"Hi." I slide the DataSlate onto my bedside table and pull up the covers. I don't think he's been in this room since I moved in.

He sits down on the edge of my bed and picks up the poetry book. I've gotten careless about leaving it out. I hold my breath as Dad reads the title. He opens his mouth as if he's going to say something, but then closes it. He turns a few pages, and I can tell he's trying hard not to frown at it. Then he puts it down. "Sorry I've been so busy lately. I haven't even had a chance to ask how you've been doing with the move. You like Placid Meadows?"

"Sure. It's great."

He looks back at the book on my nightstand, but then reaches for my DataSlate next to it. My whole insides turn to ice. "Is your work at Eye on Tomorrow going well?"

"Yeah," I say, frantically trying to think of what I can add. What would make this sound like an ordinary father-daughter summer camp conversation? What can I say so it will never occur to him that I know what I know? "It's fantastic. The library, especially."

"Sure is. That's a top-notch facility, all around." He looks down at the DataSlate. *Don't turn it on. Don't turn it on.* "Dad, I'm really tired, okay?"

"Okay." He turns the DataSlate over in his hands and pauses, and a breath catches in my throat.

But he puts it down, the screen still empty black, and walks to the door. "Night, Jaden."

"Night."

I listen to the click of the door, his footsteps on the hardwood floor of the hallway outside my room, the groan of the spiral staircase as he heads back down to Mirielle.

And then I reach for my DataSlate. The screen lights up, and I hold my breath until the menu loads.

The files are there.

They copied before I unplugged Dad's computer.

Every last one.

I breathe out.

It is all here. The real storm dissipation simulation report. The fake one. All the data that goes with those, and the full StormBank.

I open one of the files to make sure it's intact, and out pour the details of twin tornadoes that hit Gainesville, Texas, in April of 1936. There's less information for this storm than for more recent tornadoes, but the file still paints a vivid picture.

The debris in the streets was ten feet deep.

The image swirls in my mind—whipping winds and flying windows—until I shake my head and close the file. I have to try and get to sleep.

I create a new folder, drag the files inside, and start to type a label. I can't call it "Family Photos" like Dad. That's a folder he might open if he picked up my DataSlate in one of his good-father moods. Instead, I name it "Poetry" and turn off the light.

Tomorrow at camp, I'll try to get permission to run this data through the Sim Dome. After it works and I have what we need, I'll go see Alex and tell him, and he won't look at me that awful way he looked at me before. I can't wave a magic wand and make Newton okay again, but I can give him this.

I stare at the rectangle of blue-white light the moon casts through my skylight onto the carpeted floor. I try to sleep, but funnel clouds swirl behind my closed eyes.

I turn the lamp back on and reach for the book of poems.

"Geometry" would make my head spin faster tonight, so I flip through the pages for something calmer, quieter, and I find one called "Adolescence." It is about a hot summer night, like this one, about a girl hiding with someone, her cousin, maybe, behind her grandmother's porch. And the older girl whispers secrets to her in the quiet night and firefly light, tells her how soft a boy's lips can be, like the skin of a baby.

I close the book and look up at the ceiling, where there are no fireflies, only straight rows of perfectly round, recessed lights that never flicker.

Amelia kissed a boy once. It was Nico Groves, and it was winter, not summer. She was waiting for her mom to pick her up after a dance at the StormSafe teen center, and she says one minute he was talking to her about his new air-drum kit and the next minute he kissed her right there on the sidewalk. His lips were chapped, rough, she said. She never mentioned baby's skin, but I think she liked it anyway.

I fall asleep thinking about fireflies. And strawberries with raindrop seeds.

First thing in the morning, I hop on my bike, and with the wind blowing my hair from my face, I can think clearly again. I'll go straight to

Van when I get to camp, let him know I need time in the Sim Dome. And then . . . what? I wish Mom were here. My eyes burn thinking about her, how much I miss her, how much I need her.

Maybe today will be the day she answers. With tears spilling down my cheeks, I stop my bike and pull out my DataSlate. I can't help hoping. Maybe, maybe, maybe.

But there are no video-messages. No text messages. Nothing.

I pull up her contact page and press RECORD to try one more time. "Hi, Mom," I say into the screen, and then I am sobbing. All at once, I can't hold it in anymore, and I cry and pictures flash through my head like some awful horror movie. The storm at the barn. Swirling feathers and dust. Newton whimpering in pain. And the look on Alex's face. Two weeks' worth of numbers and funnel clouds and secrets explode inside me, and I drop the DataSlate to my side, my arm hanging limp. And I cry.

I *can't* face all this by myself. But the more I think about it all, the more I realize what's happening, the more I realize I am absolutely alone.

When I'm empty from crying, I breathe in. I pick up the DataSlate—it's still recording—and I take a deep breath. "Mom." My voice breaks. "I *need* you to come home."

I stare at the red record light. I should delete this and do it over. But deep down, I know it won't matter. She'll never get it anyway; it'll be like all the rest, so I just send it. I start pedaling again, and my tears dry in the wind. They leave thin, salty trails down my cheeks.

When I pull into the Eye on Tomorrow campus, I squeeze the

brakes so hard I almost go flying with my backpack over the handle-bars. Alex's mom is pulling away in the truck.

My heart jumps. Alex is here. He must be inside already.

I wave to his mother, and she gives a small, sad wave back before she drives away.

When I get to the auditorium, Alex isn't in his usual spot. He's in the back, way off to one side, a seat that has *don't-sit-by-me* written all over it.

I go to him anyway.

"Can I sit with you?"

His face is impossible to read. Empty like a cloud-gray sky. He shrugs. I take it as a yes and sit down.

I'm terrified to ask, but I force the words out. "How's Newton?"

"Not good."

My throat tightens, and I wait. *Please don't let him be dead.* "Alex?"

He looks straight ahead. "His leg's not healing right, so they have to amputate. He's having surgery this afternoon."

"Oh, Alex, I hope it goes okay." But really, nothing is okay.

I blink away tears as Van jogs down the aisle to the front. He says it's time for another holo-sim lecture, since we're at a turning point where most groups should be switching from theoretical research to practical applications.

When Dad rises out of the floor, my stomach twists.

I turn toward Alex. "I went up to StormSafe with my dad," I whisper. He doesn't respond, and his eyes are focused up front, but I keep talking over Dad's lecture on responsibility and ethics.

"I have . . . stuff from his computer. I have it here, on my DataSlate, and I was going to try and run the sim again. And then I was going to go find you and talk to you."

Alex folds his arms in front of him.

"But you're here." I turn to face front again because I'm too afraid to see his reaction to the last thing I need to say. "Maybe we could work together again?"

Before he can answer, the lights come on. Dad is gone, erased. If only it were that easy.

"All right," Van announces. "Go wherever you need to go today. I know for most of you, that's the lab, but if you have more to do in the library, that's okay, too."

"Library?" I whisper over my shoulder to Alex, hoping he'll say yes.

He doesn't say anything to me on the way out.

But Van does. "Jaden, I need a few minutes with you, okay? I've been trying to check in with all the first years for a quick conference."

Without asking, Alex lifts my backpack from my shoulders. "I'll take this to the library for you. You can meet me there when you're through."

I consider grabbing it back, but I'm so relieved he's talking to me that I just nod and watch him walk out the door.

"So," Van says, motioning me to take a seat again in the empty theater. "Things are going well?"

I nod. "Mostly, I guess."

Van smiles a little. "I know your partner was extremely frustrated when your last Sim Dome experience didn't go as he'd planned, but that's all part of the process. Have you . . . decided to go in another direction now?"

"Kind of, yeah." I consider telling him now about the new data but decide it's too risky. It will make more sense if I share it with him after we try the Sim Dome again, after I have real proof. "Can we get time in the dome soon?"

"I think so." He swipes through a few pages on his DataSlate until he gets to a weekly calendar. "Maybe Thursday? I'll check the master schedule and let you know."

"Thanks."

Van looks at my empty hands. "I was going to do a DataSlate scan. We're required to check in every couple weeks with students who carry them on campus. Don't you usually have yours with you?"

"I do. But Alex took my stuff to the library."

"No problem. I'll catch up with you later." Van stands and heads for the door. "I'm impressed with your work so far, Jaden." He holds it open for me, and the sunshine streams in from outside. It's going to be hot again. Storm weather later on.

"Thanks."

"I'm serious." He gives me a friendly cuff on the shoulder as I turn to head to the library. "If you're not StormSafe scientist material, I don't know who is."

"Hey, Jaden!" Risha races up to me on the quad after Van walks away. "Hold out your hand and close your eyes. I have a present for you."

I do what she says, and two little glass jars drop into my palm. "Same print?"

She nods. "Save them for a rainy day."

Tomas waves from the Finger Factory steps, just as Van walks up to the building. He stands close to Tomas, talking, and Tomas looks down at the steps.

"He's been hanging around Van a lot, huh?"

Risha nods. "Van's kind of taken Tomas under his wing. He says he might know somebody who can pull some strings and get his mom into a treatment center sooner." She gives me a quick hug. "I'll talk to you later, okay?" And she runs off.

Alex is back at our library table as if nothing happened. If it weren't for the healing cuts, the fading bruises on his face and arms, I might be able to pretend it didn't.

He points to a pile of books next to him. My DataSlate is on top. "I unpacked your stuff. I thought we could do a little more work on supercell formation today before we redesign the sim."

I reach for my DataSlate. "Alex, we don't need to do more research," I whisper. "I have whole folders full of—"

He puts a hand over my mouth—gentle but firm—and sweeps his eyes over toward the ceiling. *Shhh.* "Later," he whispers. "Not here."

I'm four or five pages into the supercell reading when the door opens and Van walks in from outside. "Hey, Jaden. Okay if we do that DataSlate scan now?"

"Sure." I hand it to him and get back to my notes.

"Are you kidding?" Alex hisses, staring at me from behind a thick meteorology textbook. "He's going to find those files."

"No, he won't," I whisper. "They're hidden."

"Not very well."

"How do *you* know how well they're hidden?"

"Jaden, that DataSlate's only got one storage chip and there's a search function. You can't hide anything."

"It's *fine.*"

He frowns but goes back to his reading. Van is back with the DataSlate in less than half an hour. "All set, Jaden. Looking good."

"Thanks." I take it from him and set it next to the pile of books. "Any chance that Sim Dome spot worked out for us?"

He nods. "You're penciled in for Thursday, first thing at nine."

"Great," Alex says, and looks at his watch. "I know we're not done until noon, but is it okay if I leave now?" He looks up at Van. "My dog's having surgery, and I want to be there. Plus we still have a huge mess to clean up."

Van puts a hand on Alex's shoulder. "You do what you need to do, man. We're glad to see you back. Let me know if there's anything I can do to help."

Alex packs up, and they walk out together as a bank of clouds moves in from the west and swallows up the sun. My mood dims along with it. How can he leave when we didn't even get a chance to talk?

But then I remember the barn, and the house, and his family and the millions of pieces that need to be put back together.

I remember Newton.

And I feel ridiculous for thinking that Alex talking to me—no matter what it's about—would be more important.

I read through another chapter of one of the reference books, but my heart isn't in it this afternoon, so I reach for my DataSlate instead and pull up a notes page.

The Poetry file is still there, lurking in the corner of the screen, looking innocent.

The library clock ticks—twenty minutes left for today. Not enough time to start research from a new source, so instead, I decide I'll read through the entries in the StormBank file more thoroughly. Part of me—probably the same part that wants to believe in fairies and mermaids and unicorns—still hopes there's an explanation, that my father isn't what all this makes him look like.

Another part of me is afraid. Afraid that even though there are no fairies or mermaids or unicorns, there *are* human monsters. Afraid that my father might be one of them.

But maybe, maybe, maybe. Maybe there is something I'm missing, something more. Something to explain it all away.

I click on the Poetry folder.

It is completely empty.

The files are gone.

Chapter 21

The Sim Dome and reception building are blurry through my tears as I head for my bike, but I recognize the burly figure walking toward me.

Van says nothing about me crying, but his mouth twists into a little smile. "Enjoy your weekend, Jaden. Don't work too hard."

I want to scream. I want to turn around and run after him and push him to the ground.

He deleted the files! He stole them from me! I want to tear them back out of his hands, but I know they're not there. They're not anywhere I'll ever find them again.

And I can't say a word. Because I stole the files first.

Van must know that.

Soon, so will Dad, if he doesn't already.

I pedal home as hard as I can, pumping so hard my legs burn, but no matter how hard I push, I can't outpace the voices in my head.

Stupid.

How could you bring it without making a backup?

Failure.

I slam the door, hard, before I realize Mirielle's waiting for me in the kitchen. "My goodness, Jaden! It must be sweltering outside. You are all . . . eesh . . ." She makes a face and shakes her hands. "Have a drink of cold water and put on some clean clothes so we can pick up Aunt Linda and go."

The ballet.

All I want to do is close myself in my room and think about how to undo this mess, this stupid mess I made.

Instead, I am going to the ballet.

Mirielle hands me a glass of water. Excuses race through my brain like data scrolling on a storm map, and my mouth is about to choose one when I remember the other part of tonight's plan.

I'd love to see all my girls for an early dinner.

We're eating with Dad. At StormSafe.

It's crazy to think I might have another chance to get onto that computer, but I think it anyway.

I need to get that file back. Maybe I'll have a chance tonight. Unless Van has already told Dad what I did.

And *then* what? My stomach twists in fear—but fear of *what*? Am I really afraid of my own father? I shake the thought from my head and take a long drink of water.

"I'll be right down." On the way to my room, I pass Grandma Athena. I fight an urge to stop and talk with her, ask her what I should do. She might have been the only one who'd understand.

I race up the stairs, drop my backpack, and pull out the glass jars from Risha. I open my dresser drawer, shove one of the jars inside a sock and push it to the back of the drawer. I change my clothes and tuck the other jar into my pocket. I keep moving, moving, moving as if I can outrace my own thoughts by rushing around my room, but my twisting insides follow me from the closet to the dresser to the door. It's true. I'm afraid of him.

I check my DataSlate. Nothing from Mom.

Nothing at all.

I tuck it back into my bag and race down to the kitchen. "I'm ready."

The ballet is in a public school basement—a concrete cave of a room with horrible acoustics, but no one seems to mind. Mirielle's wearing a long, black dress with a jingly silver necklace that Remi keeps trying to put in her mouth, and Aunt Linda has on a gauzy white blouse and denim skirt. The best I could do was a clean pair of jeans, but people are dressed every which way, and somehow, no one in the folding-chair audience looks out of place.

The dancers aren't as smooth or as talented as the ones on TV. Their costumes aren't as elaborate, but energy pulses through their bodies, and there is something about them—some spirit or will or determination—that makes it impossible for me to look away. Their movements are fierce and gentle, all at once, and when I applaud at the end of the hour-long performance, my cheeks are wet.

"Remi needs a quick diaper change before we meet your father," Mirielle says, standing up.

Aunt Linda and I join the rest of the audience folding up chairs and leaning them against the old wooden stage. Watching the dancers was like a dream—but now that the soothing orchestra sounds have been replaced by clanging metal, I'm awake, and everything is still wrong. Has Van told Dad yet what I did?

"Wasn't that wonderful?" Aunt Linda leans a chair against the stage, starting a new row. "Just the spirit of those dancers . . ."

I toss another one against hers. "Yeah . . ."

"What's on your mind, Jaden?" Aunt Linda reaches for the chair I've just stacked upside down and flips it the right way. "Seems like you're somewhere else."

"Do you know much about Dad's work at StormSafe?" I blurt out.

She leans against the stage and pushes her hands deep into the pockets of her skirt. "Well . . . yes and no. What are you wondering?"

"Well, I . . ." I need to tell someone. And somehow, I trust her. "I was on the computer in Dad's office. . . ."

She raises her eyebrows, but I don't stop talking.

"There are files on there about the tornadoes. About controlling them."

She nods. "You know that's his area of research, right? Always has been. He's been fascinated by the idea of weather manipulation since he was a boy, back when your grandmother was studying it."

"That's what she was doing? I thought it was secret." But now that it's not, I understand a little more. Dad's password, his crazy focus on all this, makes so much more sense. "Dad's a lot like her, isn't he?"

"Very much. So much it scares me." Her mouth tightens into a grimace.

"He scares me, too." There. I said it out loud.

Aunt Linda's eyes fill with concern, and she leans close. "Jaden, did something happen?"

Yes, something did. Something *is* happening, a whole whirlwind of somethings that I can't sort out. But I shake my head. "No. Nothing really. It's just . . ." The chairs are all picked up, and most people are leaving. Mirielle's done changing Remi but is talking with one of the dancers in the hallway. I don't understand enough about what I saw in Dad's office to even start explaining, so I don't try. "It feels like StormSafe has taken over his brain or something. Like he's . . . possessed." The word sounds silly, and I expect Aunt Linda to brush it off, but she doesn't.

Instead, she pulls herself up to sit on the stage and looks out at the empty room. "Your dad had a lot to deal with at a terribly young age."

"I know. Mom told me Grandma died when he was twelve."

She shakes her head. "Your father lost his mother long before that." She looks at me. "I'm going to tell you something because . . ." She bites her lip. "Because you need to know where your dad comes from. But more than that, you need to know that I'm here if you ever need someone. Do you understand that?"

I nod. But somehow, her words make me more afraid, not less. Does she think I'm not *safe* living with Dad?

Aunt Linda looks back out at the empty room as if she's staring through time. "Athena was part of a group of elite scientists working to harness weather for military purposes. To control the winds and the rain. That job was everything she'd dreamed about when she was in school. She'd never planned to have a child so soon."

I nod. "You told me she was gone a lot."

"All the time. The project started when your dad was a few months old; your grandfather was away serving in the military, and Athena would leave your dad with me for months and months at a time. When the war in Afghanistan expanded to Iraq, she was gone more than ever. She'd come home and take him back for a little while to cuddle him and play mother. As he got older and could understand, she'd do little science experiments with him and tell him about the exciting work she was doing. Then she'd take off again. He cried every time she left."

Out in the hallway, Mirielle sways back and forth with Remi as she chats. It's hard to imagine Dad ever being small. Or crying.

"It seemed like it would never end. Even as the troops were being pulled out of Iraq, Athena kept canceling visits home, writing e-mails instead, telling us she was on the verge of a huge breakthrough."

I climb up to sit next to Aunt Linda on the stage. The old varnished wood feels warm and shiny-smooth under my hands. "What was the breakthrough?"

"I don't know. The next news we heard was that your grandfather's helicopter had crashed in the mountains between Afghanistan and Pakistan. It was awful for everyone, but most of all your dad, because Athena barely took a break for the funeral. She poured herself into her work and almost never slept from what I heard. We saw her once more, when it all fell apart."

"Was she home visiting when she had that car accident?"

"It wasn't an accident, Jaden." Aunt Linda blinks fast, and tears streak down her cheeks. "Less than a year after your grandfather died, the government declared Athena's research project a failed effort and canceled it." She shakes her head, and even though it all happened so long ago, I reach out for her hand. "She must have felt like she couldn't go on after she lost her husband and her life's work one after the other. There was a huge storm the day she came home, tornadoes dropping all over the county, but she drove through it from the airport. She had supper with us and told us the project was canceled but not to worry; she'd finish the job on her own terms. She was so calm." Aunt Linda shakes her head slowly. "But her eyes looked far away, like she was already someplace else. She gave your dad a present."

A worn wooden image flashes through my mind. Words in fancy script.

Stormy. Rain. Change.

"A barometer?"

She nods. "He carried it everywhere. He loved it."

"He still does."

Aunt Linda closes her eyes, and I wait. "And then she left. The weather was wild, but I couldn't stop her. She walked out the door and drove away. The next morning, the police found her car at the bottom of a ravine. The storms that night were . . . Pieces of her laptop computer and papers were scattered over half the county. But they never found her body."

I shiver and picture Grandma Athena's ghostly photo in the frame. I don't know how I will sit in the living room again.

"There you are! Sorry I was so long visiting," Mirielle calls from across the room, and starts walking our way.

"I thought you should know," Aunt Linda tells me quietly, as she eases herself down from the stage. "A person never really gets over something like that. And your dad . . ." She pauses. "If you ever need me, I'll be there for you."

"Ready to go?" Mirielle steps up, bouncing Remi on her hip. "Let's get some dinner."

By the time we drop off Aunt Linda at her house and drive up to StormSafe, it's quarter to five. Dad meets us at the door. "I can't stop for dinner. Sorry. Something's come up." His body language makes it clear we're not invited in.

"Don't be silly, Stephen." Mirielle switches Remi to her other hip. "What is this thing that is so important?"

Dad lifts his DataSlate up so quickly I'm afraid it'll hit Remi, but it misses. She reaches for it and laughs, but Dad doesn't even look at her. "Were you even listening when I told you about the problem with funding for Phase Two?" he says in a voice that's getting louder and tighter by the second. "It hasn't gone away."

"But surely you can take a break. You need to eat." Mirielle reaches out for Dad's arm but he yanks it back.

"What I *need* to do is get back to work. Now." He speaks to her as if she's four years old. "I will see you in the morning."

She glares at him, and for a second, I see a fire in Mirielle that I never would have guessed was there. But then she turns and heads for the HV.

I follow her and feel the weight of my DataSlate in my backpack. Heavy with everything I've lost and with what I learned tonight. What Aunt Linda told me about Grandma makes me wonder how damaged Dad might be, and what he's capable of. What I saw and heard in his office . . . I can't begin to sort it all out now. I can't even look back at the data because it's gone.

It's a quiet drive home until we turn into the Placid Meadows gate. Mirielle flashes Lou her resident card, and as the gate starts to swing open, I see movement in the brush near the main road.

"Mirielle, wait!" She's already started pulling into Placid Meadows but stops and looks over at me. "I . . . it's nice out, and I could use some air. I'm going to get out here and walk back, okay?" I pull my backpack over my shoulder.

She raises her eyebrows. "You won't be long?"

"No, and I'm not hungry yet anyway. I may go to the park or something, see if Risha's around. If that's okay."

"Of course." I watch her pull away and wait until Lou is back in his booth playing a game on his DataSlate. Then I duck back out the gate and into the trees.

"Alex?" I whisper as loud as I dare.

"Here." A hand closes on my wrist and tugs me deeper into the brush, behind a big old tree stump that's turned into a nursery for mushrooms and moss. I lean against it, and the dampness seeps through my jeans.

"What are you doing?" I ask, looking at the DataSlate in his hands. "And . . . how's Newton?"

He takes a deep breath. "He made it through the surgery okay. He's gotta stay quiet for a couple days, and then I guess he'll learn to get around on three legs." The rest of his air rushes out. He leans against the tree stump, close enough that our knees brush. "Jaden, I have to tell you something."

"What?"

Alex squeezes his eyes shut for a second, then looks straight at me. "I stole files from your DataSlate."

I grab his arm. "What?! That was *you*?"

He closes his eyes again. "When you stayed back to talk to Van this morning and I took it to the library for you? I . . . copied some files."

I stare at the DataSlate in his hands, almost afraid to hope. "You copied them onto there?"

He nods. "I know it was a crappy thing to do, but—"

"And you have them on there, *now*?"

"I felt like I *had* to, Jaden. I didn't know at first what you'd found, but I figured it was important, and I was right. This information . . . It's *exactly* what we need." His eyes plead with me to understand what he says next. "I didn't know if you'd show me or not. He is your dad, after all. But I had to do it. For *my* dad. And everybody else in my family. This is our lives, Jaden, it's—"

"But why would you erase the files from my device? Why not

leave them in case I was going to try to help, too? I *was*, you know."

His eyes cloud with confusion. "I didn't erase anything. I only copied it."

"You did so—when I turned it on after—" I interrupt my own thought: after Van borrowed it for the check, after Van said good-bye to me, smiling. It *was* him. "Never mind. It was Van."

Alex's eyes puzzle back and forth for a few seconds, and then his face falls open with understanding. "He erased your files."

I nod and shift my weight. A sharp edge of the tree stump is sticking into my hip, so I stand up and walk over to a pair of close-together cedars that didn't get cut down. "I don't know how he could have known, why he chose that day to check . . . and I can't believe I was dumb enough not to back them up. But . . ." I look at the DataSlate in his hands. "You copied everything?"

He hands it to me. "Everything."

I click on the folder, but Alex tugs my sleeve. "Not here."

"Well, I can't take it home. Not after—"

An HV turns into the gate, and I cover the DataSlate's screen with my jacket so we can't be seen.

"We need to go someplace to look at this, where we can talk about it." Alex ducks under a branch and starts heading out of the woods.

I follow him, my shoes squishing into the damp leaf litter beneath the trees. "There's campus if we can wait until tomorrow, but—"

He holds a branch out of my way and grabs my arm as I start to pass. "We *can't* wait, Jaden. *This* can't wait." Even in the shadows, intensity flashes in his eyes. "It's waited too long already."

He's right. "Then let's go now."

"To campus? It's closed for the afternoon. Everything will be locked. The outside gate, even."

I pull the jar from my pocket. "I have the right fingerprint to get in."

Alex's eyes get huge. "Your dad's?"

"Risha made it for me."

He looks at me, hard. "You're willing to do this? To risk it?"

"Yes." I am terrified, but I mean it. "My dad's gone, working on some . . . I don't know . . . but something that made him cancel dinner. He won't be home for hours, maybe not even until tomorrow. We'll have the library and the Sim Dome and whatever else we need. Come on."

This time I lift up the branch, and Alex starts to duck under, but then he stops and stands straight again, his face inches from mine in the woodsy darkness, and whispers, "Thank you."

He leans in, and his lips touch mine, gentle as the breeze, warm as summer grass.

He pulls away and ducks under the branch, a shadow walking in front of me. I put two fingers to my tingling lips and follow him out of the trees.

Chapter 22

I wave to Lou as we walk past the gate, but as soon as he looks away, we run all the way to the house. The straps of my backpack dig into my shoulders, and by the time we creep into the garage, my hair is damp with sweat.

We lift bikes from the rack, coast down the driveway, and pedal down the street. As we pass Risha's house, I squeeze the hand brakes. "Wait. Let's get Risha, okay?" Alex nods and waits for me at the bottom of the driveway.

Risha answers the doorbell two seconds after the first ring, as if she'd been waiting for us instead of eating dinner with her family.

"Jaden!" She pulls me into a hug that smells like curry, and I whisper what's happening. I tell her everything we know and step back and wait for her look of shock, but it never comes. "Whatever you need," she says, already heading to the garage for her bike. "Count me in."

We pedal the last few blocks. The breeze has died down to nothing, and the air sticks to my skin.

When we pull up to the locked front gate of Eye on Tomorrow,

I pull the jar from my pocket, wrap Dad's print around my fingertip, and press it to the biometrics panel. "I guess this counts as a rainy day, huh?" Risha looks pleased when it works on the first try. The light turns green, and the gate swings open.

"Come with me," Alex whispers, and heads straight for the library.

"Not the library, Alex. It's not—"

"Shhh. I know where we can go."

We follow the path to the library, but instead of reaching for the door, Alex veers off around the side of the building. In the back, old-fashioned fire-escape stairs lead up to the roof.

"Oh, good call. I haven't been up here since I came for my orientation tour a couple of years ago," Risha says.

She and Alex take the steps two at a time, and by the time I catch up to them at the top of the fifth flight, I'm panting. When I look up, my breath catches in my throat.

The roof is enormous and . . . amazing. A gravel pathway winds through patches of garden with lush red and pink flowers. And flowers aren't the only things growing out of the patches of green. What looks at first like some kind of sculpture garden is actually a line of old-style anemometers. They remind me of little kids' pinwheel toys, twirling and dancing in the wind, spinning like little girls in fancy dresses. I'm dizzy just watching them.

"What is all this?" I ask.

"Ms. Walpole's outdoor classroom for the community education center." He looks up at the hazy sky. "No cameras in the ceiling here."

"They run weather programs for younger kids up here," Risha says.

Alex takes my backpack and Risha's and tosses them onto a picnic table near the stairs.

"It's incredible." And beautiful, in a way I wouldn't have expected.

With the weight of my bag off my shoulders, I almost forget for a minute why we're here. I walk to the edge of the roof and look out over miles of land that used to be full of people, buzzing with lives. The roads are so quiet now it's spooky. An abandoned water tower rises up out of the dirt like a spider grown too tall to be stable, whose legs might crumble into dust any minute. The old university campus is being renovated into another energy farm. There's a scattering of patched-up homes where people are still trying to pretend this is a fine place to live, to raise a family. Will it ever be again?

"Hey, we have to get to work, but come check this out first." Alex crosses the roof to a circle of tall rectangular stones, all standing on edge and pointing at the open sky. In the center is an angled, steel rod. "It's a gnomon," he says. "Like a pointer. The whole thing is a sundial. The ancients used them—"

"—to tell time with the shadows. I know." I walk around the circle, running my hand over the rough stones. They feel so old, so yesterday, to be part of a camp with a focus on tomorrow. "Why is this here?"

"History of earth science. History of weather." Risha walks the shadow cast by the gnomon as if it's a balance beam. "Van laughs at it, but Ms. Walpole's in charge of the rooftop classroom and always says you can't just know where you're going. You need to know where you came from, too. Alex, remember that one time—"

"*Shhhh!*" He holds up his hand to quiet her, then closes his eyes, listening.

I hear it, too. Footsteps clanging on the metal fire escape stairs. I duck behind one of the stone sundial markers and hold my breath. Risha and Alex huddle behind the next one in the circle.

The thumping, clanging steps get louder—then change to the sounds of crunching gravel. Someone is on the roof.

The footsteps get louder. Closer. And pause.

I peer out from behind the marker and see a long shadow falling across the pathway. The shadow turns, and I can make out a pony-tail. Van.

A DataSlate chimes and I duck back behind the stone. My stomach twists so violently I want to cry out. We left our backpacks on the picnic table. Van had to have heard that. He'll find them, find our DataSlates, and know we're here. And there's no way for us to get past him because the only entrance to the roof is that one set of—

"Yeah, what's up?" Van's voice rings out over the quiet roof. I peer out from behind the marker again, enough this time to see not only his shadow but the real Van, talking into a DataSlate. It was his. Not ours.

"I know. I'm leaving now. I was on my way out and heard noise on the library roof, so I came up to check it out. Musta been crows or something." He shoves his hand in his pocket and turns, and I pull my head back behind the stone. *Don't come over here. Don't come over here.*

His shoes crunch on the gravel again, but I can't tell if they're coming closer or going away. Another pause.

"Well, you'll be happy enough when you hear what I found out from my young friend Tomas today. Mr. Hazen's accepting our offer." Another pause. "I know. I told you he's a good kid . . . yeah . . . and he headed off a real mess letting me know about your little security breach. . . . No, he has no idea what it was really about. I just sent him to listen in on them, told him I was trying to keep his buddy out of trouble and needed his help. It's all good. And I told you I took the DataSlate and deleted it just in case. I don't think she would have understood it anyway."

I look at Alex, and the hurt in his face tells me that he's put the pieces together, too. Tomas. Waiting outside the first aid clinic while Alex and I talked. That's how Van knew I'd stolen Dad's files. And now his family is selling their farm, too.

"So here's where we are on the other thing," Van says. "I promised Tomas you'd hook his mom up with that clinic in New York as soon as they sign the contracts. I told you I'd take care of it." A pause. Then he laughs. "Okay, I'm sure the wind did some convincing, too, but hey. Done is done. And now we can move forward." More gravel crunching. Getting closer this time.

I look over at Risha. Her brown eyes are huge. And scared. Behind her, Alex has his eyes closed as if he's praying. Or maybe he can't stand to look at Van.

"Well, I don't think they'll be an issue for long." The footsteps move away again. "Yeah, I know it's gonna be a busy night. I'm on my way."

The footsteps crunch all the way back to the stairs—then pause near what must be the picnic table. Did he see our back-packs? My neck prickles with fear, but I lean out just far enough to see Van bending over near the gate, picking a stone out of his shoe. Then he starts down the stairs, and his footsteps clang away to quiet.

By the time I turn back to Risha and Alex, my neck is stiff from being twisted around so long, and Van must be long, long gone. Risha unfolds her legs and crawls to the edge of the roof to peer toward the gate.

"His HV's gone," she whispers.

Alex stares off into the clouds. On his cheek, the shiny trail of a tear ends in a smudge of dirt, where he must have wiped it away.

"Alex," I say quietly. "He couldn't have known what he was *really* telling Van about the DataSlate. Tomas must have . . ." I don't know what to say.

"Don't." He blinks fast and hard a few times, then stands up and turns away from me. "I don't want to talk about him."

"Alex, put yourself in his shoes for a minute." Risha follows him across the roof. "His mom is sick, and they need help. She needs treatment. What were they supposed to do?"

I should follow them, should say something to make it better, but I'm the one whose father has done all this. I'm the reason Tomas's family and Alex's are under pressure to give up the life their families have had for years. I'm the reason we're hiding up here on a roof and—

"Jaden, come on." They're back at the picnic table, and Risha is motioning for me. Even though guilt is churning in my stomach, I stand up and go to them.

"Let's just do this." Alex powers up his DataSlate and blinks hard. It's as if he's pulled a shade down over all his feelings about Tomas. "We came here to figure this out. Let's do it."

Holding the DataSlate between us, he clicks the first folder on the list, and numbers pour out like milk spilling from a cup.

"So what we have here is . . ." His dark eyes are focused, his jaw clenched in concentration. I peel my eyes away from his face to watch the stream of numbers rushing down the screen. "This is data for . . ." He frowns and taps the folder, labeled 6-17-2010.

Inside are four documents: CONDITIONS PRECEDING, STORM DATA, SUMMARY/RESULTS, and APPLICATIONS. I tap on SUMMARY/RESULTS, and a document fills the screen.

An EF4 tornado touched down near Deer Creek, Minnesota, on June 17, 2010, destroying several houses along Otter Tail County Road 143. One fatality was reported, and damage to trees, farms, and vehicles was extensive.

I watch Alex read, and slowly, like stars appearing through clouds, I see him begin to understand. "This data is unbelievable," he whispers. "Every detail. Atmospheric pressure, updraft activity. Everything."

He scrolls through the other folders and shakes his head. "This is crazy. It's . . . it looks like he's been *collecting* storms." He hands me the DataSlate. "Tell me what you see then."

What I see . . . makes my head spin. All the dates I had time to look at in Dad's office are here.

5-7-1840

5-27-1896

6-12-1899

3-18-1925

4-5-1936

6-9-1953

5-4-2007

There are more current folders, too. The more recent the storm, the more data fills the folder.

4-1-2019

10-10-2020

3-15-2022

9-1-2031

5-30-2050

It's like turning pages in a history book, past to present, closer and closer to today. When my eyes reach the bottom of the screen, I gasp. The final date in the list is from the day Risha and I hid in the old barn storm cellar. The day Alex's family farm blew away.

I look more closely, and other dates start to stand out, too.

10-10-2020.

That's the date of the worst storm ever to hit Paris. It was a year before city traffic was back to normal, another three before they finished rebuilding the Eiffel Tower.

4-1-2019.

Mom's talked about this one, too—the April Fool's Day storm that hit Vermont when she was in high school.

Alex reaches past me and touches the 6-17-2010 file again. "Jaden, *look.*" His voice shakes with anger as he taps open the documents inside, one after another. CONDITIONS PRECEDING has a narrative of the weather conditions leading up to the storms. STORM DATA has a table of temperatures, pressure gradients, and wind speeds. Where did Dad get all this? And why? *Why?*

The APPLICATIONS folder is full of projections for how the data and other information from a storm might be used "in future research and development."

"Future research and development?" My voice shakes.

Alex pulls the DataSlate from me. He taps through, opening the dated folders. Each one holds the recipe for a perfect storm.

He points to one of the number-filled boxes. "This is *everything.* Everything you'd need to . . ."

It's too awful to be real, but he's waiting, so I whisper the words anyway.

"Everything you'd need to make it happen again." As soon as I say the words aloud, I know it's true. And that thought that's wormed its way into my brain changes everything I thought I knew about my father. "He's collected all these monster storms . . ."

Alex nods, his jaw set. "So he can bring them back."

"This doesn't make sense," Risha says slowly. "It's not like he can *make* the weather. He just sends it . . . away from here."

"And *toward* somebody else." Alex's hand goes to the scar on his forehead, and he brushes his thumb against it. "He's turning existing storms into monsters, intensifying them with this historical storm data, and then redirecting them."

"But why would he want to do that?" Risha says. "There's no point."

I wish with everything I am that I could agree with her. But I know better. So does Alex.

"No point?" Alex stands so quickly he almost knocks the DataSlate from the table. "You don't think they see a point in sending storms toward the farms?" He flings his arm toward the stairs Van climbed down a few minutes ago. "There's a point."

She doesn't want to believe it; I can tell from her face. But it's too clear to miss. The more tornadoes hit the farms, the more people have to buy DNA-ture. The more damage, the more danger, and the more reason to give up and clear the way for Phase Two of Placid Meadows.

"It's about the land," I say quietly. "Placid Meadows, Phase Two."

"It can't be," Risha says, shaking her head. "Jaden, there's no way he'd do this. It's not like your father needs the money."

"It's not about money." I think about what Aunt Linda told me about Grandma, how she ignored everything except her research. How she even forgot about being a mother. "He's obsessed. Obsessed

with getting that land, with building Phase Two of Placid Meadows."
I almost whisper the words, but I know in my bones they're true.

Risha stares at me. "Who could care so much about a project
they'd forget about *people*?"

I know the answer to her question. My father. And a long time
ago, his mother, too. But I don't say so out loud. I just shrug.

"I still can't believe . . ." Risha looks at me. She wants it to be a
mistake, almost as much as I do. "Jaden . . . your dad's spent most of
his life trying to disperse storms, hasn't he? Wasn't he figuring out
how to *stop* a tornado's rotation?"

"He *was*." I can't stop staring at the screen, can't stop my stomach from churning with truth. "It looks like he's moved on." Finally,
I tear my eyes from the columns of numbers and look up at Alex.
The words feel like I could choke on them. "The recent storms have
all been hitting the farms, haven't they?"

"Four since last month. Worst few weeks we've ever had."
He stares off to the west, where clouds are gathering again on the
horizon. "My dad kept saying, 'Somebody up there ain't happy with
us.'" He chokes out a cold laugh. "I guess he was right."

I push the heels of my hands into my closed eyes so hard that
lights dance. Explosions of yellow and blue. I hear more tapping on
the DataSlate. Risha's sigh. Finally, I open my eyes and take a shaky
breath. "We need to tell somebody."

Alex's voice is bitter. "*Who*, Jaden? Who do we need to tell? The
police your father probably has in his pocket? Or maybe we should
report him to *Van*? He's good at taking care of things. And he's been
so helpful with our work in the Sim Dome."

"That's it!" I grab Alex's DataSlate and pull my own from my backpack so I can start copying the data. "Let me get this transferred so we have a second copy, just in case. We'll go to the Sim Dome and run the command codes from this file to show what it is. It will prove what my father has been doing with the storms. We'll keep a data record of the whole thing. Nobody will have tampered with those results because no one expects us to have this." I hold up the DataSlates as the files copy. "If this is really a code to re-create the storm, then we'll have evidence."

Chapter 23

My hands shake as I plug my DataSlate into the computer port inside the clear safety glass of the Sim Dome observation box. "There. It's loading."

I'm praying this works. And at the same time, I'm trying not to think about what I'm doing to my own father—what the world will find out about him—if it does.

I'm still wearing Dad's fingerprint tissue. It's weird, like part of him is here watching us. Risha stopped me when I started to peel it off, though. She's right; we may need it again depending on what happens.

"It's all set." Alex nudges me, and I look down at the computer screen.

DATA LOADED

Below it, a green button reads: BEGIN SIMULATION.

My finger hovers above the touch pad. Will this work?

We chose the ten-ten-twenty storm; it will be the easiest to recognize. Once we see how closely it follows the real event, the triple tornadoes that converged on Paris on October 10, 2020, we'll have a better idea what we're dealing with here.

"Go on," Alex whispers. He holds up his DataSlate, its red record light flashing. "Let's see what we've got."

I tap the button, the gentlest tap. But like that old saying about a butterfly flapping its wings and triggering a storm on the other side of the world, a quiet tap is all it takes.

Alex, Risha, and I stand behind the safety glass and watch.

Storm clouds gather in the dome above us first, and the sim lights cast the familiar yellow-gray, just-before-a-storm glow.

"Rotation's starting." Alex's eyes are trained on the part of the cloud where the vapor has begun to swirl in slow, ominous circles over our heads.

The cloud grows, the funnel forms, and faux trees bend in the wind. Then a swirling, gray rope touches down.

"There's one," I whisper. It whips through a neighborhood like a moody robber, stealing some houses, leaving others untouched.

"Two." Risha points to the edge of the town, where a second funnel cloud is forming. This one starts as a loose, smoky swirl; then a tighter, more organized vortex grows up from the ground like a plant that's been nurtured and watered and fed all the right things.

I wasn't even born when the real 10-10-20 storm hit, but I've heard so much about it that seeing these twin tornadoes converge is like watching a movie I've already seen a hundred times.

Swirling dust.

Flattened buildings.

Trees flying through the air, roots first.

All of it.

Now the third tornado forms and makes a beeline for its siblings.

Within seconds, the three have merged into a wide, churning block of chaos. It starts a slow, steady course in our direction, sucking up entire houses so only their flat, chalky foundations remain.

The monster storm is almost to the edge of the Sim Dome, where I know it will be sucked back up into the ceiling.

Alex leans down over the DataSlate and starts poking at buttons.

"What are you doing?" I ask. "We have to let this one finish before you view another one."

"I'm not calling up another one." Alex doesn't look up at me; his fingers tap the touch screen furiously. "I'm entering the last command code that was listed in the folder."

"What does it do?" I ask.

"That," says Alex, tapping a few more times, "is what I want to know." He tilts the DataSlate in my direction so I can see the page he's brought up. It says SI CODE.

"S-I?" I stare at the letters, but no words form in my brain.

"S for storm?" Risha tips her head. "And I . . . I don't know."

Alex taps INTRODUCE VARIABLE and suddenly, the huge tornado turns back from the edge of the dome, almost as if it's a living thing and knows what it needs to stay alive. It grows and swirls back through the Sim Community, fueled by destruction, leveling nearly everything it missed the first time.

Finally, on the other side, the growling black cloud climbs back up into the sky.

We are all quiet, staring at what remains.

A few scattered boards. Some flat foundations. There isn't much.

There wasn't much left of the Champs-Élysées or Eiffel Tower back in 2020, either.

But that tornado had slipped back into the clouds after a single pass through the city. This one swept through twice, stronger the second time around. It had grown, intensified.

And suddenly, the letters have words to go with them.

S.I.

Storm Intensification.

Here is the evidence. My father *has* been re-creating storms.

Bringing old monsters back from the dead.

Feeding them numbers to make them stronger, bigger.

Deadlier.

"Intensity. That command intensified the storm." I shake my head as Alex bends down over the DataSlate again. "Did you hear me? You recorded, right? That simulation proves everything."

"We need more than one," Alex says, scrolling through the list of dates, whispering the storm dates one by one. Finally, he clicks on the first folder we opened—for the 2010 Minnesota storm. "Let's run this one."

He chooses a set of data, but before anything can load, a weather alert sounds its shrill, blaring tones over and over, and the warning appears on screen.

Issued: 7:09 PM, June 29

The National Storm Center has issued a SEVERE TORNADO WARNING for all of Kingfisher, Oklahoma, Lincoln, and Logan counties. A powerful storm has been identified via radar and is making its way east. This system has already spawned several powerful tornadoes. Residents are advised to take shelter in safe rooms immediately. More information will be released as it becomes available.

Alex taps the screen to pull up the latest radar images.

"Whoa . . ." I suck in my breath and stare at the green and red blob. It's one of the most organized storm systems I've ever seen—on a screen or in real life.

I look out at the battered Sim Community and wonder whose real-life town will look like this tonight. Whose car will lift from the pavement, hurtle through the air, and wrap itself around a tree? Whose house will be ripped from its foundation and dashed to pieces? "Put a track on it."

Alex taps a button on the DataSlate to bring up the storm's projected path.

The track makes it pass north of Placid Meadows—everything

does—but then the storm's path swings east, and Alex's body tenses beside me.

"The farm," he whispers. "It's going straight for the farm." He squints at the screen, then looks up at me, his eyes bright with fear.

"It's okay, Alex. Their alert will have gone off, too," Risha says. "They're probably already in the safe room."

Alex wheels around to face her. "There *is* no alert at my house. Mom and Dad's DataSlates are still buried under the wooden beams from the porch. And the safe room . . . the safe room door hasn't even been replaced yet." He stands so fast his chair clatters over. He grabs his DataSlate, trips over the backpacks on the floor, scoops his up, and flings open the door. "I have to go warn them."

I catch his sleeve. "Wait!" My throat is dry, and the colors of the radar are still dancing in front of my eyes.

"*What?*"

I swallow hard. The storm is enormous. What if it's one of Dad's? The thought makes me want to pound my fists and scream. But more than that, it makes me want to help. I unplug my DataSlate from the system and shove it into my backpack.

"I'm coming with you."

Chapter 24

I race for our bikes leaning against the library, but Alex grabs my elbow. "No bikes. We can't take them through the gap in the fence."

"I'll come too." Risha's voice wavers in a way I've never heard before. "Just . . . let me check in with my parents so they don't freak."

"There's no time. But go. Track the storm from your house; it'll help in case we can't get a strong signal out there once it gets bad." I give her a quick, tight hug. "Keep your DataSlate on. We'll call."

I turn and run with Alex out the gate, all the way to the fence.

"When you ran that track on the storm, how fast was it moving? How long do we have?" I ask as he climbs through to the other side.

"Looked like twenty minutes, max."

By the time we reach the tree that bridges the river, my heart sounds like thunder in my ears. We have to slow down to cross.

One foot.

Then the next ahead of it.

The river is swollen and fast.

Thunder booms to the north, and in front of me, Alex teeters.

"Careful!" I grab the strap of his backpack to steady him. He reaches back to take my hand and doesn't let go, even after we've reached solid ground on the other side. We run, and he squeezes my hand as if holding on will keep the storm away.

But it doesn't.

When we reach the farm, loose bits of roofing from the last storm are flying up from the ground like ghosts out of a grave. The chickens are out of the temporary pen Alex and his dad built, clucking around in a panic. A stack of wood that used to be barn walls and hayloft floor groans in the wind and topples, and the chickens scatter in an explosion of feathers.

"Mom! Dad! Julia!" Alex calls into the trailer his uncle brought over so they'd have somewhere to sleep while they rebuilt. There's no answer. "Newton!"

"They had to have gotten the warning somehow! They must've left already!" I shout over a gust of wind that pushes me toward the remains of the house.

Alex runs to the trailer door and flings it open, still shouting. He tugs it shut, but the wind blasts it back open and rips the flimsy aluminum door from its frame. It clatters across the dust and comes to rest against an uprooted tree from the last storm.

"Alex, they're gone! I'm sure they're safe somewhere!"

But he's not listening. His eyes are focused beyond me, off to the north, and his mouth is gaping open.

I turn around in time to see the sky shape itself into a nightmare.

A wall of death-black cloud sits on the horizon. Slow-swirling charcoal fingers reach down from it. They point to the ground, hungry for dust and trees and buildings. The fingers close into thick fists, swirling, churning toward the farms.

I watch, transfixed, as the drifting clouds organize themselves into a thick funnel, spinning faster and faster, stretching closer and closer to earth until it touches, and there's an explosion of dirt and tree limbs, a second swirling circle around the tornado.

The monster barrels on toward two houses, a silo, a barn.

"No. No," I whisper, as if it might hear me and change its mind. As if anything with a soul could tear the roof off a house, hurl the walls off into fields, and keep marching on.

The tornado plows through a field, sucks up barn pieces. Nourished by splintered wood and twisted tractor metal, it grows. And I feel like I'm shrinking, about to be swallowed up. Was this the kind of storm Grandma Athena drove out into the night she died?

A flash of blue-bright-white pops at the edge of the funnel. An electrical explosion? A natural gas line?

A shower of sparks rains out one side of the surging mass of dark cloud. Pieces of roof and support beams and window frames swirl around the heart of the storm, tossed aside every so often when it's sick of playing with them.

Whose house was that?

Did they make it to a safe room?

Is the safe room still there?

"Come on!" Alex starts to run."We have to get to shelter!"

I shout over the wind,"I thought your safe room door was—"

"Watch it!" Alex grabs my arm and yanks so hard I fall backward into the swirling dirt, just in time to miss being blindsided by a piece of barn siding that whips past in the wind. I land on my back-pack, and a corner of my DataSlate jabs into my shoulder blade. I cry out, half in pain, half in fear that it's broken. But there's no time to check. Alex pulls me up, and we start running again.

"Our safe room's no good." He ducks into the trees past the clearing where the gazebo used to be. "We need to get to Tomas's place. We'll bang on the door and hope they hear."

Over our heads, trees bend and groan, grinding against one another in the wind. When they can't bend any more, a loud, deep crack splits the air, then smaller cracks as a tree falls, snapping branches in its path.

We burst out of the clearing in time to see the door ripped from the barn at Tomas's farm. It flies and bounces, top over bottom, cartwheeling across the field.

"Over here!" Alex pulls me toward the farmhouse door and bangs with both fists. "Tomas! Mr. Hazen! TOMAS!!"

Alex jiggles the lock one last time, then backs up to the drive-way. "Stand back." He runs, throws his shoulder at the door. There's a sick thud of flesh and bone on a solid surface but no crack of wood splintering.

"Hold on!" I run to the barn, though the opening where the door used to be, and look wildly around. Flying branches have already smashed two windows, and wind screams through the broken glass, churning loose hay into a frenzy.

There! Still hanging on the wall is an ax, and I lunge for it, trying not to think of what the storm at Alex's barn did to the tools on the wall, how it collected them like a cache of weapons and drove them into the wood, blades first.

"Here!" I run back out and practically throw it into Alex's hands. He raises it over his head and swings.

THWACK!

The wood splinters on the first hit.

He aims lower, closer to the lock.

THWACK!

THWACK!

Beads of sweat fly from his forehead in the wind, and his breathing is fast and heavy, but he swings again—

THWACK!

—and the door makes a loud *CRACK!*

He kicks once, twice, and the third time it falls. "Go!" He pushes me ahead of him. "To the right and down!"

The safe room door is obvious—the only one plated in double-reinforced steel.

It's locked.

Alex shoves me aside and bangs until the heels of his hands start bleeding.

"They can't hear!" I scream, because the wind here is louder. "We need to go someplace else!"

"There is nowhere else!" Alex shouts.

I see the wooden board a fraction of a second before it hits the window. "Alex!"

I pull him down on top of me as it crashes through the glass.

The board flies over us and pierces the video screen in the living room.

"We have to go!" I pull him toward the door.

"The truck!" Next to the barn is a green pickup, miraculously, still unharmed, and we push back out into the wind. The whirling dust stings my eyes, and tears dry on my face as I run.

"Get in!" Alex screams, and runs to the driver's side.

I reach for the handle and fight the wind to pull open the door, but this is no shelter. Even a smaller tornado could pick it up and fling it a quarter of a mile.

I force the door closed, panting, and stare through the windshield.

My heart drops right into my stomach.

The tornado is closer, wider, swirling faster than before.

Right behind it is a second one.

Not far off to the left is a third.

All of them, NF5's, at least.

All of them heading straight for us.

Chapter 25

The truck's engine rumbles to life. "You have *keys*?" I stare. It's an old-time ignition—no fingerprint panel.

"These keys are always in the truck! Hold on!" Alex flings his backpack onto the seat between us, yanks the truck into reverse, and jerks us away from the barn. The tires spin, and we fly down the driveway onto the main road, away from the storm.

The DataSlate in my backpack pokes into my hurt shoulder, but I leave it on. Somehow, I can't let go of it right now, even to put it next to me on the seat. I reach for my seat belt, and Alex almost laughs—as if seat belts will protect us from the storm—but he puts his on, too.

"Where are we going?" I ask.

"I don't know." His jaw looked so set, his eyes burned with so much confidence driving out of there that I was sure he'd have an answer, but he's as terrified as I am, and for a moment, all that matters is easing that fear for him. I try to make my voice as light as it can possibly be with three tornadoes gunning for us in the rear-view mirror.

"Since when do fourteen-year-olds drive?"

He brakes to go around a sharp turn. "I've been driving this thing since I was eleven. Tomas and I'd sneak out and run it up and down the dirt roads while his dad was working in the barn." He almost smiles.

"Well, I guess that comes in handy when—"

He slams on the brakes so we don't hit a twisted piece of swing set that must have blown out of someone's yard. The seat belt catches me, and my shoulder stings.

"You okay?" Alex asks.

I don't answer. I'm staring at the piece of swing set, three twisted metal support bars coming off a crosspiece that still has a swing attached. The painted wooden seat is splintered, but not so much that you can't see the painted handprints that decorate it.

A big green hand. A smaller blue hand. And two tiny prints, pink and purple.

Whose handprints are these? Are they safe?

How many more swing sets and barns and houses will be swallowed up before this night is through?

Alex drives around it, and I twist in my seat to look back.

The three tornadoes are lined up, still coming our way, but something is different. It looks like they've slowed down, maybe even stopped. Will they die out before they get to Alex's farm? *Oh, please, please.* I stare out the rear window at the funnels growing more distant.

But instead of relief, I feel a chill of terror. They may have stopped, but they are growing. Churning with more intense energy. And they are coming together.

Oh, God, make them stop, make them stop. I try to pray them away, will them to be sucked back up into the sky before they do any more harm. But even as I pray, I recognize what is happening . . . three tornadoes that merge. The monster that hit Paris in 2020. A sick feeling swirls in my gut.

This is no act of God.

"Alex, look."

He puts a shaking hand over my seat and twists to stare behind him. "Ten-ten-twenty," he breathes.

Stalled for a moment, the three tornadoes dance, whirling, crunching, spinning closer together and apart, together and apart, until two of them touch, like tops spinning on a table that collide. But these tornadoes don't stop spinning; they swallow each other up, fatter, stronger, and hungrier. Even though they're not here yet, the wind is picking up.

"We have to get out of here!" Alex throws the truck into gear. "Maybe we can get back to the campus, or maybe—"

"Alex! You *know* this storm!" The truck shakes in a gust of wind, and I fling my arm back, pointing at the swelling monster behind us. "You know what it did in '20. It's going to start moving again any minute. It's going do the same thing unless somebody stops it!"

"We have to find shelter!" he screams. "We can't stop that thing! I'm taking us back to campus, or Risha's place, or—"

He turns to the left, back toward the entrance to Placid Meadows, but I reach over, grab the steering wheel, and jerk it to the right instead, toward the curve in the road that leads to StormSafe.

"What are you doing?!"

"Just go!" A thick branch flies out of the woods toward the driver's side window. Alex stomps on the accelerator, and instead of bursting through the glass, the branch clangs into the metal truck bed.

"Go!" I urge him on, and he keeps driving until we reach the first sign for StormSafe. Then he slams on the brakes. "Jaden, what are you *doing*? We need shelter, and this locked compound isn't it. We'll be trapped outside, and even if we get in, what are we supposed to do?" He pounds his hand on the steering wheel and winces. "We need to get to a safe room now! We can't stop this thing!"

"Maybe we can't!" Tears stream down my face. Tears for Tomas and his family, whose house will probably be gone within seconds once the storm starts its march forward again. Tears for Alex's parents and Julia and Newton, wherever they are. Tears for the little girls whose swing set blew into the road. Tears for this whole world, where no one can even go outside without the risk that they might be swallowed up into the sky.

And tears for myself.

Burning, shameful tears because I know the truth, that my father has waved his magic wand at this sad, hot, churning world and made it even worse.

"Maybe we *can't*! But look at it, Alex! It's going to come! We're not going to make it anywhere safe. There's no time. And when the third tornado merges—"

"Stop it! We don't *know* that's what—"

"Yes, we *do!*" I swipe at the tears in my eyes and scream over the roar of the storm. "You *know* what's going to happen! We have to find my father!"

"Your *father?*" His eyes are furious. "You think your father is going to help?"

"Listen, please. We have to . . . we can *talk* to him. Once he knows it's out . . . that people know, he'll have to—"

"Have to *what*, Jaden? *Kill* us?" he spits out.

"Stop!" I scream. "Just stop!" I choke back sobs and press my hands into my eyes to make it all vanish.

It doesn't. And all I can do, all I can hope to do, is try.

"I know you think he's a horrible human being." My voice shakes. "And right now, I do, too. But he's my *father*, Alex. My father, who used to throw me up in the air and sing me to sleep and"—I swallow hard—"and love me, the same way your dad loves you. We have to find him. He can fix this . . . he . . . he *has* to! He *will!*"

I let my head sink back into my hands, but I can still hear Alex's angry, ragged breaths. And then his voice.

"I don't believe it. Not for a second."

"But we have to at least—"

"What we have to do is get out of here!" He yanks the truck's gearshift into reverse.

"Stop!" I scream.

And he does. But he looks at me with eyes that are colder than any weather I've ever seen. "I'm leaving. *Now.*"

I squeeze my eyes shut tight for a second, then open them, throw off my seat belt, and reach for the door handle. The wind flings it open, and I hear Alex shout "No!" but the wind swallows his voice, and I jump down before I can think about it. Before I can think how stupid and dangerous it is. Before I can think about flying tree limbs or barn pieces or the three tornadoes that are about to merge into a single, churning monster and come for me.

I don't think about any of it, and I don't look back. I just run.

The wet strap from my backpack flies loose and slaps at my face over and over. I tighten it and keep running. The wind batters me back and forth across the road, like a cat playing with a half-dead mouse. If there were traffic, if there were anyone else crazy enough to be out, I'd have been run over a dozen times by now.

But I keep running. My backpack thumps against me, soaked, heavier with every step.

Horizontal rain stings my face, and my wet clothes cling. I've sucked in so much water with every desperate breath, it's a wonder I'm not drowning.

Another tree branch flies into the road a few feet in front of me, and I leap aside to keep from tripping.

My backpack strap flies loose again. I can't run with it slapping at me, and I can't keep stopping to tighten it, so I pull out my Data-Slate. As quickly as I can, I stuff it into the waistband in the back of my jeans and pull my shirt down over it. I fling the backpack off into the wind and step back onto the road, but an HV is barreling around a curve, so I leap back into the brush just in time to avoid being flattened by the only other person crazy enough to be out.

When its taillights are lost in the blur of rain, I step back out and run as fast as I can. My lungs are full of needles. My legs are burning. And my heart is breaking, wondering where Alex has gone. Whether he'll make it.

But all I can do is run.

Finally, I round the last curve, and the big steel-and-glass building looms up out of the gray.

The storm is raging, growling, roaring behind me, but I force myself to slow down as I near the entrance.

It's after hours.

The gate is closed and unmanned. But there are HVs in the lot.

I unfold my hand, cramped from being clenched in a fist so long. The bio-print is wrinkled and wet, half falling off, but I stretch it, smooth it as much as I can, and raise my finger to the bio-scan.

The gate slides open with a grinding sound, and a snapped-off pine bough goes flying through ahead of me, as if it had been waiting.

Inside, I stand dripping and panting in front of the gleaming building, unscathed by the winds howling just down the road.

Dad's office on the top floor is dark, but the lights on the ground level glow through the pounding rain. A silhouette passes across a window, and I duck behind one of the shrubs along the sidewalk. The shape passes down the long hallway toward the wood-paneled conference room at the end.

At first I can't believe there's still power in the midst of this storm, but then I remember it's StormSafe. No matter how big this storm grows when the three winding ropes merge, it will never get past the gate. Dad will make sure of that much.

Dad.

I have to find Dad.

I look back. The third tornado swirls closer to the first two. Closer—then away—as if they are dancing. But I know how this dance will end if it goes on.

I have to find Dad.

I crawl out from the bushes and hold my breath, watching the windows of the reception area. There's no activity—just quiet yellow rectangles—so I creep forward and peer inside.

Even the reception desk is empty. Are they all still in that meeting Dad was busy with earlier, when we were supposed to have dinner? And how could that have been just an hour and a half ago, when it feels like the whole world has changed?

I drop to the ground and crawl along the wall. Mud soaks through my pants, and my knees are caked with it by the time I reach what would be the end of the long hallway—the conference room.

I hold my breath and rise up enough so my eyes clear the edge of the window.

The fat leather chairs are all full except for one at the end. On one side of the table are two women I don't recognize. I don't let myself stop to stare, to wonder if one of them is the DataSlate woman whose voice I heard that night in the office. I have to find Dad. Four men face the other way, so I'm looking at the backs of their heads. The first three don't look familiar, but the last one has Van's thick ponytail.

There are papers at the empty seat. And a half-empty bottle of BioWake Cola.

Where's Dad?

I stand up, and my eyes dart from the main headquarters to the outbuildings, trying to remember what was what from our tour.

The buildings are all dark, except for the little one way down at the edge of the property where a rectangle of light glows in the lone window. Dad said it was only a storage room. Why would he be there now?

I run through rain-soaked shrubs, grass that's surrendered to the mud, until I'm crouched by the door. Even though it is made of reinforced steel, low notes of Mozart ooze out around the edges, and I know I've found him.

I reach for the door but feel a rush of fear. I pull my hand back before it touches the cool metal handle.

Who is this man behind the door?

I squeeze my eyes shut and let rain and tears wash my face clean of Alex's harsh words.

He is still my father.

I take a deep breath and hope the air filling my lungs can fill me with something stronger. Faith enough to believe.

He is still my father.

He has the same passion for science.

He still makes funny faces at babies and likes ice cream with sprinkles.

He still loves Mozart.

And I am trying to believe that he still loves me.

I raise my trembling hand to the door and turn the handle.

It's unlocked.

There is no bio-scan on this door.

No excuse not to keep going, to talk to him.

Halfway open, the door hinges let out a low groan, and I freeze, but the only sounds are Mozart and the faint clicking of quick fingers on a computer keyboard in a far corner.

I step inside and stand still as death. My heart explodes in my chest, thumping so loud in my throat and my ears, I'm surprised I can still hear the music.

The steel door swings silently shut behind me.

This room looks a lot like Dad's office, with its giant flat-screen monitors. They swirl with bright green-and-red radar images, but I can't tell if the storm is still stalled.

I try to quiet my breathing.

On the other side of the monitors, the keyboard sound grows louder, as if someone is banging on the keys. Frustrated. Or excited.

What is he doing?

Maybe—

I feel hope rising inside me. Hope that he's calling off the storms on his own. Maybe he never meant to create this nightmare. Maybe—

The tapping stops. There is a sharp huff of breath. A slamming sound, like a book being thrown onto a counter. And my heart goes wild all over again.

What was I thinking coming here?

There is still time for me to go back through the reinforced door, to go back to the reception area and wait out the storm. Time for me to play dumb and pretend I was out wandering and had to rush for shelter when I saw the tornado. Time for me to run.

But I don't. I can do this.

Dad, I'll say, *I came tonight because I know. I know everything. About your files and the storms and the farms. We need to make this right. Everything can be okay again. I need your help.*

I take a long breath and step toward the monitors.

The typing on the other side stops, and my heart stops for a second, too, but I make my feet keep moving.

The Mozart rises to a crescendo. I step around the wall of weather data.

And I freeze.

The person at the computer is not my father.

But she has the same charcoal eyes.

She speaks in a voice I've heard twice before. Once on Dad's DataSlate. And once in real life . . . in his office here at StormSafe the night I came to help with Remi.

"I thought you might show up." She stands to look at me, tucking in a sky-blue blouse that feels out of place with her dark eyes and sharp chin. Her skin is tight and pale. "Stephen said you'd never put it all together, but as usual, he was wrong." She chuckles but there's no warmth in her laugh. "Never underestimate a Meggs woman." She shakes her head, tucks a curl of gray hair behind one ear, and narrows her eyes. "You don't know who I am, do you?"

Somehow, I make my head move up and down, because I do know.

I walk by her photograph every day on my way to bed.

I know. Even though it's impossible.

"You're Grandma Athena."

Chapter 26

Smart as a whip, just like they said." She cackles, sits, and spins her chair back toward the computer, and pecks at the keyboard so hard her fingers must hurt.

"Grandma Athena." I whisper the words and wonder how they could be true. But there is no mistaking the woman in front of me, no mistaking the intensity of her eyes.

"Shhh! Be quiet." Her voice is like ice. Cold. Sharp. "There's something not quite . . ." She trails off, reaches for a DataSlate, and frowns down at it. Her fingers fly, writing a message to someone, and I hear the chime that means it's sent. She calls up a radar screen, and I try to peer over her shoulder, but all I catch is a flash of green before she slams it down on the counter. "Gah! Weakening like nobody's business. Sloppy." She wheels around to face me again. "I know why you're here."

I shake my head weakly. How could this woman, this stranger, know anything about me? How could she even be alive?

She smiles, a thin, chapped line across her face, as if she's read my mind. "You look like you've seen a ghost." She whirls around in the chair again, dashes off a sequence of something on the keyboard. "Why isn't he answering?" She picks up the DataSlate, tosses it back on the desk, and stands to face me. "You thought I was dead."

"Well, yeah. They said . . . I mean, the car accident . . ."

"Brilliant, wasn't it? They knew I'd never give up. They knew I'd never rest until—"

My head is spinning. "*Who* knew you'd never rest?"

"Our *fine* and *dedicated* government leaders." She spits the words; they drip with sarcasm. "They canceled my project, the fools, but they couldn't take back what I'd already learned. I was this close." She holds up her thumb and forefingers, a hair's width apart. "This close to a breakthrough, when they cut the funding and threatened to throw me in prison if I didn't step back from my research. They didn't care that your grandfather had given his life for his country or that I was about to create a weapon so powerful that no American would have to die in battle ever again." Her eyes drift off somewhere behind me, somewhere a long time ago. "They never understood the possibilities. The power we can have."

Her eyes focus on me again. "That's why I had to die."

"You faked the car crash?"

"Oh, there was nothing fake about the crash. That car exploded at the bottom of the gorge like nothing you've ever seen."

"But you weren't in it."

"The car was rigged. Empty. I was on a plane headed for Russia. Viktor, a colleague I'd met at one of the international symposiums, assured me that his government would be happy to fund my work.

It went beautifully, and a few years ago, I sent for your father. He was overjoyed to find me alive. And he was eager to help."

She grabs the DataSlate from the desk again and looks as if she's about to throw it through the lone window. "Though he's proving to be rather worthless tonight."

"I just . . ." I shake my head, trying to loosen the nest of cobwebs sticking my thoughts together. "I can't believe you're here."

"Oh, Jaden. Never trust a death certificate unless you've seen the body for yourself." She grins, a smile so cold it makes me shiver. I take a step backward, toward the door. "But you should know that. You're a smart girl, aren't you?"

It felt like a rhetorical question, but she stares at me, waiting for an answer.

"Well, yeah, I guess."

"How smart?" Her eyes burn into me, and my throat is dry enough to catch fire.

She stands, clutching the DataSlate so tightly the tendons in her hands stick out. She takes a step toward me.

"What do you mean?" I step back. My knees wobble.

"Knock off the big eyes, Jaden. I know why you're here. You stole your father's data, ran a simulation or two with it, and figured out we're in the business of storm creation and enhancement, and not storm dissipation. Now you've come here to save the world. Am I correct?" She steps toward me again. Her eyes keep switching from brown to gray to black, like a river all churned up.

"I . . ." My DataSlate presses against my back. Can she see it under my wet shirt? My head spins with the impossibility of it all. Of her knowing what I did. Of her even being here. Alive.

Another step forward. "I knew you'd be trouble from the minute I walked in on you in your father's office. So stupid of him to leave you alone. I told him so, but he said you were too young, too green and book-smart to be any threat to the program." Another step. "He was wrong, wasn't he?"

A gust of wind rattles the window. I want to fling it open, leap out, and run. This woman, my grandmother, feels like the most dangerous person I have ever met. And yet I stand here rooted to the floor. Is it because I need answers more than safety? "How do you know all this?"

"How do you think?" She turns to the closest monitor, taps the screen once, twice, and an image of the Eye on Tomorrow quad appears. She taps again. It changes to the inside of the library, looking down on the table where Alex and I always sat. Our table, where Ms. Walpole put her finger to her lips to let us know we weren't alone. But there must have been more cameras, more microphones than she knew about.

Another tap, and the inside of the Sim Dome appears. Grandma Athena double-taps, and there is sound. The quiet hum of the fans; otherwise, the empty room is quiet. But I know what she must have heard earlier, and even thinking about it makes me feel like something's pressing on my chest, squeezing out all the air.

"You've been spying on us?" I glare at her.

"Spying?" She laughs again, a cackle that chills my blood. "It's not spying, my dear, when you install cameras in facilities that you own. Why on earth do you think we've poured so much money into Eye on Tomorrow if not to know where our brightest young minds are leading one another?"

Eye on Tomorrow. The multimillion dollar campus. The high-tech equipment. It's never been about encouraging problem solving and exceptional thinking. It's about controlling it.

I stare at the screen. The safety-glass cube where I sat, so close to Alex, working together, figuring all this out with our carefully designed scientific experiments.

Grandma Athena was the variable we never could have imagined.

"It's almost charming, really." She stands and walks to the big screen. "How you put your brainy little heads together and thought you'd found the magic formula." She taps it twice, and there's video of the Placid Meadows gate. She zooms in then, to a shadowy but perfectly clear image of Alex and me in the woods near the entrance.

Grandma Athena smiles a bitter smile as Alex steps closer to me. "Just like Romeo and Juliet, star-crossed lovers caught in a storm." She crosses her arms over her DataSlate as Alex leans into me on the video and kisses me, and at that moment, anger fills me like wind.

"No!" I scream and fly at the monitor with my hands out-stretched. It barely moves half an inch.

Grandma Athena's laugh is like dry sandpaper, and I can't control myself. I lunge toward her, but her wiry body is livelier than it looks. She leaps to the side, and I stumble into the desk.

The DataSlate lets out a high warning tone in her hands. Hers is set so loud she doesn't hear mine, muffled under my clothes.

Grandma Athena stares at the screen, completely unconcerned about where I am or what I might do.

I hate her.

I hate that this stranger with my father's eyes knows me well enough to know I will not come at her again.

Instead, I peer over her shoulder at the radar alert that fills the screen, and what I see makes me want to explode.

The three tornadoes have merged into one. One churning, raging, chewing-up, spitting-out monster.

"Finally." Grandma Athena taps the DataSlate screen, hard and fast, then harder and faster when it doesn't seem to do what she wants the first time. "Why isn't it tracking? And where the devil is Stephen?"

She punches out a message, then stares at it with eyes so intense I'm surprised it doesn't burst into flames. Her fingers grow white, tightening around the DataSlate as if that will make it respond, and a whole minute ticks by.

Finally, she grunts, a sharp, irritated sound, and pulls open a desk drawer. From inside, she takes a slender metal rod, no longer than my forearm. She presses a button on the side, and the tip glows ice blue. "Do you know what this is?"

My blank stare answers, and she goes on. "A company in Russia makes them. It's a Shock Wand, capable of delivering a high-powered, deeply debilitating electrical charge. A fatal one, if it's turned up a bit. I'm going to find your father." She levels it straight at me. "You will stay here." She nods toward a painted green chair in the corner of the room. "Sit down."

I hesitate a second too long. She jerks the wand, and a sharp current of pain runs through my shoulder where the tip grazes me.

"Now!" she says. I move away from the door and sit.

She lowers the wand long enough to reach under the desk and pull out a length of thick rope—the kind you use to tie a boat to a mooring—and flits around the chair like some tiny evil bird, pulling the rope tighter and tighter, lashing me to it, pinning my arms to my sides. She leans in, tugs the rope into a tighter knot. It scratches against my rib cage, right through my shirt.

I glare at her, and for the first time, she smiles. "You know, your father showed me video files of you when he came to Russia."

She's tied me to a chair, and now she wants to reminisce? "What videos?"

"Just some footage of the two of you, reading stories, playing on the porch. But I could tell you were a spirited child. I'd wondered about you, and then I felt like I was finally able to know you a bit."

You don't know me at all, I think. But what I say is, "I wish I had known you were alive."

For a second, her face softens, and it feels like my only chance.

"Grandma, please let me go," I say. "You can't do this. You can't just—"

She slaps me across the cheek, hard and sharp. "Don't even think of telling me what I can and can't do," she whispers, her coffee-scented breath hot on my face. "I lost my husband in battle because America's weapons weren't strong enough to end the war. I have worked my whole life to change that, to build what we've created here. Nothing else matters now. Nothing."

She fumbles with a set of old-fashioned metal keys and heads for the door. I need to keep her here, keep her talking. "How come there's no bio-scan here?" I blurt out.

"Because you need fingerprints to make them work." She holds up one hand. Her fingertips are all scar tissue. "I burned them off when I moved away—too hard to disappear otherwise." She fiddles with the keys again, laughing under her breath.

She is insane. Absolutely insane.

Still . . . she's my grandmother. How could I not matter? Not at all?

My cheek still burns, but I squeeze my eyes shut. "You don't want to do this."

"Oh, I do," she says quietly.

"Grandma, *please!*"

The words seem to press a button inside her—the wrong one—and her face hardens, though her voice stays quiet. "Stay where you are, or you'll be sorry." She raises the Shock Wand to remind me how sorry. "I'll be back." She grabs her DataSlate and takes one last look at the screen on the desktop computer, still swirling with green-and-red radar images. "Here." She turns it so it's facing my chair. "You can watch the radar while you wait for me to come back."

Chapter 27

She leaves and pulls the door closed with a heavy *thunk*. I hear the *snick* of her key in the lock, and I am trapped in what must be the only room Dad's fingerprint can't open.

My legs aren't tied, so I straddle the chair and try to wiggle free. If I can get even a little slack, I might be able to get out.

But Grandma is as good at knots as she is at meteorology. The only way I can even stand is if the chair comes with me. I throw my weight forward so the back legs come up off the floor. I do it again. And again, rocking back and forth until the chair tips forward, and I'm standing with it lashed to my back.

I turn and twist, but the sharp fibers of the rope cut into my wrists, and the knots only get tighter as sweat drips into my eyes.

I let the chair clunk back to the floor and sit again, facing away from the table. If I curl my fingers in and stretch, I can feel the knot that binds my hands. I finger the rough edges of rope—is there anything here that might unravel? I tug my hands apart, but again, the ropes dig into my skin, and I feel the stickiness of blood between my wrists.

There has to be something in this awful room that can set me free. A pair of scissors. A box cutter. Anything.

I rock forward to stand again and make a slow turn with the chair on my back. There's not much here. The desk. The chair. The monitors. And a single frame on the wall, a photograph of a storm at night. Lightning blazes out in crazy jags from the bottom of a dark cloud, and the sky below it glows yellow-blue. At the bottom of the photograph in silver letters against the black silhouette of the mountains is a quote.

I believe in one thing only, the power of human will.
—Joseph Stalin

The photograph, the lightning, the words, are so full of my grandmother's terrifying spirit, I have to look away.

I have to *get* away. *How?*

I turn full circle, back to the desk. There's only one drawer across the top. I wiggle around until my fingers, stretched out as far as they can behind my back, close around the knob.

I pull it open and turn to look. Empty, except for a few pens and a slip of paper the size of a credit card that reads "Bio-scan override code: 4687291." This must be how Grandma gets into areas like Dad's office without a fingerprint scan. It's nothing that can help me now, not in this room with Grandma's olden-days lock, but I wiggle the paper scrap into my back pocket before I let the chair thump to the floor again.

Out of breath, I sit, helpless, and stare at the computer screen's radar swirls. My eyes burn with tears, and the colors blur together, but then I see something that nearly makes my heart stop. I blink—hard, over and over—until the tears spill out so I can see.

The storm is moving again.

No. No. No.

Let me be reading it wrong. Please. Please let me be wrong.

I throw all my weight forward, too fast this time. The chair's legs fly out from under me, and I fall. My temple cracks against the corner of the desk before I hit the floor on my side.

Lying there, my head throbbing, my arm radiating pain underneath me, all I can see is the hook of that storm. It is still growing.

I ignore the pain in my shoulder, throw all my weight forward, and roll onto my knees with the chair on my back. My forehead presses against the cold concrete floor, and I summon every bit of strength I have to push up with my legs. Up, up, until I'm standing before the desk again, facing the screen.

The storm is moving again, headed straight toward Alex's farm.

I want to scream, but instead I spin around and smash the chair into the edge of the desk. Some way, some how, I have to get loose. Without any idea what I'll do or where I'll go or how I could possibly fix this, I throw my weight at the desk again.

The chair smashes into it, over and over and over, until my wrists feel broken and I have to stop. The splintering noises I pray for never come; there's only the hard, cold thunk of solid wood on wood, over and over and over.

My DataSlate has worked its way out of my jeans. It clunks off the edge of the desk to the floor. The jolt turns it on, and the screen blinks up at me.

Dad's files.

Dad's files are here.

If this little rectangle of titanium and wires holds the power to turn this storm toward the farms, it must also hold the power to turn it back.

If I can get to the computer in Dad's office, I can try to reverse what they've done.

The lightning in Grandma's picture blurs and dances through my tears, and it makes me want to smash the photo, smash everything Grandma's ever done, onto this polished concrete floor.

Suddenly, the power of *my* will feels strong enough to shatter glass.

Glass.

I stare at the reflection of the radar in the glass that covers Grandma's storm.

This. This is what I need.

The picture hangs at eye level, so the lower edge of the frame is even with my chest. I sidestep over to it, knees bent so my shoulder is pressed against the wall. I spring upward as hard and fast as I can.

My shoulder knocks the picture up, off its hanger. It bounces off me onto the floor and shatters.

Jagged shards of glass cover the floor. They crunch under my feet as I make my way to the biggest, sharpest piece. I kick it into a far corner where there aren't so many shards, lower myself to my knees, then roll onto my side. Writhing and twisting and wiggling, I back my way into the corner until my fingers touch sharp, cool edges.

I'm facing the desk, but I try not to let my eyes fall on the radar screen as I maneuver the glass between my wrists and little by little, pick at the rough fibers of the rope. I can't see how much progress I'm making, and it feels like it's already been too long when there's a thump at the door, and I freeze.

My heart wants to burst out of my chest and run, but I hold my breath and wait.

There's another thud and a scraping sound—a tree branch or piece of roofing the wind has thrown against the building—and only then do I let myself look at the computer screen again.

The whole county is swallowed up in green and red, and the hook of that monster is inching closer to Alex's farm.

I can't afford to be careful anymore. Every time the glass slips, I feel the warmth of blood spilling from the cuts in my hands. But the rope is weakening; it's starting to give. I keep slicing back and forth until there's a muffled pop, and my hands—finally—are free.

Cutting the rope that binds my chest is faster with two hands, and soon the chair clatters to the floor. I grab the DataSlate with blood-smeared hands, fly to the door, and grab the handle.

Locked from the outside with Grandma's keys.

This time, I scream.

I scream long and loud, and even though I know the window must be StormSafe indestructible, I slam the DataSlate onto the desk, grab the chair that held me captive, and fling it at the glass.

It shatters. Shatters into a million pieces.

The wind swoops in with a howling whistle, and for a second, I can only stare. I guess you don't need safety glass if you believe the storms will always stay away.

I grab my DataSlate, climb out the window, and run for the main building.

Chapter 28

The lights are still on, but the conference room is empty, and when I peer in the main doors, the reception desk is quiet, too. Dad's print wore off my finger long ago, so I tuck the DataSlate under my arm, pull Grandma's override card from my pocket, and look up to the sky.

Please work. Please.

I punch in the numbers and hold my breath until there's a beep and a click, and I push open the door. I run for the elevator, tap in the numbers there, and again, the beep of clearance—of course she would have access to everything.

My skin prickles as I press the button for the top floor and wait, willing it to rise faster, willing this office to be empty when I get to the top.

The DataSlate chimes in my hands and scares me so much I almost drop it. The message is short, from Risha:

Alex is here. Where are you?!?

Six words. But they are from Risha. And the tears I've been fighting for hours come back in a flood. Maybe because the cold, awful fear that something happened to Alex has melted now. Maybe because for the first time since he drove away, I feel like I am not alone.

I write back:

StormSafe HQ.

Even as I'm entering the text, I can't believe what I'm about to do. Break into my father's office. Hack into his computer. And—*please, let it work*—reverse his awful commands.

The elevator dings, and I finish:

In Dad's office—trying to retrack storm.

I tuck the DataSlate back into my pants as the door opens.

The only light comes from the wall of radar screens. They cast a green glow over the beige carpet, and shadows swirl on the walls.

I head straight for Dad's desk. The computer is logged off, but sure enough, right next to the bio-scanner is a data panel, and when I punch in the code from Grandma's card, the welcome screen appears.

ATHENA MEGGS, FULL CLEARANCE

It believes that I'm her.

A message pops up on the screen: DISABLE REMOTE ACCESS? CANCEL OR OK. I click on OK. Now everything will be up to me, and the thought makes me want to run, but I stay.

My hand trembles as I tap the screen, scrolling through folders and files, looking for the program to remotely operate the satellites.

I call up a search and type in everything I can think of: satellite, dissipation, redirection, downdraft, warming.

Nothing.

I pull up a database of the entire server and start scanning, but there must be thousands of files here. Programs with names I don't recognize. Documents full of numerical models, charts, and statistics. I'm not even halfway through the list, when my DataSlate chimes again.

It's Risha. Three words this time.

We are coming.

Another sob rises in my throat. I'm relieved and thankful and terrified, and before I can type back, I whirl around to look at the radar.

The main storm is moving slowly, giving people plenty of time to watch and be afraid and understand what nightmare is coming.

And it's spawned a slew of baby tornadoes, all over the county.

No matter how desperate I am for help, no matter how hungry I am for someone to be here with me, I can't let them do it. There is no way Risha and Alex can get here safely. None.

No! Storm is too big. Stay there.

I send the message and get an immediate auto-reply.

RECIPIENT NOT AVAILABLE

"No!" I shout, and my voice echoes in the empty office. The only answer is the hum of the computers that are my only hope.

I turn back to the screen on Dad's desk.

Be here. Be here. I scroll through the last half of the files. There must be a thousand documents and databases, and nothing that gives any clue it might be the program that whispers to satellites, tells them where to send their energy, how to turn away a storm.

What am I doing here? I bang my fist on the desk. Looking for answers in this jumble of files is like searching for a single blade of grass swirling in a storm. But I keep looking. What else can I do?

Finally, near the end of the list of folders, my eyes land on one labeled REDIRECTION and I click it open. There are fifty files, maybe more. I tap the one called SAT INPUT—it takes forever to open—and scan the screen that appears.

At the top are three satellite icons, each labeled with latitude and longitude.

With a trembling finger, I point to one of the satellites—which one? I can only guess—and tap.

The screen fills with scrolling numbers that make me want to put my head down and cry. It's some manic feed of temperatures, humidity, atmospheric pressure, cyclonic measurements, and who knows what else. What am I supposed to do with all this?

I swallow hard, reach for my DataSlate, and pull up the page with Dad's redirection codes. There must be a hundred different sequences.

I choose one.

I choose, because the only alternative is doing nothing.

Please let it work.

Please let it work.

I chant the words over and over, like some magical mantra, as I type in the code, number by letter by number. One wrong stroke, and I could make it bigger instead of turning it away.

When the last string of numbers is lined up at the bottom of the page, I hold my finger over the on-screen button.

EXECUTE SATELLITE COMMAND

I can barely breathe. *What if I've done it wrong? Who am I to even think I can do this?*

Before the voices in my head can get louder, I hold my breath and tap.

The screen flashes white, then blurs with a wild scroll of numbers, commands set into motion.

I look up at the ceiling and imagine the satellite miles overhead, stopping in its course, turning, rotating, blasting heat energy down, down, down into the cloud that gave birth to this monster.

When the numbers stop streaming, the screen reads.

COMMAND EXECUTED

Nothing more.

Did it work? I stand and run to the window, but there's no way to tell if anything's better. The wind is still blowing the rain at the building in horizontal sheets.

Stop. Stop. Stop.

A gust of wind rattles the window. It reminds me of another window, the one I threw the chair through, and I can't help wondering if Grandma Athena has come back to find it yet. If she's wondering where I escaped.

Or if she already knows.

I look up at the ceiling. No cameras, at least not that I can see. But no matter what, I'm running out of time.

I turn back to the radar image of the storm. It's actually slowed and—Is it possible? Do I dare hope?—looks like it's turning around. I tap the screen twice to put a track on the storm. The dotted line moves back across the screen.

"No!!"

Straight for Placid Meadows.

Placid Meadows, where concrete houses and storms that never cross the fence make everyone feel safe enough to ignore the warnings.

Placid Meadows, where toddlers giggle and shout nursery rhymes at the sky, even as the dark clouds swirl.

Placid Meadows, where Mirielle is probably nursing Remi on the couch right now.

Where Risha and her family and Alex are about to be—

"No!" I yell at the screen. "No! No! No!!!"

But the storm on the screen swells into something broader, stronger than it was even half an hour ago.

I leap back into the chair at Dad's computer and pull up the folder again, but all of these numbers mean nothing. Do I dare even try?

Above the humming of the computer and the beating of my heart and the rain pounding the window, I hear another sound that makes my heart freeze in my chest.

The elevator door sliding open.

I dive under the desk, shaking, and wait.

Chapter 29

Jaden! Are you here? Jaden!"

Alex's voice washes over me, and I scramble out from under the desk. "Over here!"

They are soaking wet, both of them. Risha's hair is plastered to her forehead, and Alex's face shines with rainwater or sweat, or both, as he takes in the huge room.

"How did you get in here?"

Risha holds up her finger. Her hand is shaking. "I made another print this week. Just in case."

"You guys, I tried to tell you not to come. The storm is—"

"We couldn't even see it until we were out of Placid Meadows." Risha's whole body is trembling. "Jaden, it was . . . It had to have been an NF-7 at least, it was just—"

"We're fine," Alex interrupts. "But for a minute there . . ." He shakes his head. "We thought we were okay, but then it turned, and I had to gun the truck, but we made it. I could tell it was still growing, so—" He stops when he sees the radar on the big screen. I watch him process the mix of images, the moving blobs of green and red, and

I hold my breath, waiting for him to see the path this storm is on now. He curses, and Risha rushes over to face a radar image of something too terrible for words.

She lets out a scream that shatters my heart like the glass in Grandma's picture. The scream of someone whose whole world is about to be destroyed. The scream of someone who knows she may never see her parents again.

She drops to the floor, sobbing.

I run to her, put my arms around her. Her body is hot with fear, cold with rain and air-conditioning, and she shakes harder.

"Risha, call on your DataSlate. Warn them!"

She tries twice but can't get a message through.

I jump to my feet and grab Alex's hand. "We have to stop it."

He steps up to the computer. "Where's the program to redirect? We'll have to find a track that—"

"No!"

He wheels around, bewildered. "Jaden, if we don't change this course, then—"

"Changing it won't help. We have to stop it. We have to kill this storm." I say the words out loud, even though I know they're impossible.

Alex shakes his head. "We can't. We never got to run the simulation successfully. We have no idea what the outcome would be, and we—"

"We have to try, Alex! Look!" I fling my arm toward the radar wall, where Risha is still crumpled on the floor. "We have to try. Otherwise, we're sending it *at* somebody, and even if that's not us, it's still somebody, and then we're just like—" The words get stuck in my throat. "Just like my father."

Alex closes his eyes, squeezes them tight, and I can almost see thoughts swirling behind his dark lashes. Finally, he shakes his head and opens them. "We can't take that chance. What if we end up making it worse?"

"But what if—"

"Jaden, no. There's no precedent for this. There's no research to support it. There's no—just, no!" He bends down and starts scrolling through the folders still up on Dad's screen. The dozens of data files with different codes. "Did you use one of these before?"

"Yes. And look what happened, Alex! We can't do this again. We have to—"

"Just wait!" He holds up one hand and keeps scrolling with the other. Risha has managed to pull herself together enough to stand behind us, her face red and puffy. Alex pulls her forward so she can see the screen, too. "There has to be a path here that doesn't hit any developed areas. Everybody, look. There has to be."

"Which one?" I throw my hands up. "Alex, there must be two hundred separate codes there. We can't keep trying them all until— There's no time for this!"

"Wait." Risha reaches a thin arm between us and scrolls back up through the list. Her bracelets clink together, and her eyes focus on the data scrolling past on the screen. The numbers, the patterns seem to calm her. "Which one did you run before, Jaden?"

"I don't even know. About halfway down, maybe?"

She scrolls halfway and leans in, squinting at the numbers. Then she picks up her DataSlate, calls up a map, taps at it a few times. "Yes," she whispers, and leans in to point at the computer screen again. "These numbers . . ." She runs her finger down the center part of the list. ". . . are all sequential in terms of geographic coordinates." She taps at one of them. "This must be the code you ran. It corresponds with the latitude and longitude of Placid Meadows."

"So that means . . ." I pull up a map of Logan County on the DataSlate and choose the satellite view, the one that shows all the roads and buildings. "If we can find a path without people . . ." In my mind, I draw imaginary lines from where the storm is now, trying every direction. But eventually, no matter which way it goes, the storm is going to hit someone. "It won't work. No path goes on forever."

"It doesn't have to. Hold on." Alex pulls up Dad's historical storms database. "The path just needs to be long enough for the storm's energy to run out. No tornado can last forever, and we already know what this one's got in it. It's already happened once." He calls up the 10-10-20 storm and runs his finger down the screen, stopping at a line close to the bottom. "Thirty-eight miles. We need a path that's empty for thirty-eight miles."

I look down at the map in my hands. It feels impossibly full of buildings. The path might as well be a million miles. "I can't—" The wind gusts, and the sound of rain on the roof turns harder, louder, like someone throwing stones. Hail.

"We have to hurry!" Alex brings the redirection folder back up. "I'll get this ready so when you find the coordinates, we can just do it."

Risha leans in to look at the DataSlate, so close her hair brushes against mine. "What about here?" She drags the line I've drawn a bit farther southeast, and we zoom in to see the track. It would take the storm mostly through woods near one of the energy farms, then past what looks like a few orchards from the satellite view, and close—too close—to one old farmhouse.

"That won't work." I point to the energy farm.

"They all have huge safe rooms," Alex says. "They'll get a warning."

"What about that house?" I point.

"It's not perfect, but we have to do something. That's the only building in the path," Risha argues. "It's thirty miles out. The storm will be starting to weaken, and they'll have plenty of warning time."

She starts to pull the DataSlate from me, but I hold on. "But it's still somebody's—"

"Jaden, will you look!" She lets go and points to the radar wall, where the storm on its current path is churning toward Placid Meadows. Ten minutes, maybe less, from swallowing up Risha's family. From Mirielle and Remi, who are sure they're safe inside the gates. None of them will ever see it coming.

I hand her the DataSlate, and she slides it onto the desk in front of Alex.

"Okay . . ." The computer screen reflects in his dark eyes. "What am I looking for here?"

Risha reads him the coordinates, and he scrolls down the list of command codes until he hits the one that matches. "Here?"

She double-checks it. "That's it."

He clicks it open, copies the code, and taps back to the command entry field. "Jaden, you just typed it in here before?"

"Yeah. Then run it." I look away from the screen, toward the radar, and hear his fingers tap against it.

Then quiet. Except for all of our breathing. All of our hoping.

Then the hum of the computer processing.

Risha and Alex turn to watch the radar. We hold our breath, and it feels like all of the air in the room has gone still while we wait.

The storm on the screen inches closer to Placid Meadows.

"Why isn't it turning?" Risha's voice trembles.

"It will." I take her hand, and she squeezes so hard she crushes my fingers, but I don't let go. "It should. Any second."

But it doesn't.

"It's not going to stop." She doesn't scream or cry or yell at the screen. Her voice is flat, as if she's already died with them. "It's going to hit them."

Turn, turn, turn, I think, staring at the ceiling, imagining the satellites miles above us. Why aren't they doing their job? "Wait, look!" Alex's voice brings me back to the screen, and just as the storm is about to hit the fence, it slows, like it did that day in the park, the day Risha and I listened as the moms and kids shouted their rhyme to the sky. It listened.

And it's listening now.

"Oh, thank God, thank God!" Risha's tears flow again, this time tears of thankfulness. She takes a deep breath and walks to the window. Her fingers trace raindrops down the glass.

Alex sinks back into the chair as if the storm sucked away all his energy when it turned.

I stay at the radar screen, watching the storm pick up its pace, starting a race in its new direction, ready to devour the new meal set before it.

I pick up my DataSlate and zoom in to follow its path as it moves.

The trees planted alongside Placid Meadows. When the sun comes up tomorrow, they'll be in splinters scattered over miles.

Better trees than farms, though.

I follow the path past the energy farm. Criminals or not, I hope they all get to their safe room in time.

I swipe the screen through ten, twenty, thirty miles of woods until the trees thin and arrange themselves into lines, and I know this is the orchard that the storm will level soon—in twenty minutes, maybe twenty-five.

Past the orchard and just a hair off to the east is the one house still in the path.

I zoom into the satellite view, hoping in a corner of my heart that I'll see a FOR SALE sign or already-broken windows and an empty garage to tell me no one lives there.

In another corner lives the cold, raw fear of what else I might see. Cars in the driveway. Dogs on a leash, waiting for someone to come play. Swing sets and tricycles.

I take a deep breath and zoom in as far as the satellite view allows.

And there is something I hadn't imagined even in the darkest corner of my heart.

A house with peeling white paint.

A stable and a brown mare.

A split-rail fence that I reached over with a handful of sugar cubes.

A rickety farm stand with a sign that I can't read in the satellite image, a sign I don't need to see to know that it offers sweet raspberries, fresh peaches, and compliments.

This is Aunt Linda's house.

And we have just sent a storm to swallow it up.

Chapter 30

This can't be happening. Not now. Not when it was all supposed to be over. I let out a moan.

"What?" Alex jumps from the chair, but even his shoulder brushing mine can't warm the chill that's settled on me.

"This house." I tap the screen, and it zooms in closer. The wreath Mom sent last Christmas is still on the door. A bird has built a nest in its gentle curve. "It's my great-aunt Linda's."

Aunt Linda, who fed me pie in that kitchen. Who gave me the poetry book, the one thing that's made Oklahoma feel a little like home. Who told me the truth.

Alex's face darkens. He stares at the screen, processing the information, then hands the DataSlate to me. "Call her. She may not even be home."

I nod and bring up her contact page. The call goes through, straight to Aunt Linda's video-mail, and I've never been more relieved. "Leave a message!" she says, but I don't. If she were home, she'd have answered.

"Feel better?" Alex asks, and I nod.

But then my DataSlate dings with a new message. "That's weird," I say. "I've had it on all day."

"We've probably been getting interference," Risha says, turning away from the window. "I couldn't get through before." Her eyes have relaxed some; they aren't as puffy, and her breathing is finally back to normal. "My DataSlate never connects right on storm nights."

"It's my father." Where is he? Is he on his way up here? I need to know, but I can't bring myself to open the message. Can't make myself let him into this room, even if it's only a recording. I can't help imagining him, looking right through the dark, shiny screen, seeing us here, seeing everything we've done.

But Alex is insistent. "Play it."

So I do.

Dad's face fills the screen. He's not 3-D like he is on the holo-sim at Eye on Tomorrow, but otherwise, it's just as realistic.

Only where did he record this? The shelf behind him is full of old dishes. He's definitely not here at StormSafe. And it's not our house in Placid Meadows, either.

"Jaden," Dad says from the screen in my hands. "I know where you are." He puts a hand up toward the camera in a gesture meant to keep me from freaking out, meant to keep me from throwing the DataSlate across the room and running like I want to. "I need you to stay there for now. You're not in trouble, and I—" He takes a deep breath, and instead of the usual fire in his eyes, the focused intensity, there is something else. Are they shining with *tears*? "I don't want you in danger. I can explain things to you later. It's not what it looks like." His voice breaks, and he looks down.

Alex laughs a quick, bitter laugh and walks away, but Risha stays by me and listens as Dad goes on. "But no matter what, I'm sure you're going to want to go home with Mom. She's on her way here now. So as I said, please stay where you are. Mom will be here in"—he looks at his watch—"ten to fifteen minutes, and after she and I talk, she'll be right there to pick you up."

The screen goes black.

Mom?

Mom is in town? Does that mean she was getting all my messages but couldn't respond? Did she get the last one? Does she already know what Dad has done?

And Grandma! Does Mom know Grandma Athena is alive?

Where *is* Grandma Athena now? I picture her bony fingers, curled around the Shock Wand, and I shiver.

"We can't stay here." I run to the window, where the rain should be letting up, but it's swirling harder, faster in the wind. "My grandmother might come back."

"Your grandmother?" Risha looks bewildered, and I realize I never told them. There was no time. There is no time now.

"We just—we have to go."

"Now that the storm's gone, let's go back to your house. Wouldn't that make more sense than you waiting here for them to come pick you up?"

"They're not *at* the house." It wasn't Dad and Mirielle's house in the video; there are no painted plates in Mirielle's shiny steel kitchen.

But where are they? I rewind the video-message and zoom in to see the background more clearly.

A wooden shelf.

Faded red apples on the wallpaper.

I suck in my breath. Not there. No.

Then I see the coffee mug with Emily Dickinson's face and know it's real.

Dad is at Aunt Linda's house.

And Mom is on her way. Or *was* . . . I check the time-stamp on the video. 7:22 PM. It's 7:45 now. Plenty of time for Mom to have arrived, sat down at Linda's big, wooden kitchen table with a cup of tea. Time for her to be devoured by a giant storm.

I lunge toward the radar screen. The storm is racing forward, showing no signs of weakening.

Alex points to the DataSlate in my hands. "Try calling again." His voice is so steady and calm I could scream.

I pull up Aunt Linda's contact page again.

No response.

I call up Mom's.

Nothing.

And Dad's.

Nothing.

I slam the DataSlate down on the desk and start typing blindly at the computer keyboard.

"Jaden, what are you doing?! You can't just—"

"Yes, I can!" I swipe at the tears filling my eyes, blurring my vision, and pull up the last sequence of numbers we entered, the code to turn the storm. I feed it back to the machine in reverse order. If we sent this storm to Aunt Linda's, then we can take it away, erase its path as if it never planned to flatten the white farmhouse at all. As if it never found this course toward the building with everyone I love inside.

That is the story I tell myself, and I am willing it to be true.

I finish the code, press the command button before Alex can protest again, and turn to watch the radar screen.

Like before, the storm inches forward a few more seconds before it slows and then stops, and then changes direction. And only then do I realize I was holding my breath. Aunt Linda is safe. My mother is safe. My father is . . . safe.

"Are you *insane*?!" Alex pushes me from the computer and starts entering code. "You have it coming right back at us!"

I stare at the radar image.

The storm had been so real when it was chasing us down the road, but between then and now, it's started to feel like something artificial. Something that lives in the colors of a map instead of in the real world.

My eyes trace its new path, back through the woods, along the road, around a curve, and up the driveway to the compound where we sit watching. It is headed straight for StormSafe. Straight for us.

It feels real again.

"What have you *done*?" Alex is tapping the computer screen but can't get back to the page that will let him redirect the storm.

"I had to do something!" My throat closes tight. I slump against the window and watch the clouds swirling above us. Then I whirl back to Alex. "Wait! Stop the redirection codes—what we need to do here—it's what we've needed to do all along! We have to run the dissipation code instead."

Risha shakes her head. "But that's not—"

"Not tested, I know! But it's all we have. Otherwise we can keep turning this storm around and redirecting it every two minutes, and we're going to end up with more people in danger. We have to—" I'm so certain of what I'm about to say that it surprises even me. "We have to take it out."

Chapter 31

Alex doesn't say a word. He walks to the window, presses his forehead to the glass, and closes his eyes.

Risha stares at the computer screen with big eyes, as if she expects it to make the decision all by itself.

"We have to do this." I say it again and look at my watch. For another six minutes, the storm will be swallowing up nothing but forest and fields before it gets back to the populated area. We have six minutes. "There is no. Other. Choice."

Finally, Alex turns away from the window. "It goes against everything we know. Running untested code to drive a real satellite? Testing an unproven theory on an event that's already in progress? Jaden, it's just—"

"It's our only chance! Look!" I fling a hand at the radar screen. The storm hasn't weakened; if anything, it's feeding off the chaos of being directed and redirected in a way nature never intended. "We can't keep recoding it over and over again. There's always going to be somebody in the way, and I can't—" I choke on the words, but I force them out. "I can't be responsible for this anymore."

Risha steps to my side, so we're both facing Alex. "She's right. How close were you to figuring this out?"

"More than close." Alex taps his fingers against the glass. "We . . . I'm sure we have it. But we haven't run a simulation, and—"

"We have it right, Alex. You know we do."

"I know. I'm just afraid that—" He whirls around to face me. "There's another Sim Dome here, right? We could run the code there first and then as long as—"

A gust of wind shakes the building and interrupts him before I have a chance to do it myself. There is no time.

"Where's the code?" Risha asks.

The windows shudder and rattle.

Windows. *The windows jerk free to hover near the ceiling . . .*

I call up the file and stare hard at the numbers, and somehow, they whisper back to me.

Yes. This. Yes.

Almost like a poem.

The ceiling floats away with a sigh.

This is what we need to do. It will work. It *has* to work.

I hand Risha my DataSlate and watch her dark eyes flicking up and down the rows of numbers. She gives one quick, sharp nod when they add up. "This looks perfect. I say we do it."

But Alex doesn't move from the window. I walk over to him and slowly, tentatively, put a hand on his arm.

Still gazing out at the storm, he nods. "You're right." He turns and heads for the computer, but just as I'm about to follow him, a flash of sky blue catches my eye through the rain and I stare out the window.

The rain pours down in sheets, and the wind has picked up enough to send branches whipping down from the treetops and roofing shingles flying like playing cards. The sky is even darker off to the north. The storm is coming. We need to move, to act now if we're even going to try to disperse it, but I can't take my eyes off the figure in blue, making her way through the torrents, toward the main door of the building.

"Hurry. She's coming," I whisper, even though Risha and Alex don't know who she is, and there's no time to explain. I shake my head to clear my thoughts, push off from the window, and rush to join them at the computer. Alex has already keyed in half of the long string of numbers. He hands me the DataSlate.

"Read me the next line, starting at oh-four-six-dash-two-seven-one," he says.

"Oh-four-six . . ." My eyes focus on the numbers, but in my mind, I'm picturing Grandma Athena pushing her way through the wind to the front door. Does she know the bio-scan override code by memory? She's probably in by now, probably through the door with her Shock Wand.

"Jaden!" Alex's sharp voice brings me back to the numbers. He's almost shouting now to be heard over the wind's steady, whooshing roar.

"Sorry. It was oh-four-six-dash-two-seven-one . . ."

A *thunk* against the window makes me jump. I almost drop the DataSlate but manage to fumble it in my hands and get hold of it again. "What *was* that?"

"Piece of the roof came off, it looked like." Risha takes the

DataSlate from my shaking hands and reads Alex another line of numbers. She's about to start the next line when the lights flicker and go out.

The computer's hum dies, and all we can hear is the growing roar from outside.

The windows shake.

There are more clunks and scrapes from the roof, as if pieces of it are breaking free to escape from the cruel winds.

Risha's free hand finds mine, and I hold on.

"The generator will kick in any second." Alex waits. "There has to be a generator. There must be, right?"

My heart sinks. There doesn't have to be a generator because there wasn't supposed to be a need for one. The storms were never supposed to come here.

Dad didn't count on this.

There is no generator. Only the faint glow of the DataSlate.

I let go of Risha's sweaty hand and go to the window. There, eight stories down and off into the trees, is the only other light in the compound. It is the building where I found Grandma Athena.

It must have a generator. And it has a computer.

"There's a light on down there; it's the only building with power!"

"We can't go out there!" Alex shouts.

"It's moving faster!" Risha holds up her DataSlate with a radar image. The storm is coming.

"We *have* to leave! Otherwise, we're trapped on the eighth floor of a glass building!" I scream. "Come on!"

We run, dodging desks and radar screens, past the elevators—there's no hope of them working now—and to the fire exit door that leads to the stairs.

"This way!" I tug it open. "Here!"

Behind us, there's a tremendous crash of glass on glass, and even though I can't see it, I know that one of the windows we'd been looking through is gone, shattered.

When the stairway door closes behind us, everything goes dark.

I've been clinging to Alex's hand but I let go so I can turn on my DataSlate and give us at least a little light.

Risha stumbles behind me. I feel her hands on my back, catching herself, and I grab the railing and hold on. I stumble down a few steps, but Alex reaches back to steady me, and we go down, down, down, until finally, there are no more stairs to descend.

"Ready?" I turn off the DataSlate, tuck it into the back of my jeans, and reach for the door handle.

"Wait!" Alex shouts into the darkness. "That's going to lead straight outside. Do you know where we're going?"

"The building's to the left—maybe thirty yards. We'll have to run!"

"And hold on to each other!" Risha screams.

"I've got my shoulder against the door!" Alex shouts. "On the count of three, you turn the handle, and I'll push it open, and then we need to grab on to one another and go!"

"I'm ready!" I try to ignore the noise from beyond the door, the wind that sounds ever more like that legendary freight train, ever more like a monster from mythology, ready to swallow us up. "All set?"

"Do it!" Alex shouts.

I turn the handle and we push, but nothing happens. Even when I hear Alex grunt from the effort of pushing, pushing his whole body against the door, it doesn't move except to pop open for a split second to mock us and then slam shut.

"Again! Together!" Alex cries. "One!"

The door is cold against my shoulder.

"Two!"

I think about three. Think that *if* we are successful, *if* this goes the right way, we'll fly out of here into a monster storm, and then what?

"Three!"

The door pops open like before, but this time, we are pushing, all of us, and we keep it from slamming shut. Then a swirl of wind comes, and the door that we could barely push open all together flies off its hinges as if it's nothing more than the lid of a shoe box.

And we are out.

Thrown into the wildest storm I have ever seen.

Forget freight trains. Forget Greek monsters.

It feels like the atmosphere itself has come to life, furious, ready to whip us all off the face of the earth in revenge.

Alex is shouting something at me, but I can't hear.

"What?" I scream, but it's no use. Our voices are sucked into the sky. Alex grabs my upper arm tight and pulls me away from the door. His fingers dig into my flesh so hard it hurts, and thank God for that. It feels like I'll be carried off if he ever lets go.

"This way!" I scream, but he can't hear, so I point frantically toward the outbuilding, its light flickering through the rain. I push into the wind and pull Alex along.

The closer we get, the more my stomach clenches. Is she in there?

From the second Alex and I made it out the door, I have been waiting, watching for that glimpse of sky blue. Where is she?

Alex suddenly yanks his hand away from me and pushes Risha to the side. A branch flies close to her head. But it misses her, and we press forward through the blinding rain.

I tug Alex's sleeve and point to the cold yellow light flickering through the rain. I pull Alex and Risha in that direction.

The wind blows rain into my face. I raise an arm to wipe my eyes and finally see the squat little building with its shiny steel door.

Is Grandma waiting on the other side?

There's no time to wonder, no time to worry. The solar energy panels on the next building crackle and send up a shower of sparks.

Alex reaches for the door handle, yanks it open, and pulls Risha and me inside so fast we tumble on top of him. The wind screams through the room, celebrating its newly conquered territory.

The steel door swings open and bangs shut wildly in the wind, and every time it flies open, there are great green flashes of lightning outside. Faster and faster, closer together.

The storm is coming for us.

As if it knows our plans.

And desperately wants us to fail.

But at least our voices are back. "It's over here, hurry!" I lead Alex and Risha around the radar screen to the computer desk where I first saw her. The chair I threw is still toppled on its side in a heap of broken glass. The wind's whipping through the broken window in weird whistling-glass noises. And perhaps the most eerie thing of all is the computer.

Still humming quietly against the wall.

Waiting for Grandma to come back. Where is she now?

Alex kneels down in front of it and starts pressing keys. "Here's the program. Got numbers for me?"

I pull out the DataSlate and start reading numbers, leaning over him. "Oh-four-six-dash-two-seven-one."

"Got it."

"Then five-four-zero—"

The wind shifts, and sheets of rain pour in the broken window. It stings our faces, soaks the floor and the desk.

"It's going to short out the equipment!" Risha screams. She tries to use her skinny body to shield the computer. "Hurry up!"

"FIVE-FOUR-ZERO-TWO-SEVEN!" I scream. There's a terrible scraping, crunching sound above us that can only be pieces of roof, giving up to the wind. But Alex keeps punching in numbers. I can see the strain in his eyes, the urgent effort to focus on getting this right.

The wind is blowing in the open window so hard we can barely stand.

"Then ZERO-ZERO-ONE-ZERO-FIVE— Watch out!!" I drop the DataSlate and throw my body against Risha to shove her out of the way of the radar wall, toppling in a great shattering of glass to the concrete floor.

"Jaden, what's next?!" Alex shouts.

I grab the DataSlate. Thank God it didn't break. "NINE-FOUR-THREE-ZERO-TWO!" I force myself to keep my head down, keep reading numbers, no matter what falls around me, no matter how many branches fly past my head. No matter how sure I am that we will fail. I keep going.

"SIX-FOUR—" The wall behind us explodes in a deep rumble and tears away from the rest of the structure. The wind howls in victory. The roar of the storm is louder, the lightning more frequent; it feels like we'll be hit any second. When I look up, I see why.

I stop shouting numbers because it's too late.

It's here.

"Get down!" Alex screams and tries to pull me under the heavy wooden desk, but I can only stare at the great raging whirlwind bearing down on the main building we just left.

The storm pushes forward. A violent cloud of debris swirls around its base, branches and shrubs, shingles and twisted HV parts, bits of people's lives that will never come together again.

When it reaches the main StormSafe building, it pauses.

Just for a split second.

As if whole walls of glass are a delicacy it wants to savor.

Then it plunges into the first wall. The glass crunches like falling icicles, and the shining pieces are sucked into the vortex and become part of the tornado, sharp and fast.

In twenty seconds, the building is gone.

"Get down, it's coming!" Alex pulls my arm so hard I fall to the ground beside him.

Risha drops and flattens herself next to us. "Ow!" she cries, rubbing her side. She must have landed on something. Broken glass? "You guys, look!" She bends over and pulls with all her weight on a latch screwed into one of the floorboards. "Storm shelter!" The door swings open, and we pile down a steep set of steps behind her.

It is nothing like the storm cellar at Alex's barn. No daybed. No food. But it has metal bars poured into the concrete, for holding on. And on a heavy desk in the corner, it has the one thing we need most right now.

A computer.

I race to it, wait for a home screen to load, and squeeze my eyes shut as tight as I can, as if refusing to watch will keep the tornado from jumping the last stretch of lawn, keep it from coming here where I've brought Alex and Risha.

The wind screams overhead, and I scream back. "No!!"

Because I know now what is about to happen if we cannot destroy this storm.

It is going to kill us.

Storm cellar or not. It's too big. Too strong.

It will devour us. Me, and the two people who are here with me. *Because* of me.

I squeeze my eyes shut tighter.

Please, please, please, don't let them die because of me.

When I open my eyes, the computer has booted up, and I find the file Alex was working on upstairs. "It auto-saved!" For once, it feels like someone might be on our side. "Get the last line of numbers, quick!"

Alex pages through DataSlate screens, one after another.

"Hurry up!"

The wind and rain, already impossibly loud, scream louder, and there's clunking, clanking coming from over our heads. Something— lots of somethings—being flung around like play toys, until finally, in an almighty howl of wind, the whole of the little building— everything above us, is ripped from the foundation and sucked into the sky.

I fall to the floor, grab on to one of the metal bars, and hold on. But impossibly, the wind lets up, and when I dare to peek into the screaming, high-whistling swirl above me, all I can do is stare.

The storm has lifted up; the tornado is no longer touching down, though it's close, and it is absolutely, directly on top of us.

The air feels heavy, like every last molecule of oxygen has been sucked into the sky, and this gray cloud has us encircled like a tomb.

Blue lightning flashes from the sides of the tornado. We are surrounded by a circular wall of clouds and electricity.

"We're inside," I whisper, and only then do I become aware of Alex and Risha on the ground next to me, staring into the sky, too.

"It's . . . it's beautiful," Risha says. But she is also the first to get her wits back. "But it's still moving. It could touch back down any second, and we'll have the other side to deal with. *Finish!* While we still have the computer!"

It's a miracle it still works; if the winds had raged on the ground a half-second more, it would be up there, swirling over our heads.

But it's here, and I crawl to it. There are two lines left to copy from the DataSlate. Alex reads, and I enter them with shaking, blood-stained hands.

"SEVEN-THREE-ONE," he finishes.

I stare at the columns of numbers and let my finger hover over the words EXECUTE COMMAND.

What if?

What if we are wrong?

This storm over our heads will go . . . where? And will we strengthen it along the way?

Alex's hand presses down gently on my shoulder. "It will work."

I tap the button.

Drop to my knees.

And wait.

The wind starts to blow again as the second wall of the storm moves over us.

Let it work. Please let it work.

I keep my head down and listen. I send all my hopes up into the sky.

Wind howls. Rain pelts down. The computer flies off the desk—"Look out!"—and Risha yanks Alex out of the way the instant before it explodes in a shower of sparks on the concrete floor.

We huddle close and hold on, waiting for the wind to rip us apart.

But it doesn't happen. The monster never quite comes back.

There are more distant pops from electrical explosions in blown circuits and transmitters. Branches and bits of ceiling and roofing and God knows what else bang and scrape against the one wall that remains.

But the sounds start to fade.

And we are still here.

We lift our heads and watch the storm sweep away from us, back toward Placid Meadows.

"No, no!" Risha says, and starts to lunge for the computer, in pieces on the floor now.

"No, wait." Alex's eyes are trained on the top of the storm cloud. "It's going to be okay. Watch."

And yes. The churning gray monster is tired. It slugs away from us another quarter of a mile, stirring up dust and last year's leaves.

And finally, it lifts its tail up from the ground and snakes back up into its cloud.

And is gone.

Chapter 32

There are no words to describe this sound.

The quiet after a storm has gone.

The absence of everything—birds chirping, HV motors idling, air conditioners humming.

Here in this broken shelter full of leaves and branches, shattered glass, and bits of buildings the tornado threw at us as it passed, there is almost total quiet.

Only the sound of our breathing—Alex and Risha and me, huddling together.

It feels like time should have stopped when the storm rose back into the sky, like this problem should be solved forever now that it's gone.

But I know it's not.

I know the storms will come again, on the next day when the clouds start swirling and the conditions are just right. They will come.

But right now, it's too soon to talk of next times. I am too thankful to do anything except stay here with my head on Alex's shoulder, breathing this same air with him, holding on to Risha's hand, and feeling her bracelets, cool against my wrist.

Alex is the first to speak. "Thank God we had the numbers right."

A few minutes later, Risha is the second.

"Look." She points up, out of the shelter. We uncurl ourselves like fern fronds in spring and stretch our necks up, up to the line her finger traces toward the clouds in the east.

A smudge of broken rainbow leans against the storm-bruised sky, faint color in the day's last light. I stare hard at it, willing the colors to brighten.

They don't.

I am thankful anyway. Because hope has to start somewhere. And a glimmer is better than nothing at all.

It is the sound of tires crunching over broken boards and branches that finally brings us up out of the shelter to meet Aunt Linda's blue farm truck. Mom jumps out and looks as if she can't decide whether to hug us or kill us.

"Jaden!" She flies at me and pulls me into a hug that comes dangerously close to accomplishing the latter, but I manage to push away so I don't suffocate.

"You got my messages!"

Her eyes fill with tears. "I'm sorry I didn't come home sooner. I thought you were probably getting used to everything. A new house and Mirielle and—"

"Mirielle! Remi! Are they okay? Were they with you and Dad? Or are they home at Placid Meadows? And where's Dad?"

My stomach tightens. Is he okay? Is he back in his office at Placid Meadows sending down another storm?

Mom presses her hands against her eyes and shakes her head a little. "Mirielle and Remi are fine. They're safe. So is Dad, but . . . there's . . . we have a lot to talk about, Jaden." She moves her hands and smiles a weak, exhausted smile. "And I need to say hello to your friends, too."

"This is Risha. And Alex." I wait while she shakes their hands. "Mom, where is everybody? What's going on?"

"What's going on," she says, "is that we need to get the three of you someplace safe, where we can clean up those cuts, and you can eat something." She looks at my matted hair. "And take a shower. Pile in." She opens the truck door. "We'll talk on the way back to Linda's house."

Chapter 33

Dear Dad,
* I hope things are going okay for you. I wish...*

I stop and stare out the window, where fat raindrops are starting to fall, pelting the red leaves on our sugar maple in the yard. A long time ago, I used to love the way September storms would make Vermont's autumn leaves shine.

Thunder rumbles, and I set the pencil down.

It feels weird writing to him like this instead of talking at my DataSlate for a video-message, but it makes sense that one of Dad's restrictions at the energy farm includes the use of any electronic communication devices.

At first when Dad turned himself in and came clean about the technology he developed with Grandma Athena, it didn't look like he'd be doing time.

After all, it was the government that opened the floodgates on weather manipulation research when it changed the laws and even paid StormSafe to redirect hurricanes in the Gulf when they were headed for populated areas. They wanted Dad's technology, so they pretty much gave him free reign, extended his patent for the Sim Dome, and didn't ask questions about how he made Placid Meadows so safe. It was the National Storm Center that funded Dad's tornado dissipation project when he came back from Russia. Weather manipulation won't be a crime until the new legislation takes effect next year.

But lying under oath has always been against the law, and Dad had testified before Congress about the failure of his dissipation research. He lied about the project he scrapped so he could go on to something bigger, technology that would let him rule the storms instead of simply sending them home to the clouds. The project Grandma Athena had always dreamed of. What she'd given up her life to do. And Dad finally got the attention he never had from her when he was a kid.

It's crazy that after all he did, all the lives he destroyed with his pet storms, that it was the lying that landed him on one of those energy farm bikes, sentenced to pedal for power in the sun for the next five years, paying back in sweat what he stole from society with his crimes.

Only he can never really pay it back. I think of Alex and Tomas whose family farms were ravaged and almost stolen away, of the countless people who lost their homes in Dad's redirected storms. Of Newton.

Thank God for Ms. Walpole, who helped Tomas's family get their farm deed back, along with a settlement so StormSafe will pay for his mother's treatment in New York, and then some. He and Alex have had a chance to talk, too. I was right; Tomas trusted Van and had no idea what he and my father were doing.

Lightning flashes, and my stomach twists, even though the only storms around tonight are small ones. I run my hand over the cover of the poetry book I brought home with me from Dad's, and I breathe in slowly. It will be a long time before my heart remembers that storms aren't all evil. That they can be ordinary rain, with thunder and lightning and a bit of wind.

I pick up the pencil again.

Set it down.

What do you write to someone who is so much like you and yet nothing like you at all? What do you say to a parent who is no one that you want to grow up to be?

And what can I say about this summer that was supposed to be our time to reconnect?

I've only been home—real home with Mom—two months, but Eye on Tomorrow already seems like forever ago. Placid Meadows, the campus, the playground . . . they all feel like memories of some high-definition dream.

That afternoon when the storm was raging, when we crouched clinging to metal bars in the storm cellar, I wanted to wake up like Dorothy from *The Wizard of Oz* and find a cold compress on my forehead because it was never real.

Just a dream.

Did Dad ever really want to know me again? Or was I there like all the others—another Eye on Tomorrow kid to watch and shape and ultimately hire to help keep secrets?

Mom unloaded the truth on the way back to Aunt Linda's house that night. When she left for Costa Rica, she hadn't known how Dad's research was evolving, how his interests had taken such a dark turn. When she finally got my message—the video-message of me crying by the side of the road—she called Mirielle, who broke into Dad's office—I still don't know how but it doesn't surprise me that she figured it out—and pieced together what was happening. That's when she learned, all at once, that her dead mother-in-law was alive and that her husband was not doing the work he said he was.

She told Mom everything. And Mom borrowed an HV, drove straight to the airport, and caught the next flight home.

Aunt Linda had picked her up at the airport, and when Dad met them at her house, Mom gave him a raging earful about the promises he'd made to her, to me, about my summer and keeping me safe.

And that's when Grandma Athena's message got through. Her face appeared on Dad's DataSlate, right there in Aunt Linda's kitchen, talking about how the storm wasn't performing as they'd planned, how she locked me in the outbuilding. I was more of a problem than he'd imagined, she said, and so the two of them would need to talk. Dad swore up and down to Mom that she never really would have hurt me. I don't think I believe it.

Dear Dad,
    I hope things are going okay for you. I wish
this summer could have been different. I really
wish...

I roll the pencil between my fingers, then snap it in half.

Thunder rumbles again, and rain pours down my window in thick rivers. Everything outside looks warped and blurry and wet.

What do I wish? I wish Eye on Tomorrow had been real, a legitimate opportunity for kids like me and Risha, Tomas and Alex, to collaborate and solve this world's problems.

I wish Dad was the father he used to be, or pretended to be anyway, the dad with the strong shoulders and rainbow sprinkles.

I wish that his corporation never existed. That he'd never gone to Russia and found Grandma Athena.

I wish I had a grandmother like Risha's, who stirred curry stews and kissed my head, instead of one who tied me to chairs.

And yet . . . I wish I'd had a chance to talk with her, really talk with her, about her life and her ideas and her choices, before she died.

I pick up a jagged pencil piece and turn it over in my hands.

It's been two months, but we haven't had a funeral yet. Mom and I will have to go make arrangements because with Dad locked up, we're the only ones who can take care of her burial.

Mom's waiting to book plane tickets. The storm was so huge it's taken them weeks to clear the debris. If Grandma had entered the main StormSafe building, or if she were right outside, she'd have been buried under a mountain of glass and steel when the tornado hit.

"Jaden?" Mom knocks at my bedroom door, then walks in with a pile of clean clothes and balances it on my dresser. "Done with the letter?"

I push the paper away. "I don't think I have anything to say."

I run my finger over the end of the pencil piece, then pick up the other one and try to fit them back together, but splintery edges stick out. Breaks are never truly clean.

"Did he really used to love me?" I try to say it as if I don't care, but my shuddery voice gives everything away.

"Yes." Her eyes are sad. "He really did and he still does, Jaden."

I almost laugh.

"Truly." Mom puts a hand on each of my cheeks so I have no choice but to look right at her. "It wasn't until that night you were in danger—you, his little girl—that he could finally see what he had done. Remember what he looked like when he called you on the videophone?"

I nod. I remember. I could never forget the first time I ever saw my father cry.

"He loves you. Nothing excuses what he's done, but he's damaged, Jaden. His thinking. Athena is—was—I can't get used to the idea of having her alive and now gone again—she was larger than life somehow. It's like . . . I don't know . . . like she had some spell cast over him."

"Yeah," I whisper. And I almost understand. I know that feeling of wanting a parent back so badly. Wanting to be celebrated and loved. It's a feeling he never really knew. Mom pushes my hair behind my ear, and all at once, I'm filled up with tears at how lucky I am that I do know.

The house videophone buzzes in the hallway, and as Mom leaves to answer it, my DataSlate dings with a video-message from Alex.

"Hey, Jaden! I gotta show you what came in the mail today."

Video-Alex holds up a fat off-white envelope, and I cheer, even though I know he can't hear me. "All *right*!" Risha and I both got similar envelopes two days ago, invitations to spend three weeks interning at the National Storm Center's new weather modification research facility this winter, and permission documents for Mom to sign. According to the paperwork, Ms. Walpole recommended all three of us, based on our "outstanding commitment to research." Everything in the NSC envelope makes me hope this is the program that Eye on Tomorrow was supposed to be.

"So I guess I'll be seeing you in a couple months!" Video-Alex winks, and the screen goes black.

I stare out the window and smile at the rain, just thin trickles down the glass now, and the clouds are thinning. It really was a small storm this time. Nothing more.

I pick up the longer of the two pencil pieces and go back to Dad's letter.

I ask him about Mirielle and Remi. They've been to visit him, Mom says, even though Mirielle isn't sure if she'll stay or take Remi back to France. I write a few lines about school, about the new schedule I'm on this fall with home connection three days a week and morning classes in person the other two. I ask how things are at the energy farm, then erase that because they're probably not great.

I'm about to sign it when Mom comes back through the door. The lines in her face are tight.

"Who was on the videophone?" I ask.

"Logan County Sheriff's office. They finished clearing all the debris from StormSafe, and Grandma . . ." Mom pauses.

They must have found the body.

Mom bites her lip. "I'm . . . not sure how to tell you this."

I stare at her for a second. Does she think I'm going to be that upset over losing a grandmother I never knew, until the night she almost killed me? "Mom, it's okay. I was there when the building went down. I know she never could have survived. Is the funeral going to be soon?"

"We'll go down for a service on Monday," Mom says. "Closed casket."

I nod, remembering the flying debris, the minefield of broken glass and twisted metal that night. "Her body was in pretty bad shape, huh?"

Mom shakes her head. "They didn't find her body."

A million thoughts swim through my head. The storm was huge; it could have picked her up and dropped her anywhere. But one thought rises to the surface—not so much a thought in words as a mental movie of Grandma Athena, standing in the outbuilding, her mouth a straight line, her hands on her hips.

Her laugh.

Never trust a death certificate.

Could she possibly have survived that monster?

My stomach twists.

Could she still be out there somewhere?

Mom goes on. "We can still have the service. But closed casket. It's not a problem."

Not a problem. I let Mom go on thinking that. She's probably right.

"When will we leave?"

"Sunday. You should call your friends. You'll have some time to see them, too." Mom leaves and closes the door behind her.

An image of Grandma's face floats through my mind, but I imagine the wind blowing it away like Risha's dandelion fluff. Like the magical numbers on her bracelet, zeros and ones, swirling through the air until the ceiling lifts away, and they arrange themselves into something that makes sense, into a world mended and whole again.

But it took decades to make this mess. It will take time for us to go back.

No. To move forward.

It'll take time and research and work. And hope. Failing and trying again and probably wanting to scream because it can't happen fast enough. It won't be impossible, but it will feel that way sometimes; I already know that. And I know I want to be part of it. I need to be.

I reach for my DataSlate to call Alex and Risha. Outside, the sun streams through a gap in the clouds. Puddles glimmer on the sidewalk, and half a rainbow arcs over the woods. This one is brighter than before.

And today feels like a good day to start.

Acknowledgments

Many thanks to all whose work, research, and support helped me to write this book, especially Dr. Howard Bluestein from the University of Oklahoma's School of Meteorology, who took time out of a stormy week in September 2010 to meet with me and answer my long list of questions, most of which began with the words, "So what if . . ." Dr. Bluestein also reviewed sections of this manuscript for scientific accuracy relating to the formation of tornadoes (even though the actual weather manipulation that happens in the book isn't possible at this time). His meteorological expertise is most appreciated, and any errors that remain are my responsibility alone.

I'm grateful to senior meteorology student Tim Marquis for the weather school and National Severe Storms Laboratory tour that provided much of the inspiration for the Eye on Tomorrow campus. The following books were also helpful: *Tornado Alley: Monster Storms of the Great Plains* by Howard B. Bluestein (Oxford University Press, 2006), *The Tornado: Nature's Ultimate Windstorm* by Thomas P. Grazulis (University of Oklahoma Press, 2003), and *Storm Warning: The Story of a Killer Tornado* by Nancy Mathis (Touchstone, 2008).

Acknowledgments

As someone who loves both science and art, I am fascinated by the idea of intersections between the two. Richard Holmes's *The Age of Wonder: How the Romantic Generation Discovered the Beauty and Terror of Science* (Pantheon, 2009) got me thinking about it in new ways.

I am grateful to poet Rita Dove for the gift of her work and for permission to include the excerpt from "Geometry" that Jaden reads in her faded paper book.

Thanks to student beta-reader Theo Gardner-Puschak for sharing his thoughts on the manuscript and to critique partners and writer friends Loree Griffin Burns, Eric Luper, Liza Martz, Ammi-Joan Paquette, Marjorie Light, Stephanie Gorin, and Linda Urban. You all make me a more thoughtful writer, and I'm grateful for your friendship.

Thanks to my agent, Jennifer Laughran, for supporting my writing, helping me weather storms, and generally being amazing; to my brilliant editor, Mary Kate Castellani, for asking just the right questions; and to Emily Easton, Beth Eller, Katie Fee, Kate Lied, Amanda Hong, Nicole Gastonguay, and the rest of the team at Walker/Bloomsbury, and to cover illustrator Vincent Chong.

A special thanks to Elizabeth Bluemle and Josie Leavitt of Flying Pig Bookstore, Marc and Sarah Galvin of The Bookstore Plus, and all the other independent booksellers who work hard for authors, books, kids, and communities every day. You rock.

Finally, thanks to Tom, Jake, and Ella. I saved you for last because the very best part of this book journey is sharing it with you.

4-13